Black Lipstick Kisses

I was being spanked, and it was not at all what I'd expected. In the occasional darker moment I had imagined punishment, not being spanked, but whipped in some dungeon or crypt, with evil men revelling in my pain. I had thought spanking would be a lesser version of the same, not the gradual bottom warming my sexy, oh-so-straight MP was giving me. It was dirty, but closer to worship than punishment.

He turned his full attention to my bottom, holding me around the waist and slapping my cheeks with his fingertips, just hard enough to make my skin sting. Soon I was in a rosy haze of pleasure, not so very far from orgasm. He was going to make me come, but in his own good time, at once enjoying my body and taking his revenge for me tormenting him. Until then all I could do was lie there and let myself be brought slowly, slowly higher, my dignity forgotten as I surrendered to the delicious thrill of my first spanking.

Black Lipstick Kisses
Monica Belle

BLACK LACE

Black Lace books contain sexual fantasies.
In real life always practise safe sex.

First published in 2004 by
Black Lace
Thames Wharf Studios
Rainville Road
London W6 9HA

Typeset by SetSystems Ltd, Saffron Walden, Essex
Printed and bound by Mackays of Chatham PLC

ISBN 0 352 33885 7

1

There was a man in my graveyard.

He had to be over six foot, because he was at eye level with the inscription on Lisbet Stride's tomb, and I have to look up a little to read it. It was hard to pick out detail from forty feet above his head, but he was slender, pale, with a mop of floppy black hair, and dressed entirely in black, save for a tie-pin that glinted in the brilliant sunlight: intriguing.

For a while I was content to watch, simply admiring the lithe, easy way he moved among the monuments and wondering what he was up to. He had a small pad, and would pause occasionally to sketch a detail: the grotesque black iron faces on the gate of the Braidault family mausoleum, the rusting semaphore installed by Major Inkerman Goodwell in case he woke up, the entwined angels lifting Lisbet Stride to heaven. Very intriguing.

I still wasn't going to do anything about it, not until he'd finished drawing the green man over the main door and began to investigate the corrugated iron sheets blocking it off. If he came inside, Lilitu was going to get him, and he was much too good looking for that. I had to stop him, but that was a problem. All I had on was a layer of factor 50. No clothes, no shoes, no make-up. Lilitu would have finished him before I was ready, bones and all. I pulled my head back a little, making sure all he could see was my face and a lot of black hair, and called down.

'I wouldn't do that if I were you.'

He looked up, startled for just an instant until he realised that there was a woman's head among the row of gargoyles on the parapet. I smiled. He spoke.

'No?'

'No.'

'Why not?'

'My dog will attack you.'

'Ah. What sort of dog is he?'

'She is a Doberman.'

'Ah.'

There was a pause as he stepped back from the sheet of corrugated iron he had been trying to pull free. When he spoke again his tone was rather different, enquiring.

'I was hoping to do some drawing inside. There are supposed to be some heads on the rood screen, which is the high wooden partition . . .'

'I know what a rood screen is.'

'Well, this is Victorian High Gothic, with seven heads representing . . .'

'Representing the seven deadly sins, carved by Isaac Foyle. I know.'

'You do? Maybe you've heard of me then. I'm Michael Merrick. I draw for *Illuminatus, Black Dog*.'

'Cool. Don't move.'

I drew back. This guy I had to meet, but not stark naked. Stark naked was better than casual, so he was just going to have to wait, and I was hoping he would. I'd seen his art, beautifully drawn pictures that pulled you right into the page, usually dark, sometimes disturbing, occasionally arousing, always immaculate. I'd read his work too, and loved the way he could turn a conventional idea completely on its head. People like that don't turn up at All Angels every day. Graffiti writers maybe, but not *bona fide* Gothic artists.

In two minutes I was down in the vestry, my 'flat', once reserved for priests and choristers to don their robes, now just right for me and Lilitu. The deal is simple. I keep out the vandals and taggers, the drunks and junkies, the lovers and perverts: anyone else who thinks an abandoned church is a good place to disport themselves. In return I live for free, company water provided.

In twenty minutes I was dressed, heeled black boots, black fishnets, black skirt, black belt, black top, black collar, black gloves, even little black silk panties. After all, you never know, and the idea of seducing a man only to have him discover I'm in granny pants is too much. I decided against a bra, determined to tease at the very least. A touch of rose attar served for scent.

In twenty minutes I was made up, my eyes large and dark, the lids touched with deep green, my lips glossy black, my face pale. For jewellery I went for silver set with green tourmaline, not my birthstone but a match to my eyes, and not too much, just four rings, a necklace and ear-rings, pentacles and black suns. A green lavabell for my tummy button and a plain stud for my tongue were the final touches.

I left by the rectory door to find Michael still at the front, sketching. Rather than speak to him, I perched myself on the flat top of Eliza Dobson's tomb and rested my chin in one hand, waiting. He must have sensed me, because he turned almost immediately, smiling as he fixed me with piercing steel-grey eyes. I let him come to me, unmoving as I took him in.

He was certainly six foot, cool and handsome, but with his loose hair and the large amethyst tie-pin giving him a faintly louche touch. I'd thought he was about my age, but a trace of line at his eyes and mouth suggested a little more, while he certainly seemed to have the confidence of maturity, arrogance even. He spoke as he reached me.

'Here lieth the mortal remains of Eliza Dobson, 1827 to 1895. You look remarkably good for a woman dead over a hundred years.'

'She would not have been amused. Eliza Dobson, spinster of this parish and a noted philanthropist dedicated to the cleanliness and chastity of London's poor. Quite mad too; apparently she used to sit the drunks and dollymops in leg irons while she lectured them on their vices.'

He nodded thoughtfully.

'Are you going to let me inside? Introduce yourself maybe?'

'I'm Dusk.'

He gave a nod, maybe of appreciation, maybe sceptical. I was not going to disillusion him. Angela I keep in reserve for the mundane. I slid from the top of the tomb and walked to the main door, not wishing to take him through the vestry and shatter any hope I might have of maintaining my mystique. He followed cautiously, a sensible choice, as the moment I'd slid the lower section of corrugated iron aside Lilitu's toothy snout poked out, followed by the rest of her. Her eyes immediately fixed on Michael, but I'd taken a firm grip on her collar and begun to scratch her behind the ears.

'Michael, meet Lilitu. Lilitu, meet Michael, who is not prey.'

Michael stepped a little closer.

'You named your dog after a Babylonian demoness?'

'It suits her.'

'Well, yes.'

I ducked in through the hole, pulling Lilitu behind me. Michael followed, into the cool dimness of the porch and then the nave, to look around with an expression of rapture. I let him take it all in, and for all my familiarity it was hard not to stare myself. Above us great Gothic arches rose to bosses carved as angels, demons and green men high above us. The shattered stained glass produced a dozen rich colours, with bright streamers of sunlight breaking through the holes to illuminate dust motes in the still air. Ranks of decaying pews lined the nave, with the striking black and white checkerboard of the floor tiles now spattered with pigeon droppings. Nearby, the arch that led to the tower and crypt, the interior chapels and tombs, each individual, each familiar.

'Wonderful.'

He didn't speak the word, but sighed it. I immediately felt a touch of pride, for all that I had contributed nothing to the place, and only held its picturesque decay in check. It was still mine, at least for now, and it was impossible not to feel good when a man I had so long admired for his Goth art seemed awestruck by where I lived. To have him awestruck by me would have been better still.

If he was, he wasn't showing it, very cool an instant after he'd got over the initial image. He didn't speak as he began to explore, taking in everything, and occasionally shaking his head in delight at some particularly fine detail, and also pieces of picturesque decay. Only at the sight of the scaffolding inside the tower did he frown, and he spoke only to ask if I had a torch so that he could explore the crypt. I obliged as best I could, with two of the big altar candles from the vestry, and finally found something I could say without looking silly as we descended the stair.

'Don't expect to be too impressed. It got a make-over sometime in the 60s, to try and bring in some money by hiring it out for meetings and stuff. It's pretty awful.'

He had stopped at the bottom of the stairs, peering in at the decaying hardboard facings, the broken fluorescent light fittings, the false ceiling sagging down to reveal black gaps. A plastic chair lay on its side at the centre of the space; otherwise it was empty, our candles barely reaching the far end. Michael shook his head, but not in delight.

'How could anyone do this? It's vandalism, pure and simple.'

'I agree.'

'Some people have no sense of history, or aesthetics for that matter. Do you mind if I do some drawing? Not here, of course.'

'Go ahead, whatever you like.'

We left the crypt and he immediately sat down on the charity box by the door and began to sketch, his eyes flicking from the paper to the body of the church. I watched as the picture grew, soft lines, then hard, an image building quickly on the page. He was capturing the atmosphere with extraordinary skill, maybe even exaggerating it, adding melancholy to the angelic faces, malevolence to the demonic, infusing the green men with an eerie mystique. With the main image in rough, he began to add details around the margin of the page, the faces of imps and angels, of beasts both wild and mythical. I wasn't going to interrupt him, but he finally spoke of his own accord, still drawing.

'This is perfect. I've a commission for a piece, the Goat of Mendes it's going to be called. There's a cabal of Satanists attempting to summon the spirits of an earlier, Regency, cabal.'

'Cool.'

'I can just see this as the interior of the ruined temple, the one the earlier cabal used. OK, so the period's wrong, but for me it's visual effect that matters.'

'I can see that. I love your work. I've got a poster of yours, with a demoness and an angel fighting over a soul.'

'"The Balanced Scale"? That was years ago, one of my first commercial pieces. I've never been that happy with it.'

'It's great! Just so . . .'

I stopped. I'd been going to say 'erotic', because I'd often seen myself as the beautiful female demoness in the picture, and let myself go over the fantasy more than once. Admitting to masturbating over his drawings seemed a bit much, but I felt a stab of annoyance for holding back as I finished, somewhat lamely.

'. . . evocative.'

He went on: 'Thanks. It certainly sold well. I was exploring ideas of good and evil then, trying to show how sometimes it can be a matter of which side you're on.'

'I've read your essay on evil forces in science fantasy, the one where you show the story as propaganda by the good guys, because they won so they get to tell the story, with the bad guys as defeated rebels. It gave me a whole new perspective.'

He grinned, flattered.

'It was a bit tongue in cheek, but yeah, it works, for Tolkein especially. I feel that's been done though, and I want to move away from it, to take a less black and white perspective, even an irrational one.'

'How do you mean?'

'I want to get away from the idea of building a main character to suit the reader's preconceptions, which is what the magazines always want. Now I've got a bit of a name for myself I can afford to be somewhat bolder, to make people think, even disturb them.'

'I think you manage that already!'

'I try. I didn't in that sense though. I'm doing one at the moment, where my main character's a typical anarchist eco-warrior type, but at the end he'll turn out to have been telling the story as he looks back at how he came to be an executive in the very corporation he tried to defeat. That's when his ex-buddies burst in, but I'll leave the ending open.'

'Well cool.'

'It's not new. Have you read *Clockwork Orange*? Not seen the film, but read the book?'

'Sure.'

He shrugged, looking a touch embarrassed, as if he had revealed himself as a charlatan, and went back to work. I felt myself warm to him, something in addition to simple physical attraction and the fascination of meeting somebody I admired. For a moment he had let his defences down, and it prompted me to do the same, allowing my mind to wander to more intimate possibilities.

As the drawing grew he paid more and more attention to the margins, filling them with fantastical details. The picture was centred on the nearest of the great roof pillars, but he had left it as a faint outline, despite the real thing being decorated with a column of grotesque little faces, which I'd have thought irresistible. At last he spoke again.

'I might even make this a cover. What do you think?'

'Sure ... great ...'

'It just needs a focus, perhaps not one of the characters, but something to get the essence of the story across.'

He turned to me with a disarming grin.

'Would you mind posing? You really look the part.'

'Sure. How do you want me?'

I'd tried to be cool, hiding my instant rush of girlish glee at being asked to pose for him, but my voice had cracked a little as I answered. He'd really got me flustered, in no time too. As he pondered my question, my wicked side was hoping he'd suggest I would be best naked – for all that my shy side was dreading exactly that. It felt nicer to be naked, shy or brazen. Finally he spoke.

'I'll have you as a spirit, I think, brooding on her fate.'

'I can do brooding.'

'Great. Lean against the pillar. Put your cheek next to the stone ... yes, like that. Raise your right arm. No, with your palm flat against the stone ... yes. Put your left hand at the front of the pillar, fingers splayed, as if you're caressing the stone. Yes, perfect, just under a face. Now closer, and stretch up a little, onto your toes.'

'Like this?'

'Yes, ideal, but it wouldn't work if you were even a fraction less slender.'

Flattery, which from him nudged the balance of my feelings further towards taking my clothes off, at least some of them.

'My clothes don't spoil your line, do they?'

'Don't worry. I can work around that.'

He began to draw, his eyes narrowed in concentration. I stayed still, horny, wanting to impress, yet feeling something of a fluffy girlie for doing so. That's just not me. I like to take charge, to be the one getting into another's head, the desirable one. He should have been the one getting slowly steamed up, not me. Bollocks to modesty. Sometimes a girl just has to do it.

'It would be better with my top off, wouldn't it?'

Before he could answer I'd pulled my top up, and over my head, leaving my necklaces. I resumed my pose, now with my bare breasts pressed to the cool stone, giving him no more than a brief glimpse of my nipples, hopefully not enough to show just how perky they were. His response was a cool nod, but he had gone ever so slightly pink. Again he began to draw, his concentration more intense than ever, only to stop suddenly and speak.

'There, I don't think we can improve on that until I'm in the studio. Thank you.'

'My pleasure.'

I stepped away from the pillar, pointedly indifferent to my partial nudity. He watched me come towards him, calm and appreciative, without a trace of embarrassment as his eyes moved down from my face. I stepped close, allowing the side of my breast to press onto the lean muscle of his arm as I inspected the picture.

It was me, but transformed into an impossibly slender creature, half merged with the pillar and with the tiles of the floor, naked beneath a gossamer shroud. The contours of my body, the lines of the pillar and the black and white check of the floor blended, light and shade. Even my hair seemed to flow into the surroundings, my face alone distinct, with an expression hard to read, maybe grieving, maybe remorseful, maybe defiant. At first glance my breast had seemed to show clearly, yet looking closer it was hard to pick the lines from those of my shroud, while another fold might or might not have suggested the lips of my pussy.

It was beautiful and flattering, yet I felt as if he'd stripped me bare, and again caught the need to exert myself. I stepped away, wondering what he'd do if I simply pushed him down on the tiles and ravished him. My wicked side wanted exactly that – him inside me as I rode him on the floor, amusing myself with his body, taking orgasm after orgasm until he was begging to be allowed to do the same. Drunk, I might just have done it, even if I did have a suspicion he'd have rolled me over after a minute or two. Sober, my shy side came to the fore and I found myself walking away from him, towards the rood screen.

He came behind, with Lilitu trotting after, now as seemingly indifferent to his presence as Michael was to my nakedness. The rood screen was extravagant even by the standards of the Victorian craze for the high Gothic, the seven faces yet more so. Isaac Foyle was said to have taken a cup of laudanum each day before beginning work, and I could believe it. The rood itself was unusually macabre in detail, and supported above eight arches rising to over twice my height, the central two joined. Each was fantastically carved, the pillars six slender caryatids, supposed saints but looking more like demons, with their hair rising in asymmetric coils from which six of the faces peered. The seventh, wrath, peered out from among flames, directly beneath the rood itself, a Hell to the Heaven above.

I admired them as Michael began to sketch, immediately impressed by his understanding of what had been going on in Isaac Foyle's head. His wrath projected fury, hatred, fear and pain, surely enough to terrify any sinner, but among the others there were hints of less orthodox attitudes, or so it seemed to me. Pride and avarice flanked wrath: the one a long, haughty face, the great hooked nose lifted high in disdain, pompous but also comic; the other shining with greed and normal enough save that it was known to be a caricature of his own father. Sloth showed a somnolent, drooping expression, the least human of the seven, but had one eye cocked slightly open, as if the slumber were merely a pretence. Envy radiated spite and yearning, but was shown with a necklace of sovereigns and skin marked with the ravages of disease. Gluttony was huge, twice the size of the others, a great moon face with bulging cheeks and pig's eyes, food running out over the lower lip. Lust was finest of all, a beautiful female face, the mouth slightly open to reveal tiny, pointed fangs, twin horns protruding from among luxurious curls. I had always wanted to be her, at least to have her fearsome sexual aggression, something I imagined Foyle, and his audience, had feared the most.

Michael had never seen them before, and was fascinated, sketching the whole screen then each face individually. I watched, delighted, yet soon biting down a growing sense of pique as he maintained his indifference to my half-naked state. Yet to dress would have broken the moment, and I stayed that way, as if it were quite unimportant. Only when he finished the last page of his sketch book did he stop and turn to me, in doing so revealing his watch. It was ten minutes to four, far later than I had realised. At four o'clock I had to be at the community centre, urgently. He smiled, and reached out, to very gently run one finger up the curve of my breast to the nipple. I felt myself flush hot, and my mouth came open in reaction as instinctive as the sudden hardening of my nipples.

His smile grew a little broader, arrogant and certain as his fingers fanned out across my breast, each one flicking over the nipple. I stood still, letting him touch me, although I wanted to throw him to the floor, unleash his penis and feed him into me; to hold him down as I rode him, to make him beg for release, to punish him for treating me so casually and for being so damn cool. I didn't, but gently detached his hand from my breast, speaking as I did so.

'Sorry. I have to go. I mean, I'm late already, for something really important. Sorry.'

It sounded pathetic, the reaction of a scared and insecure virgin, but my excuse was genuine, for all I badly wanted sex with him. My protests didn't stop him either, and his voice was wonderfully gentle as he took me in his arms, his fingers going to the nape of my neck and the curve of my bottom. I pulled back, embarrassed and thoroughly cross with myself as I tried to explain.

'I'm sorry, not now, Michael. I mean ... I'd ... can we take a rain-check on this? I really do have to go.'

'Now? Really?'

There was just a touch of temper in his voice, no more than that, but it was there. I shrugged and kissed him, then made a dash for the vestry door, praying he wouldn't follow. If he did I would have given in and had him then and there. As it was he simply slipped a card behind the carved ear of St Peter. His voice followed me as I closed the door.

'Call round if you want to.'

I was really cursing as I struggled on a new top and substituted my boots for my rollerblades, angry, bitter and very cross with myself. It was not the mood I needed to be in. We had a new MP, Stephen Byrne, some up-and-coming junior minister determined to 'do his bit for the community'. Being a politician, and therefore both soulless and a busybody, he was not content to allow All Angels to continue its elegant decay. Instead he was proposing a scheme to bid for Lottery money to have it converted into a community hall, in which people would play bingo and watch big-screen football. It was unthinkable.

Unfortunately it was all too likely to become reality. He was just the sort of person to get it done, pushy, smarmy and above all self-righteous. I hadn't met him, yet, but I'd read enough, and seen his fatuous physog staring out from enough local papers. He was a clone, undoubtedly manufactured in a factory somewhere in the Midlands, handsome but as cold as a fish: grey-haired, grey-suited and grey-minded.

I wasn't at all sure what I could do, when I was sure to be a lone voice against the creeping blandness. Even the local anarchic types weren't likely to support me, not when I'd threatened to set Lilitu on so many of them. My only real hope was that there would be objections to the desecration of the interior because it was Grade Two listed, but the council were firmly on his side. It looked hopeless, and I even considered making a detour through the market to see if I could pick up a few rotten tomatoes. It would not have helped my cause.

My intention had been to spend a couple of hours on the roof to achieve real calm, then dress sensibly, or rather, dress as he would expect a sensible young woman to. At the hall I'd have done my best intellectual young student impression and put a clear and well thought-out case for the preservation of the rood screen, the pew ends, the panelling behind the altar and other fine details of Victorian Gothic carving. Thanks to Michael Merrick and my own capricious nature, I was now going to have to make my case as mad Goth girl on rollerblades, not an image a stuffy politician was likely to be impressed by.

The community centre was as bland as All Angels was glorious, a concrete box built where a string of bombs had taken out three terraced houses in a row, dull and unimaginative as Stephen Byrne's ideas, a temple to conformity and dumbing down. It was also only two streets away, but even with my blades on I managed to be late, pushing through the heavy double doors with my head full of determination, to find it very nearly empty.

Well, not that empty, but it was a big hall and the dozen or so people there looked pretty lost among the ranks of bright-red plastic chairs. Most were nondescript suits, local councillors or something, and they were milling around any old how. A group of three were together at the far end of the room. One had the look of a site manager or something, in a blue boiler suit with a big bunch of keys in one hand. The second was a smart young woman, looking somewhat offended. The third was Stephen Byrne.

I was either very late or very early, because I'd got

the time wrong, because Michael Merrick's watch had been wrong, because the meeting had been changed, whatever. It didn't matter. I was going to speak my mind anyway, even if a firm decision had been taken. Ignoring the caretaker and the woman who was presumably a secretary, I rolled straight up to Stephen Byrne. He fixed me with a bland smile, just as one blade slipped sideways on the polished floor, to put me in a whirl of arms and legs and hair, clutching madly at the air. Then I sat down hard on my bottom, right in front of him, legs splayed, skirt up, the crotch of my black silk knickers on show.

My face was burning as he helped me up, but I let him, feeling a complete idiot and very sorry for myself. I could see he was trying not to laugh as he stood back, and it was impossible not to smile in response. He mastered himself very quickly though, and as he did, so did I. When he spoke, it was with exactly the neutral, carefully controlled tone I had expected.

'Are you all right?'

'Fine. Thanks.'

I'd tried to sound cold and formal, but it had just come out as pitiable. It was not a good start, and worse for the unexpected effect the brief touch of surprisingly hard muscle beneath his suit had had on my already keyed-up nerves. I struggled to get a grip on myself anyway, remembering that was exactly what he was, a suit, and everything that went with it. As I met his eyes I realised that the effect of rollerblading all the way from the church in about a minute flat was beginning to tell on my mascara, but I spoke anyway.

'Have I missed the meeting about All Angels Church in Coburg Road, or has it been postponed?'

'Neither. This is it.'

'It is?'

'There is a core of people here, but yes, I had antici-
pated more interest.'

So had I. I looked around the half-empty hall. He
went on.

'You know who I am, I suspect?'

'Yes. Stephen Byrne MP. I wanted to talk to you
about the project for All Angels.'

'I would be delighted, of course. May I ask your
name?'

'Angela McKie.'

'Well, Angela, as you no doubt know, I am a strong
supporter of regeneration in the local community, with
a specific focus on those most in need. In the case of
All Angels, we intend to provide an important multi-
cultural, multi-able facility, something I'm sure you
appreciate as a young woman living in the borough,
and which...'

'No. I don't.'

'I'm sorry?'

'I don't. I don't appreciate what you're trying to do
with All Angels. It's all bollocks and you know it is. All
you want are votes, really, and to get them you're
prepared to sacrifice a unique interior, which is listed,
and to replace it with ... with this!'

I swung an arm out to take in the plain, square hall,
with its flat surfaces and right-angles, ranks of identi-
cal plastic chairs and stark fluorescent light. My intentions of remaining unemotional had given way in
seconds, far too weak for the feelings inside me. For a
moment he looked genuinely surprised, then he went
on, his tone no different than before.

'I see. As a young person I would have hoped for
your support in this matter, but yes, I can see that

17

there are valid objections from the perspective of architecture and heritage. Still, these are really matters we should be discussing as a group...'

He stopped. I'd leant forward to massage my ankle, which hurt from my fall, and it took me a moment to realise that when I'd snatched a top from my pile of clean washing I had made a bad choice. He could see right down the front. I straightened up quickly, blushing again and feeling a bigger idiot than at first. He had gone ever so slightly pink, but managed to carry on.

'Here, let me help you to a seat.'

I let him take my arm and steer me to a seat in the front row of the chairs set out in front of the stage. The efficient looking secretarial type had finished talking to the caretaker and was arranging notes on a lectern, which the other people there took as a cue, seating themselves in twos and threes in the first few rows of seats. Stephen Byrne took the stand and gave a brief but unctuous self-introduction before beginning on his speech.

It was complete bollocks-speak, full of phrases like 'maximisation of utility resource', 'holistic urban progress' and 'zero tolerance of the brown-field wastage cycle'. For a while they just let him speak, presumably either because they agreed with him or because they couldn't understand a word he was saying, but finally a man in a buff-coloured suit and a lilac tie managed to get a word in.

'Do you feel that the site is appropriate with respect to local transport infrastructure, particularly in consideration of differently abled access buses?'

They spoke the same language. Stephen Byrne considered a moment, consulted the efficient-looking woman, then answered.

'The intention is to take due consideration of the needs of all sectors of the community while prioritising those designated in the council's priority target consultation paper. Indeed, the scheme is designed around those specific prioritisation issues. However, as this is an area of high urban density we are obliged to optimise ...'

I'd had enough. I interrupted, struggling to exert whatever authority I could muster after more or less flashing him.

'No, you're not obliged to optimise, or prioritise, or anything! In ten years time it won't make any difference at all, much less a hundred. We'll all be dead, but All Angels would still be there. Can't you just leave it, for once!'

He began to speak again, some new piece of drivel, more meaningless even than before. I struggled to make sense of it, but before I could get a sensible answer together somebody else began and the discussion went off on a tangent. Twice more I attempted to put my objections across, and twice more he gave me a piece of spiel before neatly avoiding the real issue. The third time I tried somebody else spoke over me, and inevitably it was his question that got answered. I could see how they thought of me, as some pushy kid full of ideals that didn't work in the real world, their real world. I gave up at that, but determined to speak to Stephen Byrne alone after the meeting. Then at least I would have a chance to say my piece, even if it obviously wasn't going to do me any good at all.

For another half-hour they droned on, not one single

other person questioning the scheme from any but a practical viewpoint. When they finally did finish, the secretary tried to hustle him away, but I had already rolled up to the lectern and short of cutting me dead he had to acknowledge me. I got a bland smile from him, and the secretary was about to make an excuse when the caretaker tapped her on the shoulder. She turned and I had my moment.

'Look, can't you see that what you're doing is ... is just pointless. You can have your community hall anywhere, but All Angels is unique. Foyle's rood screen alone is worth more than a thousand faceless community centres, and the pew ends, and...'

'Nevertheless, we must consider these things in the light of modern community needs, particularly with respect to vulnerable minorities such as the differently abled. As I was saying earlier, the All Angels project allows us the possibility of installing state of the art accessibility...'

'Oh please! What, do you think you're going to make me feel guilty? If you want your "state of the art accessibility", build new, and you can do just as you like!'

'Unfortunately the prioritisation for brown-field sites does not allow for special projects. The ministry directive...'

'So you're going to tear the heart out of All Angels because of some here-today-gone-tomorrow government directive? Hang on, does "state of the art accessibility" mean you're going to tear the floor up? You are, aren't you?'

'Well, yes, but surely the floor is of no particular importance?'

'Of no importance? Don't you realise you'll be committing desecration? The first priest of All Angels, Father James O'Donnell ... he had his heart buried somewhere beneath that floor!'

'Er ... how unusual.'

'Yes, very unusual, unique even, like the rest of it, and you want to turn it into some soulless box. Isn't there anything I can say that will make you see common sense, just for once?'

He began to reply, another torrent of bollocks-speak, then caught himself. For a moment his eyes flicked to my chest, and lower, then back to my face. When he spoke again his tone was very different, more human.

'Well, I can see you feel very strongly on this issue, Angela.'

'I do.'

'In the circumstances then I'd be happy to talk it over in detail, at the very least explain the good points of the project. You can make your own points, and who knows, you might just convince me. Perhaps I could buy you dinner?'

He was making a move on me, and it took a moment for the sheer cheek of it to sink in. It was outrageous, but I had to go. More likely than not he was just going to string me along in the hope of getting into my pants, but two can play at that game.

'I'd love to, thank you.'

I gave him a little coy glance, sure that he would have an image of me as vulnerable, naïve and more than a little ditsy building up in his head. That was just how I wanted it, for the time being. Later on he would learn otherwise. I took the card he was offering me and gave him a shy smile as he helped me up from the chair.

'Write your number on the back.'

'I don't have a phone. I'll call.'

Rather than wait for the obvious question as to why I was the only person in the known universe, or East London anyway, not to have a mobile phone, I skated off, spinning as I reached the door. It was just fast enough to make my skirt lift and give him the briefest flash of stocking tops and sheer black knickers, and he was staring openly as I gave him a little wave, and left.

He thought he had me, or was going to, but I already had him, well and good. That was if I wanted him, but it was my choice, no question. It was impossible to keep the smile from my face as I skated back to All Angels, my mind full of the possibilities raised by the last few hours. It had been quite an afternoon. I'd shown two men my breasts, one intentionally, one not. Both were good looking even if one was a suit, and both wanted to see me again.

I could play it any way I wanted, have one, have both, have neither. Stephen I wasn't sure about. I liked the game, which had an edge of danger, but he was just about old enough to be my dad. Michael I wanted, if only to break his cool and have him begging me for release. If he was still at All Angels I was going to do it too, because I was right in the mood.

He wasn't; there was only Lilitu dozing in the shade of the sycamores, which made me more determined than ever. I'd run off, sure, but it was outrageous that he hadn't bothered to wait. The idea of him lurking among the tombs, crazed with lust, really appealed, but I knew he wasn't or Lilitu would have known. It was a nice idea anyway, and it stuck in my head as I went inside to take my blades off.

I could have come to him, cool and in control, just as he had been in the church. He would have lost his patience, deciding to masturbate over what might have been, in among the yews and sycamores behind the church, his cock thick and hard in his hand. I wouldn't have spoken, but watched from close by, as silent as the wraith he had seen in me when I posed. He'd have been aching with frustrated lust, his eyes closed, picturing me in his mind, naked for him. I would have come forward, to take him in my hand, quite silent, never speaking as I eased him down to the dank earth, my mind heavy with the touch of the souls around me, mounted him, slid him into me . . .

It was going to be me taking out my own frustrated lust on myself if I wasn't careful, and there was a wry smile on my face as I fixed sweet coffee and toast, the first thing I'd had since the morning. I had turned Michael on, obviously, for all his cool, and Stephen too. Both would be thinking of me, I was sure, imagining what might have been, and what might still be. Stephen's fantasies I was sure would be quite plain, straight sex with him on top, maybe a little bondage or something else mildly kinky. Michael had imagination, and would want something dark, maybe with me in restraint, or something ritual, even a little vampirism, inspired by the fanged image on the rood screen.

The thought of expressing myself as Isaac Foyle's lust to Michael was just too much. Foyle would be shocked, but I could commune later for atonement. For now I needed my head filled with thoughts of a live, hot-blooded man, and to come as he burned in my mind. By the time my coffee mug was empty I knew I had to do it. Nobody was going to catch me, not with Lilitu on guard, and I pulled my skirt up as I sank to the floor, kneeling, my knees wide apart, imagining myself on top of Michael, beneath the rood screen, about to feed him inside me. I lifted my top, freeing my breasts to the air, my necklaces suddenly cool against my skin, my nipples hard and sensitive as my fingers found them.

I closed my eyes as I began to masturbate, stroking myself as my mind wandered. We'd come so close to sex, maybe right there on the floor of the church, surrounded by the spirits of the dead as we fucked, joined together in life. Or we could have done it on a tomb, taunting one of the Victorian worthies buried within the church, their anger and lust and envy bringing us up to ecstasy. Michael would feel it, I was sure. He'd seen me as a wraith, an ethereal being, rising from death; he had to understand.

To come over the way he had seen me was what I truly needed, and I pictured myself, as I could have been, pulling out from the face of lust, to greet his fear with an insubstantial kiss. I'd grow firmer, feeding on his energy, my sharp little teeth on his skin, pricking it as I gained substance. He'd be lost, helpless in my arms, as we sank to the floor, his body beneath mine, me drawing up his power, preparing to draw out his seed also as I slipped his penis free and into my now substantial body.

My panties came aside and I pushed my fingers into myself easily, imagining them as his cock. They went to my mouth, and back, the fantasy now burning in my head. It felt good, wonderful, just right for me, mounted on him, the salt taste of his skin in my mouth, him inside me, me draining him. I began to rub harder, squirming my hips against my hand, wishing he was really inside me, his body given over to my pleasure completely, mine to take.

I came, my body tightening as I cried out in ecstasy,

and at the last moment it wasn't Michael Merrick in my head, but Stephen Byrne beneath me, terrified yet utterly enraptured as I fed on his neck and drew his come into my body.

2

Two men, and very different. The question was, which first? Michael fascinated me, but he seemed the type to lose interest if I was too eager. With Stephen it was all a bit embarrassing because he was so much older, but there was no use denying my own interest, not after the way he had popped into my head just as I was enjoying my orgasm. Stephen's plans for All Angels decided me.

I called him on the Tuesday and fixed a date for the Friday night. By then I'd spent an hour in an Internet café and I knew a lot more about him. There were no surprises. He was married, as I'd suspected, to the daughter of one of the fat cats in his first constituency, who seemed to be a right bitch. She was high up in a food chemicals company for one thing and, to me, that alone made him fair game. There were no kids, and he lived in a fancy house in Suffolk.

As I dressed I kept having to remind myself that my real aim was to change his ideas about All Angels, but that was no reason not to look good, just the opposite. I change my look for nobody, but I wanted to make the best of the naïve image I'd already established, albeit by accident. I went for patterned tights, a thong, a dress so short and loose that the least breath of wind or 'careless' movement would give him a peep-show, no bra, heeled boots and a collar. As usual, I was dressed in all black, set off with my silver and tourmalines. I even toned down my make-up a little, more gravy and less graveyard.

He picked me up in a fuck-off big Jaguar, very new and very black. From the outset there wasn't much effort at pretending it was a business meeting. He was dressed casually for a start, the neck of his shirt open under a roll-necked jumper and cream-coloured trousers tight enough to hint at a not unimpressive bulge at the crotch. Nor was he talking political rhetoric as he had before, but normal, easy chat with the odd carefully dropped hint to show how wealthy and important he was. I soaked it up, playing the awed little girl as we picked our way through North London and onto the motorway. After slipping a CD in the sound system he put his foot down, picking up speed to just under a hundred miles per hour with the Rolling Stones on loud. It was mature yet cool, and just guaranteed to overwhelm silly little me.

The place he'd chosen was miles from anywhere, by the roadside beyond Aylesbury, and presumably selected because there was no chance of him being recognised. Again, it was not the choice of a man wanting to have a serious discussion on a heavy issue, but just right for an experienced lothario out to seduce a woman half his age. That was his intention, no question. He took my arm as we went inside and selected a table in an alcove. Before we'd even got our drinks he had taken my hand under the pretence of admiring my rings, and by the time we'd finished our starters his hand was on my knee beneath the table. I couldn't just let him seduce me, that would have been too easy, so I gently detached his fingers from my thigh and put the question.

'So, what about All Angels?'

'All Angels? Oh, don't worry about that.'

'I do worry. I don't want it ruined – no, desecrated – because that's what you're doing, even if it isn't used as a place of worship any more. And besides . . .'

He laughed and I stopped, right on the edge of pointing out that attempting to seduce young Goth chicks was not going to help either his marriage or his career.

'What's so funny?'

'You. You're so earnest. It isn't going to happen, not in a million years. All Angels is Grade Two listed, and English Heritage have vetoed any attempt to alter the interior, unless it's a complete restoration. Nobody can afford that, so I expect it'll stay as it is.'

'So why all the bollocks? Votes?'

'Yes, mainly. Prestige within the party as well, but yes, mainly votes. That's why the project is designed principally for pensioners. Do you know what the percentage of voters over sixty is in my constituency?'

'No.'

'Thirty-one, and they are more likely to vote than any other age group. That's just the start. There are a lot of new people moving into the area, and I need to keep my profile up. The longer I can keep the All Angels business going, the better, just so long as I can be seen to be supporting local residents. I don't want it to actually happen – that way I lose out on months of good publicity.'

'Oh.'

I was cross, suddenly, not with his answer, but at the realisation that he was telling the truth, and that I'd worked myself up over what was to him a tiny move in a big game. He smiled, with more than a touch of condescension.

'So don't worry about your precious church.'

'Right. Thanks, I suppose. Isn't that a bit cynical?'

He shrugged. I decided to press the point.

'What about your ideals?'

'Ideals? Ha! I used to have ideals, yes.'

He paused to dab his mouth with a serviette, then went on.

'I was going to change the world, or at least the country, make it a better place for everybody, get rid of the old class system once and for all, make for a genuine meritocracy. Before the end of my first year at uni I was toeing the party line with the rest of the hacks. Idealists don't get on. But never mind all that. Who wants to talk politics? Tell me a bit more about yourself.'

I didn't really want to, and I was feeling small and not a little stupid, so I just smiled and shrugged. By good fortune the waiter chose that moment to arrive with our main courses, and I buried myself in steak with peppercorn sauce to avoid conversation. He did the same, and my feelings slowly came around as we ate, from chagrin to a really urgent need to somehow get the upper hand on him.

My chance came sooner than I had expected. He was trying to get me drunk, surprise, surprise, and had ordered some fancy gin cocktails when we came in. I hate gin and had hardly touched mine, but he'd drunk his and ordered a bottle of strong red wine with our food. He kept wanting to top my glass up but I was just sipping, and he didn't have the patience to leave his. By the time we'd finished he had drunk almost the entire bottle and was starting to go pink in the face. He also had his hand well up my skirt, tickling my thigh just an inch from my pussy. One knuckle brushed the crotch of my panties and I gave a little involuntary shiver. I pulled back, but he'd seen, and he knew. Once more I got the little condescending smile, then his open move.

'Pudding? Coffee? Or perhaps back to London for a nightcap at my flat?'

I had to take charge.

'Not pudding, no, I couldn't eat another thing. You could eat something though, only not at your place, but at mine.'

I winked. It took a moment for what I'd said to sink in, and then he went pink, which was well satisfying. Recovering himself he turned to signal a waiter for the bill even as he pulled his car keys from his pocket, then tried to give as good as he'd got.

'Great, but you're to eat too. Fair's fair. Where do you live?'

'Don't worry, I'll drive.'

'You? Drive? That's not really . . .'

'Yes it is. You're drunk, and MPs can't do that sort of thing. I'm driving.'

'But . . .'

'I've passed my test, don't worry.'

'Yes, but, the insurance . . .'

'Live a little, will you? I won't speed and I won't hit anything, promise. Then, afterwards, you can have a nice leisurely coffee and head back as late as you like, or in the morning if you prefer.'

I gave him another wink. He swallowed and nodded, reduced from wicked seducer to quivering jelly in seconds. I reached out to take the keys from his limp fingers. He let me, and I went outside as he settled the bill. I hadn't lied. I had passed my test, at seventeen, first time of asking. OK, so that had been in a Ford

Fiesta and I hadn't driven since, but how hard could it be?

It wasn't hard at all, it was wonderful. By the time he came out I had more or less figured out the controls, successfully turning the lights on and only managed to spray water over the windscreen once. He began to give me instructions the moment he got in, but I ignored him, pulling out onto the road and putting my foot down. I was doing seventy in a few seconds, and revelling in the sheer power at my disposal, also the fact that he was clutching the seat with both hands while desperately trying to act nonchalant.

All it needed was the right music, but his 70s rock at least had pace, and helped keep me on a high all the way back to London. Getting down to the East End was less fun, and even more terrifying for him, but I made it without incident and parked the car outside the gate to All Angels graveyard. I seated myself on the bonnet, twirling the keys around one finger as he got out, looking none too happy, also puzzled. I was ripe for mischief, feeling alive and in control, in my element and well out of his. He looked around, more than a little uneasy.

'Angela, where are you taking me? I thought we were going to have coffee at your flat. Why are we stopping here, at the cemetery?'

'Surely you like a frisson of danger, Stephen? It's the thought of the dead all around me that really makes me come alive. What could be more vital than being among those who've gone before, knowing we have this one brief moment, for lust?'

I took him by the neck of his jumper, pulling him in as I trailed off, to kiss him hard on the mouth. For a moment he resisted, his eyes flicking up and down the empty street, but his instincts quickly took over, his mouth opening under mine as he took me into his arms, one hand cupping my bottom. I wriggled away and broke the kiss, laughing as I pulled him after me, towards the gate. He gave a last wistful look at his car and followed, between the high pillars with their stone griffins staring down at us and into the dimness of the yew alley beyond.

His lust got the better of him as the darkness closed around us, his hand cupping on my bottom to pull me close. I let him grope, and kiss me again, but steered him firmly on, pushing between two thick yews to where Eliza Dobson's tomb lay completely screened from the road. His face showed for a moment, dull orange in the faint glow of a far-away streetlight, then disappeared as I pushed him back against the hard stone of the tomb. I caught his voice as I fumbled for his crotch.

'Angela! Not here, not on somebody's ... ah ...'

The sigh came as my hand closed on the bulge in his trousers. He was as big as I'd hoped, and hard, his cock a rigid bar beneath the material of his trousers, straining to be let free. As I began to squeeze him he gave in, allowing me to push him over on the flat stone surface, to ease his zip down, to pull his erection free as I began to feel the outrage of the mad old bat on whose tomb we were about to have sex.

I climbed on, mounting him, his cock now hard against the crotch of my tights, pressed right on my hot spot. All I needed to do was rub and I would come, then and there, but that was not enough. I rode him, making him moan deep in his throat as I wriggled my pussy and bottom against him, feeling the fleshy bulk of his cock and balls and thinking how it was going to feel inside me. His hands came up to touch my breasts through my dress, feeling their shape and then tugging urgently at the material to get me bare. I obliged, peeling it up and off, to leave myself naked from the waist up but for my jewellery, a near naked succubus ready to take her victim into her body.

His hands found my chest again and I let him feel, lifting my arms onto my head to raise my breasts, flaunting myself, with my upper body outlined in the orange light. Fingers found my nipples, eager and trembling as he explored me, stroking and pinching as I squirmed my bottom onto his lap. I was not far from orgasm, then it hit me, suddenly, and I was arching my back and crying out in ecstasy, my clit pressed hard to his rigid shaft through panties and tights. He let me do it, squeezing my breasts as I rode him to ecstasy, wriggling on his cock, bare and wanton and free.

I went forward as the glorious peak began to fade, on top of him, wanting to be held and stroked as I came down. He was urgent, too urgent to care for my needs, his hands going not to my back but to my bottom, to pull my cheeks wide even as his cock prodded at my crotch, his fingers digging into the mesh of my tights. I managed a protest, but too late as the seat of my tights was torn wide and my thong pulled roughly from between my cheeks, baring my bottom fully to the cool night air.

He went in, easing himself up into my body with a long sigh and still gripping my bottom as he began to buck underneath me. I tried to lift up, still dizzy with my orgasm, but wanting to ride him. He wouldn't let me, holding me firmly with my bottom spread to the night and grunting as he jerked into me, faster and faster, only to stop suddenly. I thought he'd come, but a moment later he was lifting me off and swinging me down from the tomb, his erection wet with my juices and still rock hard against my belly.

I let him turn me, too high to fight, down across Eliza's tomb, bottom up. His fingers fumbled at the ruins of my tights, tearing them wide to leave the whole of my bottom sticking out from the hole in the back, whipping my thong smartly down and once more pushing himself up inside me. I took a firm grip of the far side of the tomb as he began to fuck me once more. Now it was me who surrendered, bent near-naked over the cool stone of a grave, my tights ruined to expose me for rear entry, my nipples rubbing on the engraved letters in the lid, Eliza's hymn to the virtue of chastity.

Stephen grunted, and came, pulling himself free at the last instant to spray hot come over my bottom and back, then settling it between my spread bottom cheeks to finish himself off. I stayed down, letting him enjoy my bum and feeling a little used, but impossibly horny, too much to resent what he was doing. All I could manage was a weak protest.

'Pig.'

He chuckled.

'Now for that pudding.'

For one instant I didn't realise what he meant, and then he was down behind me, his face to my bottom, licking me from behind. My mouth came open in shock, and pleasure too. He was licking my pussy, just after he'd come, something so few men will do, and from behind, something dirtier, more abandoned that I would have believed him capable of. Not that I was going to stop him, and I gave my bottom an encouraging wiggle to make sure he didn't stop.

His reaction was to burrow his tongue deep up my

pussy. I closed my eyes, relaxing, sure he would take me where I wanted to go without having to be told. He put his hands to my bottom cheeks, fondling and squeezing as his licking grew firmer, and firmer still. I slid my feet apart and lifted my chest a little, taking my breasts in hand, to stroke my nipples. I was going to come, and soon, licked to ecstasy over Eliza Dobson's tomb, on which I'd fucked.

I could sense her ghost screaming disapproval of my naked body, of the sacrilege I had committed, but most of all of the joy I took in everything she had fought so hard to repress. It was good, dark and dirty at the same time, just like what Stephen was doing to me, his tongue now on my clit, licking hard, the tip flicking over my taut bud, faster and faster. A thumb slid into my pussy, a fingertip began to tickle my bottom hole and my muscles were contracting, my orgasm rising up, and bursting in my head and sex.

As I came I screamed out loud. He kept on licking and teasing, to give me a wonderful long orgasm, pure bliss as I held the image of my naked body over the tomb with him kneeling behind me. Only when I at last went limp did he stop and pull back. I stayed where I was, quite content to be spread so blatantly in front of him after what he had given me. He gave my bum a slap as he stood up, hard enough to make me squeak and bring me out of my daze. I put a hand back to the sore spot as I pulled myself up. He laughed.

'You are well dirty, Mr Byrne.'

'Well, that makes two, Miss McKie. Now I really am going to drive you back, I insist, and I could do with that coffee.'

'You don't have to. I live here.'

3

I didn't sleep with Stephen Byrne in the end. He left in the early hours of the morning after several strong coffees and another bout of sex. It was a lot more conventional, not as much fun, but still good, and he didn't seem to be able to get enough of my bottom. Again he let me go on top first and come first, but in return insisted on me kneeling for him and going doggy. We kissed as he left, and he made me promise to call, leaving me to go to bed feeling well pleased with myself. The sex had been good, much better than I'd expected, I hadn't had to compromise my principles by threatening him, and the church looked like being safe.

His behaviour showed just how wrong it was possible to be about a man. I'd initially imagined him as cold and grey, then as conventional. To find that he was obsessed with girls' bottoms came as no great surprise, but I was taken aback by just how rude he'd been. I was going to be back for more, but I had no illusions whatever about him. What he wanted was a convenient Mistress on tap for sex. That was fine, but he was married and I wasn't going to start getting guilty about seeing other men, especially Michael Merrick. Call me a slut, but I don't get hung up on this 'finding the single perfect partner' bullshit. I like sex, and anyone who can't handle that knows where they can stick it.

I took the weekend easy. Having suffered the threat of All Angels being developed, it had become more special to me than ever, every stone, every carving, every piece of glass. The graves too, and I began to catalogue them in a lazy way, and the effect each had on my emotions, starting with Eliza Dobson. I thought about Michael Merrick too, but I was determined not to seem over-eager and didn't phone. Instead I skated round to his address on the Monday, as if I'd just been passing.

It was in a big warehouse conversion down by the docks, all old red brick and new plastic. I took off my blades in the doorway and buzzed for him. He let the catch off without bothering to ask who it was, and when I got up to his floor I found the door a touch open. I pushed in to a big, airy flat, one big room with an elevated section at the far end and a tiny bathroom and kitchen at either side of the door. A huge drawing desk occupied the long wall, with shelves, cabinets and a great litter of paper around it. On the far side was a moth-eaten settee, a stack stereo, chairs and a table under slanting windows let into the roof. There were also books, hundreds of them, some on shelves, more piled any old how on the floor. He was standing by the desk, unshaven in a black silk dressing-gown looking at a piece of artwork with an expression of brooding dissatisfaction. As the door clicked shut behind me he turned.

'What do you think?'

That was it. No greeting, no offer of a coffee, no remark on the dark, spiritual look I had spent two hours getting right. I bit down a trace of irritation as I dumped my skates on the settee and crossed to stand beside him. He continued to stare at the paper, which showed a creature half-way between a pelican and a pterodactyl apparently in earnest conversation with a man in a bizarre multi-tiered hat. It was beautifully drawn, but I had no idea what it was about and couldn't think of anything to say beyond simple flattery. He saved me the trouble.

'Fantasy art, for a calendar. Not really my thing but it sells well. When nobody had heard of me I used to try everything I could, and nine times out of ten I'd be rejected. Now I get people asking for all sorts of stuff, album covers, portraits, even adverts.'

'You don't have to accept them.'

'I don't. Not all the time, but it's hard to turn the money down.'

'I bet. This place must cost a packet.'

He shrugged.

'It has a good north light, and it's quiet. Not very inspiring though, not like All Angels. Coffee?'

'Sure. Black, two sugars.'

He nodded and moved off towards the kitchen, leaving me to look around. I'd been expecting a sort of shrine to Gothicism, black witchcraft, diabolism and all the other things he expressed so well in his drawings. Instead it was very much a work space, simple and functional. It was in his pictures that his personality and imagination were expressed, and stared from every wall. I went to look, first admiring the haunting beauty he'd projected into a picture of a black-skinned demoness crouching naked among twisted and thorny roses. Next to it was a landscape that could just have been real, with the crumbling ruins of a monastery rising above a valley shrouded in mist, the tendrils of which hinted at ghostly shapes. I was still admiring it when he came out with the coffee.

'The cover for my graphic novel version of *Nightmare Abbey*.'

'Neat. I'm not surprised you get plenty of work.'

I took a coffee and went to sit on the settee, curling my legs up to leave enough thigh bare to pique his interest, hopefully. Not that I was up for anything then and there, but his offhand attitude got me, making me determined to get his attention. He simply went back to studying the fantasy art piece, sipping his coffee with the same brooding expression as before. It was a very different reaction to Stephen Byrne's openly lecherous approach, and I found myself wondering if he had taken my rejection to heart. More likely he was just an egotist. After maybe five minutes of complete silence I broke into his reverie.

'So how's the Goat of Mendes going?'

'Fair. I just wish I could put more into it.'

'How do you mean?'

'I'm contracted to twenty episodes, each one a double-page spread, so I can only do so much in the way of plot.'

'Oh, right. So you can't just do as you like?'

'Not entirely. I can do what I like, write what I like, but that only goes so far. It still has to be a certain length and a certain format, and there are subjects I can't touch. That means I have to keep it simple.'

'So how does it go?'

'I haven't worked out all the details yet, but essentially the modern cabal believes that the Regency one were in possession of important knowledge and are trying to summon their spirits. What they don't know is that the leader of the Regency cabal, who styles himself the Goat of Mendes, was in fact an incarnation of the Devil. As I said, it's primarily a vehicle for visual effect. I open with the modern cabal meeting, a ritual, then the group drinking and talking afterwards, that's to ground it, bring the unreal closer to what's real for the reader.'

'What's the ritual?'

'I'm not certain. I thought a sacrifice, but I've done that several times. Besides, you get complaints. One time I did this scene with a black cockerel being sacrificed in an attempt to summon Satan. The editor got 47 letters of complaint about cruelty to animals. Fortyseven! Daft really, 'cause it's only a drawing, and in the same story I had a military type eaten by a demon. Nobody complained about that, not one.'

I laughed and arranged myself more comfortably on the settee, more languidly too.

'So not a sacrifice, what then? How about some exotic sex ritual?'

'No deflowering virgins. It says so in the guidelines.'

'How about male virgins?'

His morose expression vanished and he gave me a big smile.

'Now that's a thought! Different anyway. PC in a way, but still with some shock value. Hey, I think you've hit on it, and that way I can have a great closing spread. I'll make the leader of the modern cabal a Priestess, not a Priest, and finish with her having sex with the Devil while the rest of them cower back in terror. Great!'

Suddenly he was all energy, taking a moment to put the drawing he'd been working on carefully between two boards and fixing a new piece of paper into place. I watched, pleased to have him react so well to my input, but still feeling a touch short of attention. With Michael it was plain that his art came first.

He began by sketching out a faint grid, then adding figures. They were just in outline, vague, asexual things without faces. They grew quickly, bony hands, faces shadowed by hoods, the sharp contrast of candlelight, a set of scenes both forceful and disturbing as the sinister cabalists prepared a louche young man for his fate. It was wonderfully done too, and satisfying. The virgin was a drunken stag expecting sex with the beautiful, poised priestess, allowing himself to be stripped, spread on the altar and teased to erection. His face was set in idiot, drink-sodden lust right up to the moment she penetrated his anus with the monstrous dildo she'd had concealed beneath her robes. It was pretty graphic, much more so than I'd expected, and he was taking such relish in the detail I began to wonder if he was gay, or rather, bisexual. I also couldn't help but wonder which magazine he expected it to be published in. I held back the question until Michael was actually drawing in the hapless young man's straining bottom hole.

'Are they going to let you get away with that?'

'No. The one I send in will have convenient bits of shadow, hands, edges of robes, just enough to make it clear what's happening without risking an accusation of obscenity. The full version I'll have published in Belgium. Do you know about *bandes dessinées?*'

'No.'

He stepped a little to the side, reached up to a shelf for a handful of magazines and tossed them to me. I picked up the top one as he went back to his work and my mouth came open in shock. Right on the first page a beautiful girl in old-fashioned costume was having sex with two men, one from behind and one, a coachman, in her mouth. No detail had been spared, and it got worse, or better. There were orgies, lesbian and gay sex, scenes of flagellation and bondage, even a seriously weird one with a girl making love to an octopus. I could only stare, my emotions flicking between shock and arousal, disgust and delight. Some of the images were pretty gross, but I could not stop myself from turning the pages, every one, until I was left feeling seriously flustered and seriously horny.

Michael had kept working all the time I was reading, barely sparing me a glance. I wondered if he'd given me the cartoons on purpose, to turn me on, but his attitude was no different from before. The drawing had evolved though, with the seduction and buggery of the young man now in full detail, as dramatic and sexual as anything I'd just seen and considerably better drawn than most of it. He'd even managed to capture the mixture of shame and helpless ecstasy on the man's face as he came, his erect penis in the priestess's hand even as she buggered him.

It was great, and it felt good that he could be so open in front of me, but I wanted his attention, and his cock. He went on working, oblivious to me and to my feelings. I was just going to have to take him in hand, literally. He was a tempting target too. His buttocks looked firm and tight beneath the thin black silk of his robe, and while it was tied at the front I could see that it would be so, so easy to slip a hand in, to take hold of him, to tease him slowly erect.

He turned around just as I was swinging my feet off the settee.

'Would you like to model? I know I used you for the cover picture, but your face would be great for my priestess.'

'Yeah, sure.'

It came out in a croak, my plans for seduction abruptly cut off. I should have carried on, of course, offering to model for him even as I began to caress him, but the question was just too sudden. Besides, if the last occasion I had posed for him was anything to go by, the outcome would be the same. This time I had all day.

In the last few pictures the priestess had her robe open, displaying not just her breasts and belly, but the elaborate system of leather straps that held her dildo in place. It was an invitation if ever there was one, and I wasn't entirely joking as I made my suggestion.

'I suppose you've got a cowled robe and one of those strap-on things?'

'Not a strap-on, no. You'll find a robe in the third drawer down, next to my bed.'

He wasn't joking at all. I went up the stairs, wondering just exactly why he kept a cowled robe in his bedside drawer. Possibly it was just a prop, because they featured in a good many of his drawings, but then again . . .

It was black, and heavy cotton, also too big for me, the hem still spread out on the floor as I lifted it to shoulder level. He wasn't even looking as I began to undress, or not directly, but he turned me a glance and a smile as I peeled my dress off over my head. I didn't need to strip, but I was going to. It felt right. My stockings stayed, but my knickers came off, which made him lift one black eyebrow just a fraction as my pussy came bare. It felt good to get a reaction out of him, but I didn't show it, trotting down the stairs with the robe in my hand as if undressing in front of men I hardly knew was of no consequence whatsoever.

He was cool about it, inevitably, simply waiting

until I'd put the robe on and asking me to stand in a certain way. As he adjusted the front to make the folds of cotton hang the way he wanted his hand brushed my nipple, sending a little shock through me and bringing him to instant erection. If he noticed, he didn't give it away, simply finished what he was doing to leave me with the robe half-open at the front, the inner curves of my breasts, my belly and one thigh bare.

We were both near naked in a warm, drowsy atmosphere, no distractions, no reason why we shouldn't come together. It was going to happen, soon enough, maybe when he got to the point he couldn't hold his pencil steady anymore, maybe when my patience snapped and I pushed him to the ground and mounted myself on his straining erection.

Still he drew, his eyes flicking between me and the paper as the Priestess's face became mine in one picture, and a second. With the third he adjusted my robe, opening it across my breasts and belly, leaving my pussy bare and the scent of my arousal mixing with my perfume. I was trembling, little ripples moving down to between my legs as he again began to draw.

In the fourth drawing the woman whom was now my avatar had her hips pushed forward as she pressed the head of her dildo to the young man's. I was going to have to push my hips out just the same way, undoubtedly betraying the moistness of my sex. He would know I was available, physically, and surely mentally too, and if he didn't do something about it then I was going to, at any moment.

With picture three finished I opened my robe and pushed out my hips, not waiting to be asked. He had turned a little, and as he moved back his robe swayed, revealing his cock for just an instant, heavy and urgent over a pair of good-sized balls, just needing a touch to bring him to erection, my touch. Yet still he drew, cool and steady, only now I knew his indifference was a pretence. For nearly two hours I'd been slowly working myself up. I was ready and so was he.

'Look, Michael, are you going to fuck me, or do I have to fuck you?'

He turned, grinning, put his fingers to the belt of his robe and tugged. It came open, showing off his lean, smooth torso, the firm muscle of his thighs, and the bulk of cock and balls. I stepped forward, intent on mounting him, with my robe still on, a hooded Priestess taking her pleasure, naked beneath her robe. He needed just a touch of encouragement, no more, and I sank quickly down, to take hold of his beautiful big penis. My mouth was wide, then full, the taste of man filling my senses as I began to suck. Michael was swelling in my mouth, and pulling back suddenly at the sound of a key grating in the lock. He swore.

'Shit!'

I stood, instantly angry and at the same time embarrassed, searching desperately for what I was going to say to the girlfriend who was undoubtedly about to walk through the door. Only it wasn't a girlfriend, not a woman at all, but a man, as handsome as Michael, only blond, taller, a little more solid, with the same easy confidence in his face. He must have guessed what we'd been up to, because he was grinning the instant he saw me and there was laughter in his voice as he spoke.

'Don't mind me.'

He strolled into the kitchen, completely casual, in fact just as if he owned the place. I was sure there was no flatmate; the possibilities that Michael was gay, or at least bi, flicked through my head again before I realised the truth, at the same instant Michael confirmed it for me.

'My brother, Chris.'

'Oh, right. Does he normally just walk in like that?'

'He owns the flat.'

'Oh. But . . .'

'Yeah, I know, he's –'

He broke off with a gesture of irritation and went back to the drawing, now just filling in details of shadow. I was so horny that for a moment the idea of asking them if they'd like to share crossed my mind, only to be dismissed. For one thing I couldn't see it happening, and for another I'd felt a link with Michael the instant I'd seen him. Not with Chris.

It was only when Chris came out of the kitchen with an open beer in his hand that I realised I'd left the *bandes dessinées* magazines on the settee, with one open at the page showing the woman entangled with the octopus. I'd already been blushing, sure he'd guessed what had been going on, but my face grew hotter still as he picked it up, turned it sideways and then upside down, smirking all the while.

'Kinky! You ought to draw stuff like this, Mike. Aren't you going to introduce me then?'

Michael didn't answer for a moment, and he didn't look too pleased when he turned around.

'This is Dusk, she's modelling for me. Dusk, meet Chris.'

'Hi.'

'Hi, babe.'

He went back to reading the magazine, pausing only occasionally to take a sip of beer. Finally, Michael spoke up.

'Chris, I am trying to work here.'

'Yeah, sure, but there's this guy coming round to view the flat later.'

'You have to be joking!'

'You know the deal, Mike, and you're doing well now. You said so yourself. We better get some of your shit out of view and all.'

'Yeah, right.'

He put his pencil down, carefully, but I could sense his frustration as he began to tidy his work area. I was feeling the same, but there was nothing I could do and it felt silly just standing there. So I began to help, stacking the magazines and moving the chairs in an attempt to create some sort of order. In half an hour we'd succeeded, more or less. When Michael went into the kitchen Chris followed, and I was sure he was dropping a hint that I leave. I took it, dressing as best I could under my robe and making my excuses to them, only to have Michael quickly tag on. I was feeling pissed off as we went down in the lift, and in the street asked him straight out.

'So what's the deal with the flat?'

'Chris is in property, buying to let or sitting on places until he reckons he can get the best price. He's pretty generous, as it goes. I've been there two years, rent free, but he's getting a bit impatient with it.'

I nodded. It was a feeling I knew well, my own occupation of All Angels being more or less on sufferance. The difference was that if I lost it I'd be looking for squats. Technically I was already in one, but there are squats and there are squats. Feeling a bit more sympathetic, I took his arm. He accepted the gesture and began to steer me, not towards some conveniently lonely alley, which was where I needed to go in my belly if not in my head, but to a wine bar.

It was further down the dockside, a trendy new place built of polished wood and glass. Across the dock was a rank of cranes painted black, not functional, but a sort of industrial sculpture, really quite Gothic. He ordered a carafe of wine, and my irritation began to slip away as we sipped and chatted, the funny side of what had happened slowly coming to the front, and I found myself smiling.

'Lucky your brother didn't come in a few minutes later.'

'Lucky he didn't bring the clients in with him!'

'Nah, that way you get to hang onto your flat for longer.'

'Yeah, true. He reckons it's bad enough with my pictures on the walls. Apparently what really sells a place has nothing to do with practical things. According to Chris it's all down to ambience. He'll be making toast and coffee about now, to make it smell homely.'

'What could be more homely than a woman's pussy?'

For one tiny moment he actually looked shocked. I found myself smiling and blushing, embarrassed but pleased with myself at the same time. He was cool, but not that cool. There was no longer any need to act, at all.

'We could go back to All Angels?'

'Why not?'

He drained his glass and I did the same. We rose as one and left, arm in arm, all pretence gone. We were going back to All Angels and we were going to fuck, plain and simple. It was a good way, half an hour on skates, and I was in no mood for small talk.

'Have you ever had sex on a grave?'

'No, I haven't.'

'Well you're going to. I like to imagine the person's ghost watching me, maybe pleased, feeling that I'm honouring them, maybe angry at me, for committing sacrilege or for mocking them with my vitality.'

'What was the name of the tomb you were on when you came down for me, when we met?'

'Eliza Dobson. Yes, I have. Think how she'd rage, so angry yet so impotent, when in life she had all that power. I love to think of her, watching me bare, watching me enjoy a man's cock, watching me fuck, all the things she tried to suppress.'

'What if she appeared to you? Screaming at you, clawing at you with ghostly hands.'

For a moment I wondered if I should tell him, but decided it was better to keep it as fantasy, for the moment.

'Oh, yes please! I wish, I really do. I'd just fuck all the harder, put on a good rude show for her.'

'I really think you would.'

'Oh, I would, you'd better believe it.'

'That I have to draw. You in the throes of passion, underneath me . . .'

'No, on top, riding you with pride.'

'OK, as you like, naked.'

'No, not naked. Not stark naked, anyway. With some clothes on, a skirt and top maybe, but pulled up so that I'm hiding nothing.'

'Your knickers would be off though, maybe dangling from a piece of carving.'

'Perfect.'

'And her ghost rising from the tomb, maybe swirling up from under the lid . . .'

'... her face set in fury and shame and anguish ...'

'... her fine clothes decaying tatters ...'

'... her hands clawing at my body ...'

'... but only bringing you more pleasure.'

'Yes, and the wilder she got the more pleasure we'd take, feeding on her rage and spite, until we came, together. That would banish her, and soothe the souls of all her victims.'

'Her victims?'

'Oh, she used to do some horrid things, all in the name of propriety of course. The Victorians were like that.'

'Yes, I've read Acton. It always seemed so sordid, nothing to really get a grip on for a story. I like the way you see it though. You're an inspiration.'

'Just weird.'

'You're not weird.'

'Trying telling that to my parents, the other kids at school and my teachers.'

'OK, you're weird. So am I then.'

He laughed, and I grinned in response, feeling closer still. Like me he was an outsider. Like me he knew how it felt not to fit in and to refuse to try. Like me he had never gone under, and was now free from all the stifling social constraints we had to put up with. I wanted to talk, to tell him everything, and to know about him.

'You had a hard time as a kid?'

'More odd, but yes, hard at times. I'm not complaining, because without it I'd never have the richness of experience I rely on for my work.'

'Tell me.'

'Well, I'm adopted, for a start, which didn't help, but it was down to my mother, in the main. She's one of these people who is always searching for an answer and is never satisfied with what she gets. My grandparents are quite sane, but she caught religion in her teens, a bad case. I can't remember what it was when I was tiny, High Church Anglican I think, but I remember being converted to Roman Catholicism at about four, especially the candles, hundreds of them, burning in this huge church. Candlelight fascinates me, and I'm sure that's where it comes from.'

'I'm Catholic, or I was, and I know exactly what you mean about candles. I still go to confession sometimes, just for the atmosphere. Do you?'

'No. I'm not a Catholic any more, I haven't been for years, as such. I suppose I could be considered Christian, but only in the broadest sense. My mother changed her mind when I was maybe six. When we went to Scotland for a holiday she caught Calvinism. Suddenly nothing would do but we come to understand our basic wickedness, and all the candles and incense and stuff was so much popery and a sin in itself. I remember being made to feel dreadfully guilty for wanting to go into a church and light a candle to a great-uncle who had died, when just a couple of months before the same action would have earned the highest praise.'

'Confusing.'

'Just a bit. It happened again a couple of years later. I can't even remember what to, but it was another Low Church sect, and even more severe. Then there was a brief spell as Mormons, some American thing she saw on TV with lots of shouting and waving our arms about, and an evangelical group largely dedicated to harassing people on Sunday afternoons. The last lot had a particularly strong anti-sex message, remaining a virgin until marriage and all that shit. You can imagine how that went across with my hormones starting to kick in.'

'What about your dad, and Chris?'

'Dad was foreman at the local factory, and where home was concerned he'd do anything for a quiet life. My main memory of him from childhood is that he was always tired. Not mother, she never stopped, sampling different creeds as if they were brands of washing powder and never satisfied with the results. We couldn't just be part of the congregation either, she always had to try and take over the whole thing. Every time it happened it was always the great life-changing event, the crucial revelation that immediately had to be preached to the unenlightened, and of course everyone else in the family had to tag along. I've been anointed, dipped and dunked. I've been a choirboy, an altar boy, an acolyte, a supplicant, and several other things I can't remember, one of which involved kissing the toe of some seedy old sod's sandal.'

'You're lucky that's all you had to kiss. You rebelled, yeah?'

'Inevitably. It used to scramble my brains at first, but by the time I left school I had come to understand who I was, and my creed. School was another problem. It changed every time mother's religion changed. I kept myself sane by drawing, first mixing up all the imagery I was picking up, with pretty much the entire range of Christian myth at my disposal and some very peculiar ideas about priests, death and ritual. When I hit puberty I started to explore the dark side of it all, revelling in everything I was told was wrong, devils and sins expressed as anthropomorphic beings especially. I can't have been more than thirteen when I bought Isaac Foyle's biography. I loved horror comics too, and anything dirty of course, but as much because it was utterly forbidden as for the thrill. Mother used to burn them if she could find them, and I was for ever being sent to priests to discuss my "problem". It only made me keener.'

'Of course.'

'By the time I was seventeen Chris was doing well for himself – he's ten years older than me – and so I moved in with him and began to try my hand at professional art. Then there was the flat, and well, here I am. And you?'

He was being very open with me, and for once in my life I felt I could be equally open. For one thing his mother sounded worse than anything I had put up with, and I could guess that the casual way in which he had said it 'scrambled his brains' hid a lot of very real pain. It was a pain that had been echoed in myself.

'Where shall I start? Like you my mum's religious, and she had converted, but only once, to Catholicism. I suppose new converts always tend to be more zealous than those who're born to it, because that was a long time before I was born but it hadn't worn off. When I was little it seemed like we were always going to church – St George's on the Island?'

'I know it.'

'Yeah, it's a great church, but I hated it then, or at least I hated the services. It was so boring, and I'd spend my time staring at the architecture and making up little stories about the gargoyles and angels and saints. The big stained glass of St George and the dragon behind the altar was my favourite. I always sided with the dragon, and wished he could have eaten stupid St George. I never really used to take in what the priests were saying until I was maybe nine or ten, and when I did it was terrifying. There was this dreadful place called Hell, where you got tortured for ever and ever unless you were good. It wasn't just good, either, but very, very good, far better than I could ever be. I used to get terrible nightmares, imagining myself spitted on a pitchfork for pinching biscuits from the cupboard, or tossed into a lake of boiling blood for pulling another girl's hair at school.'

'Oh, Hell's not all bad, it just gets a bad press. You hadn't been reading Dante, I don't suppose?'

'Yes. That was another problem, I used to read too much. I've read the Bible from cover to cover, and there's some pretty heavy stuff there . . .'

'. . . stoned to death, burnt to death . . .'

'. . . "their blood put on their own heads", I never did understand that one, but it conjures up a gruesome picture.'

'I've drawn it.'

'That I must see. I didn't understand most of it, it just sounded awful. So I began to read other texts in the hope of it all becoming clearer, but it didn't. Mum thought it great that I was so keen, and I was always top in Bible study, but they didn't know what was going through my head. Then there was confession, but I could never understand why if you could be forgiven your sins so easily you shouldn't do them. As I got older and sex started to get involved it got worse. I wanted to do all these dreadful things, and I knew that the thought was as bad as the deed, so I did it anyway, and when I confessed one time I caught the priest tossing himself off . . .'

Michael burst out laughing, a full-blooded roar of

delight. I shrugged and smiled, blushing slightly and well pleased with his reaction.

'That was my defining moment. I realised it was all bullshit and hypocrisy, just crap designed to keep the proles down, even when the priests believe it themselves. I rejected the church, but I felt I needed something to replace it, some abstract temple in which I could be honest with myself. For instance, I felt that as a woman I should be able to acknowledge the Mother openly, not behind a veil of pretence the way the Catholics do. I realised I'd always been clawing at the temple door, but from that moment I was within. I still believe in God, or at least the idea of deity, but nobody is going to make me believe that lot speak for him. Besides, there are so many different religions, all claiming to be the only one with the real truth, and they can't all be right.'

'My thoughts exactly, but deity? Why worship a deity, God, or the Mother, or even Satan, if they provide nothing tangible in return? How can you even be sure they exist?'

'There must be some sort of spiritual force, surely? Haven't you ever felt the change in atmosphere when you go into a church or a graveyard, or even into an old house, on a battlefield perhaps. The first time I went to Northern France, on a school trip, I kept getting these sensations of melancholy and fear, so strong I was shaking. Nobody else seemed to feel it, and I swear I'd never heard of Armentieres. There has to be something ... No, there is something. You can feel it if your mind is open enough. Maybe some day I'll show you.'

We continued to talk as we walked through the East End, along streets Michael seemed to know better than

I did. Sometimes it was deep, sometimes shallow, usually strange and frequently dirty. By the time we got near All Angels we had stopped several times to kiss. In one alley Michael slid his hand into the front of my panties, only for a door to open unexpectedly just feet away from us. We ran off laughing, leaving me more ready than ever.

I heard Lilitu barking before we could see the church. It was her angry bark, and gave me an instant stab of apprehension. I ran forward, Michael following, reaching the gates just as a pair of kids carrying spray cans burst out. They fled, and no surprise, with Lilitu right behind them, her teeth bared and her chest and neck brilliant red. For one moment I thought she'd got one of them, or worse, that she was hurt, before I realised it was spray paint.

That was the end of my plans for sex with Michael. We had to find something to clean her fur safely, then do it, which took ages. The incident had completely spoiled the erotic high I'd been on, and while we might eventually have got around to it, the moment was gone and it could never have been so good. He was also keen to get back and find out if his flat had been sold from under his feet. I didn't complain. I was to be his model, and there would be a next time.

4

I'd put myself in a fine position, not for the first time. There's that old joke about men being like buses, none for ages and then they all turn up at once. It certainly seems to be true for me, because there had been nobody significant in my life for months and then both Michael and Stephen had appeared on the same day.

The sensible thing to do would have been to gently but firmly dispose of Stephen and concentrate on Michael. It was the obvious choice, and what every friend, agony aunt and busybody would have told me to do. Michael was single, more or less my age, unattached and shared a great deal with me. Stephen was old enough to be my father, married and we had very little in common.

It was not that simple. Stephen and I had fucked, and it had been good. I'd really enjoyed my feeling of power and his uncertainty as I'd pulled him into the graveyard and mounted him on Eliza Dobson's grave. He licked me too, well. I had also promised to be in touch, with the implication of more sex to come, and I knew that I wanted it.

Michael and I hadn't fucked, but from what we had done he seemed less mature in his outlook, which was hardly surprising, but almost more needful of being in control, and I do like to call the shots. Bossy or not, he shared my fantasies, and it was great to imagine the sort of ritualised sex we might get into. I'd done it with other men, fucking on tombs, in churches and once in a pentacle with black candles burning at each point, but it had always been to oblige my desires rather than to share them. It had been the same with Stephen, but with Michael it would be mutual, and so much stronger for that.

Had Michael laid any claim to me it might have been different, or not, because I hate the idea of being any man's 'girl' and exclusive to him. He hadn't, though, and he seemed pretty liberal, especially the way he'd jumped at my suggestion of a male virgin getting one up the bum from a priestess. Most straight men get pretty hung up about that sort of thing, getting it up the bum that is, not sex with priestesses. Then again, I wasn't sure he was one hundred per cent straight, something I also found exciting.

In the end I promised myself I wouldn't ring Stephen and that if he didn't come around that would be the end of it. It was an easy option, a bit of a cop out maybe, but the only decision I knew I could stick to. Michael was off to Brussels to see a *bandes dessinées* publisher for the rest of the week, but I was going to be modelling for him on the Sunday. Both of us knew what was likely to happen, and I also knew it might make a difference to my attitude to Stephen.

I spent most of Tuesday in the graveyard scrubbing graffiti off. Even with Lilitu around it had proved impossible to stop it all, although it was nothing to what it had been when I arrived. Most had given up, but I was sure that at least two of the local writers had decided it was a challenge. Either that or they were trying to provoke me personally. One signed himself 'Biggy', the other 'Snaz', which might just have been female. Girls are rare in the graff scene, most of those who do associate sticking to hip hop and other things that don't get you arrested. Biggy went in for purples and blues with a lot of fades and a silver base. Snaz preferred clashing electric blue, vivid pinks, a particular acid green and a scarlet lip motif. Both were equally skilled and an equal nuisance. I wasn't even sure which they were, or even if there really were two rather than one, because the pieces and tags always appeared when I was taking Lilitu for a walk. It had occurred to me they might live close by, close enough to watch my comings and goings, which was a little scary.

The two Lilitu had scared away were much clumsier, and had managed only the outline for two letters, Z and U, before she arrived. They had also painted the little metal flag on Major Inkerman Goodwell semaphore red, which I left, and made a few random scrawls elsewhere, which I cleaned off. Snaz had done a big piece on the rear wall which I hadn't noticed as well, and by the time I had finished I was hot and sticky, thirsty too.

I went inside for a drink and a wash, stripping out of my sweaty dungarees and climbing into the big sink to splash water over my face and body. It had been a lot of work, and I smelt of meths and paint. My mind was dwelling on ways of getting rid of Biggy and Snaz, but while I was pissed off with them it was hard to feel resentful. I'd done my share of tagging, as a kid and when I'd wanted to assert my identity as the dark and mysterious Dusk instead of plain old Angela.

Dusk had been my tag, done in black lettering as if from a medieval scroll, sometimes as a dub with a gold or silver fill. Twice I'd made it a piece, or tried to – one huge one beside a railway in black shading to deep purple with highlights of silver and dull dark green, and the other one a red and black Gothic script with deaths heads over the 'u'. I'd always been a loner, and never got that into it because everybody seemed to hate each other. The local bombing crew had held me down and tagged 'TOY' across my chest, but with my usual defiance it had only made me worse. In the end I'd earned their respect by putting my piece halfway up the sheer glass face of a twenty-storey office block. I was working for the firm who did the window cleaning, but they didn't know. About that time I'd begun to really understand myself, and as I'd moved more into my own peculiar blend of Gothicism and sex I had given up on the tagging.

So I knew how Biggy and Snaz worked, probably as a team with one keeping lookout while the other completed his piece. They could watch the cemetery gate and might even have mobiles to communicate my comings and goings, while it was no doubt possible to do the outer walls at night without disturbing Lilitu. So far they hadn't done anything inside the church, but to grow more daring is in the nature of tagging, so I was sure it was only a matter of time, and that the more I reacted to them the more determined they would get. Of course if Lilitu got one then they'd stop it, but that would lead to all sorts of trouble.

My thoughts were interrupted while I was drying myself, first by a deep growl from Lilitu, then by a knock on the vestry door. The writers were hardly going to knock for me, so I called out and was answered by a familiar voice, Stephen Byrne. I shouted for him to wait and began to dress, hurrying on my panties and dress, then slowing down. He had an image of me in his head and I wanted to keep it that way.

Stockings, boots, hair, make-up, jewellery and perfume and I was ready in a shade over half an hour, not bad for me. Lilitu had come in from the church to see what was going on, and I took a firm grip on her collar as I opened the door. Stephen was reading the inscription on Nathaniel Hawkins's stone, very smart in his suit and tie. He smiled as he saw me, flicked a worried look at Lilitu and spoke.

'What a beautiful dog. Um ... I managed to get off early today, cancelled meeting, and I thought you might like to come out for the evening?'

'Sure.'

There was no hesitation. I'd promised myself I wouldn't call him and I hadn't, but that I'd go if he came for me. Here he was. There was no hesitation, but a little guilt. As I let Lilitu free and locked the door I was telling myself I would just stick to dinner and conversation, but I knew there was no real strength in my resolve. Stephen intrigued, and if I wasn't entirely sure why, then in part at least it was because of his very respectability, and what I knew lay hidden underneath.

He'd been patient waiting, presumably an asset in a politician, and was smooth and friendly as he guided me to his car, so smooth and friendly in fact that I began to wonder if he was up to something. After all, we'd had sex, and in my experience even those guys who play the white knight at first tend to drop it after a shag or two.

We drove west, through the city and into the West End, along the front of the Houses of Parliament and in among a cluster of tall, red-brick buildings beyond, flats for the wealthy. His block had a garage beneath it, complete with security guard and automatic iron grille to keep out the mob. I could see from the way he was acting that I was meant to be impressed, and I was, a touch, even if it was all more or less what I'd been expecting.

His flat was equally impressive, furnished and decorated with restrained elegance, mahogany furniture, deep-green leather, nothing garish or cheap. It wasn't really my taste, but it was comfortable, and all very new despite the old-fashioned look, with the sweet-sharp scent of leather catching my nose as I sat down in the settee he indicated. He went into the kitchen, speaking as I heard the chink of metal on glass.

'Tonight, Angel, I treat you . . .'

'Angela, but I prefer Dusk really.'

'Angel, if I may. It suits you.'

'Suits me!?'

'A dark angel, maybe, but an angel.'

I shrugged and smiled, flattered despite myself. He was laying it on thick, but it was impossible to be anything other than amused. As he busied himself in the kitchen, just out of my sight, he went on.

'Angel or devil, tonight I treat you. Sit back and enjoy yourself while I cook you a dinner I promise you won't forget in a hurry.'

'Why? Are you going to drug me and do obscene things to my semi-conscious body?'

'Very funny. No, I'm going to treat you as I suspect you've never been treated before, as a Lady should be.'

There was more than a touch of condescension in what he was saying, and my mouth came open for a sarcastic response, only to close again. If he wanted to play the generous benefactor to my street waif, then that was up to him, and he obviously thought he was flattering. It seemed silly to make an issue of it when all he wanted to do was fill me with good things, then presumably fuck me.

He stepped out from the kitchen bearing a tray with two glasses, two plates, bread and butter, a wooden platter with some smoked salmon on it, a jar of fish eggs and a bottle of champagne. He spoke as he indicated each item.

'For my Angel, nothing but the finest. Smoked salmon, wild, from a little place I know on Loch Fyne, Avruga caviar, champagne *La Belle Epoque* 1996. Tuck in.'

'I will, thanks.'

I had no idea what it had cost, but I guessed more than I got in a week, maybe a month. Part of me wanted to point out that I was quite happy to be his Mistress without the gifts, but it was far easier to accept his offer. So I piled some of the caviar onto one of the tiny slices of brown bread and took a mouthful as he worked on the foil of the champagne bottle. The caviar was salty, nothing special really, and certainly not something I'd pay a lot for.

The bottle came open with a gentle pop, spilling a touch of froth over his hand and onto the carpet. He ignored the spill, pouring carefully with the glass tilted and handing it to me when the deep-yellow liquid had risen halfway up. He watched paternally as I took a sip, leaving me feeling I should make some remark. Unfortunately the stuff tasted like old white wine put through a soda siphon, something I'd experienced in my last year at school, only worse.

'I've never really tasted anything quite like this before.'

'It's exclusive, naturally. Only a little is made, and then only in the best years.'

'Oh.'

He settled back, his eyes on me as he sipped at his own glass, apparently enjoying the spectacle of watching me eat. I felt rather as if I was in a goldfish bowl, but it beat scrubbing tags off walls, so I helped myself to some of the salmon, which actually tasted nice. Stephen took only a tiny sample of each food and had filled my glass before his own had really been touched. Presently he got up again and returned to the kitchen, then began to lay a table in the adjoining room, carrying through more glasses, crockery, cutlery, and three bottles of different wines.

'I don't mind you getting me drunk, Stephen, but with that lot I really am going to be semi-conscious.'

'Nonsense. We don't have to finish every bottle anyway, but each course needs its own wine.'

As he began to cook, so he began to hum to himself, 'Jerusalem' of all things. He seemed thoroughly pleased with himself, doubtless confident that he had me where he wanted me. It was true, sort of, although far less because of the fuss he was making over me than the memory of how dedicated he was to my pleasure.

Whatever he was doing in the kitchen it was pretty complicated, and he paused only once, to put on some classical music very quietly and dim the lights. The taste of the champagne had improved after a couple of glasses, and I finished it along with the salmon, leaving me feeling pleasantly mellow by the time he brought out two steaming plates. He even held my chair out for me to sit down at the table.

It was an incredibly elaborate dish, and incredibly rich, with different sorts of meat and a dark red sauce, some unusual kind of rice, tiny peas and asparagus.

The wine was equally rich, red and strong, and he poured with a generous hand, both for me and himself. I didn't bother to hold back and I couldn't help but be flattered by the effort he was putting into my seduction, and was soon playing my part.

A delicious chocolate cake followed the main course, washed down with sweet golden wine, then cheese and port. By then I was completely mellowed out, ready for anything except that my tummy felt fit to burst. He had become ever more attentive and ever more confident as the meal progressed, also eager, and he was fidgeting with his empty port glass when I had finished mine. I stretched, deliberately making my dress tight over my braless breasts to show their outline and the twin bumps of my nipples.

He smiled, trying to look cool and refined, but only managing randy. I got up, slightly unsteady on my feet as I crossed to what I had already worked out was the bedroom door. Within was a big, square room, the light already on to show a huge four-poster bed, furnishings much like those elsewhere in the flat and a wide-screen TV. I laid myself down on the bed, flat on my back, too drunk and too full to pose. My vision was swimming slightly as I took in my surroundings, all very neat and restrained. There were framed prints, maybe even originals – Beardsley but not rude ones.

I heard the chink of glasses and Stephen appeared, a large brandy in each hand and lust written all over his face. All I could manage in response was a drunken smile. He put the glasses down and reached out to trace a slow line down my body, from my forehead, across the tip of my nose and my lips, over my chin and down my neck, between my breasts and lower, over my belly. He stopped just an inch short of my pussy, tickling me gently through my dress, then moved back up, to touch the stud in my tummy button.

Relaxed, too full to respond, I let him explore, content so long as he didn't climb on top of me. He was slow, and seemed fascinated with my piercing and the shape of my belly, stroking for ages before he at last moved to my breasts. My nipples were already hard, my need to be touched rising ahead of his eagerness, something so rare in men. With my breasts he gave me the same slow attention, caressing my skin through my dress, tracing the outline of each low mound and moving slowly towards the centre.

I was moaning by the time he got to my nipples, my eyes shut and my mouth wide in bliss. The tension in my stomach was still there, but had died a little, and the need to rest was being slowly pushed down by that to let my legs come apart. His touches became a little firmer, almost a massage, at once soothing and arousing. I stretched, arching my back to lift my bottom from the bed and tugged up my dress, all the way to my neck, laying myself bare to him.

Still he stroked, once more moving slowly lower with his hand as his body nestled up against mine. His mouth found my skin, kissing my shoulder, my breasts, my nipple, suckling on me. A shiver ran through me, prickling the skin of my neck and running down my spine. I wanted to touch myself, but as I moved my arms he took me gently by my wrists and raised them above my head. There was the tiniest, briefest touch of resentment, and then his hand had found the bulge of my pussy mound and I simply didn't care.

My thighs came apart, opening to his touch as he cupped my sex, one finger pressing the front of my knickers down between my lips. He began to rub, still suckling on my nipple, and before I really knew it I was pushing back, wriggling into his touch as he masturbated me. Only when I felt the hard hot flesh of his erection touch my thigh did I realise he had his cock out. Again I reached down, wanting to take him in my hand, and again my arm was gently put back above my head.

This time his hand didn't go to my pussy, but to my hip, pushing gently. I responded, rolling to the pressure and sticking my bottom out in the same movement. His hands found my pants, suddenly urgent, his patience at last gone. They were tugged down, baring my bottom. The hard shaft of his cock pushed between my cheeks, rubbing between them, the hair of his balls tickling my bottom hole. Again his hand found my belly, holding me to him. My leg rose, stretching my lowered knickers taut as I let him in, his hand to the bulge of my sex, his penis at my entrance, and in.

Immediately I was gasping in ecstasy, held firm on his cock as he began to pump into me and to rub me all at once. I took my breasts in hand, cupping them and stroking my nipples as his lips found the nape of my neck, kissing and licking at my skin. I was going to come, held and taken there by the man inside me, my pussy already tightening as he began to pump hard and deep, and I was there.

As it hit me I cried out, completely overcome by the sheer ecstasy of being brought so skilfully to orgasm as I was fucked. Even as my body went into frantic, jerking contractions the thought hit me that I was in the hands of a master, a man with a great deal of practice and dedication in the art of pleasuring women.

Then I was coming down, my body still shivering to

his firm pushes, his cock seeming huge inside me, and rough, then suddenly smooth and he had come, groaning in his passion as he emptied himself inside me with deep, hard thrusts. His fingers now locked in the flesh of my hips, his teeth open against the skin of my neck, giving one last, delicious thrill at the thought of being vampirised as I was fucked, and it was over.

I had to get back, because I was not at all happy about leaving Lilitu on her own all night. Stephen wanted me to sleep with him, but could see the sense in my argument and called a cab. He was well pleased with himself, almost preening as we drank a leisurely coffee. It had been good, but it hadn't been me.

All the way back I was thinking about it, and trying to work out why it didn't feel right. He'd been generous, considerate, sweet; maybe a bit condescending and definitely controlling, but that shouldn't have been too big a deal. I hadn't felt the same way when he'd bent me across Eliza Dobson's tomb, after all, and that had been a much more assertive act.

I couldn't really get my head around it, but I did know I wanted to regain the balance of my emotions, to get away from the feeling of being the little street girl in the rich man's house. More than that, I felt I was somehow spiritually tainted, as if I had betrayed myself.

Back at All Angels the familiar gateway seemed somehow different, less welcoming, the griffins dark and menacing in a way they had never been before. The night was absolutely still, warm and velvet black in the shadows, with yellow, orange and umber highlights absolutely static, creating strange shapes among the tombs and stones, the church itself rising above everything as a black monolith. I moved into the yew alley, thinking of the spirits all around me, and their reaction to what I'd done, the Major full of lascivious interest but a little haughty, Eliza Dobson tutting knowingly, Foyle suspicious and full of envy.

What was needed was an act of atonement, even if it was just a little sex ritual, at the least a candle burned for each of those I had deserted in favour of the soft comforts of Stephen's bed, and not just the dead, but Michael also. Better still, I would commune, but not sexually. I had enough candles, and it had been too long, far too long. As I made for the vestry door I let slip the straps of my dress and hung my head, stepping free from the little puddle of cloth, naked in the warm night.

I would kneel at the foot of Isaac Foyle's tomb in silent prayer with the candles burning all around me, communing with his spirit, but that was all. Sex had scared Foyle, as his carving of Lust on the rood screen showed. The fantastic carving of the tomb lid with its wonderfully overdone motif of cherubs and roses evoked only a sweet melancholy in me. It would also have been agony to lie on.

The mundane thought pushed into my head as I struggled to turn the key in the lock of the vestry door. Lilitu gave a welcoming snuffle from inside, and as the door swung wide her black snout thrust out, sniffing the air. She began to whine and I sniffed myself, but caught only the hot summer scents, my own perfume, flowers and plants, the cemetery mould. Lilitu knew more, far more. Somebody was out there among the graves.

Suddenly my nakedness was no longer atonement but vulnerability. I took a quick hold on Lilitu's collar before she could move off among the stones, calmed her and quickly pulled my dress back on. She was growling and sniffing the air, eager, her sleek black fur reflecting dull ochre in the dim light, and as she turned I caught her eyes shining red. The knot of fear that had started up in my stomach faded a trifle and I was about to shout out a warning when I realised that there was another scent, very faint, and it took me an instant to recognise it – solvent.

I had a tagger, maybe a oner, maybe a crew, perhaps Biggy or Snaz. Now was the time to stay silent, to get as near as I could, revealing myself only when we were feet apart. I let Lilitu pull me in among the stones, her strength far too great for me to hold the instant I allowed her forward, into the yew avenue and across it, now snuffling at the ground. A light flickered across the cemetery, from among the tangle of sycamore that hid part of the far wall, yellow and quickly extinguished. I caught a hiss, a whisper, excitement blending with fear as again the yellow light flicked on and I made out a hooded figure crouched low where the sycamores half hid the tomb of Sir Arnold Radlett.

There was a moment of ambiguity as I imagined the outraged spirit of the pompous and egotistical Sir Arnold, but I bit it down. He deserved tagging, but they were on my turf, and putting my occupation of All Angels at risk. Sympathy was out and, besides, it was too much fun.

We drew close, Lilitu now by my side, my hand clamped over her muzzle to quiet her eager whining. The temptation to simply let her slip free was so strong, but I forced it down, holding her as I sank into the shadow of a tombstone, just metres away. Again the torch flicked on, pointing downwards into a rucksack full of cans, and then I saw the writing, a full-on piece, just for a moment and still half-finished, but unmistakable – Snaz.

Again I moved forward, my heart in my mouth as the soft hiss of the aerosol sounded just feet away. He was filling using his trademark green to give a heart to fat letters of fuchsia pink, rapt in concentration, his companion admiring the work instead of looking out for trouble, trouble that was right behind them. I was two rows away, then one, biting my lip with tension as I ducked into the shadow of a stone angel. The hiss stopped, the torch came on, and off, and I stepped out from behind the tomb just as their vision would be weakest.

I'd meant to challenge them, maybe pretend to set Lilitu on them, but I caught myself at the last second, remembering just how much bloody-minded defiance I'd had when I used to tag. In place of my angry shout I gave a hollow groan, even as I ducked back behind the angel. The effect was instant: a voice, tinged with fear, then another.

'What the fuck was that?'

'Shh!'

My mouth was twitching in an uncontrollable grin, the urge to laugh impossible to control, my second attempt at a groan coming out as a weird, bubbling cackle. Both swore, and ran. It was too much for Lilitu, seeing her prey break. She lurched forward, jerking free to send me sprawling on the grass. I heard her deep growl, a thump, a scream, running feet, and I was up, yelling for her to leave off as I picked out the black bulk of her body and something grey beneath it.

5

Lilitu hadn't savaged a writer, only his hoodie, which was really just as well. I couldn't stop laughing afterwards, cackling really, but I was scared too and shaking. It took ages to get to sleep, even with Lilitu beside me, my adrenaline high and the incident running over and over in my mind. At last I drifted off to sleep with the first grey tinge of dawn shading the vestry windows.

I woke to full sunlight, and Wednesday started much the same way as Tuesday had done, with me scrubbing paint, only not before I'd climbed up the scaffolding inside the tower and run Snaz's hoodie up the flagpole. They'd dropped their bag too, full of cans, including fat-cap Molotows that cost a bomb. I knew it was only likely to rile him, and that he probably didn't have the sense to back off, but I had to do it. It felt good, and made cleaning up a lot less of a pain. When I'd finished I was still on a high, despite running sweat from the hot sun.

Even in broad daylight Sir Arnold's tomb radiated indignation, barely diminished by my scaring off the desecrators or cleaning up. He'd been a local worthy, and dedicated to law and order, believing in hard labour, flogging and even death for the most trivial offences. To have his tomb tagged would be making his spirit boil with fury, and from what I'd read I knew that he would have thought of me as an impudent guttersnipe, whatever my actions.

As I'd said to Michael, I do believe that people leave some sort of spiritual presence after death, and it was certainly the case with Sir Arnold, also Eliza Dobson. Just being near her tomb brought out my feelings of defiance, and it was the same with others. Major Goodwell I was sure had been a randy old goat, because his always gave the feeling I was being interfered with, as if my bottom was likely to be pinched or my nipples tweaked. The Braidault family made me feel homely, Lisbet Stride saintly, Isaac Foyle inspired. He was inside, in a little chapel of his own with the roof half-collapsed, creating an atmosphere I had savoured many times, and where I had intended to make my atonement before I was disturbed.

I still felt I should do it, more if anything as I was certain the tagging crew had been keeping an eye on my movements. They had fled over the back wall too, into the gardens behind, so possibly one of them even lived in the houses there. Had I not gone with Stephen, they might have stayed away, adding to my guilty feeling. More than that, I knew deep down that my need for atonement had more to do with Michael than anything else.

With Sir Arnold's tomb probably cleaner than at any time since he was put inside it I went back to the vestry to scrub myself down, naked in the big sink. As the smell of paint and meths faded I began to enjoy the feel of the cool water on my bare skin and my thoughts turned back to Michael. It was such a shame we hadn't been able to have sex, preferably on Eliza Dobson's tomb the way we had talked about it. The fantasy had been glorious and I knew the reality would have been better still, even if her ghost would only have been in my head, or not.

Knowing Michael offered so many possibilities, both sexual and artistic. The thought of my face and body appearing in the magazines I had enjoyed so much over the years was wonderful, and all the better for the fact that I would be screwing the artist. If he did the one of us fucking as Eliza Dobson's ghost clawed at our bodies it was going on my wall, framed, whatever it took to make him part with it. There was the thought of joining him in ritual lovemaking too. He would understand ideas like atonement, and help me too.

Sadly he was not on hand, but that didn't stop me imagining him in his cowled robe, standing over me as I knelt naked in prayer. Possibly he was some sort of Satanist, but simply not ready to admit it, in which case he might know all sorts of things. In any case he was sure to be able to give me penance, something he frequently put into stories. Inevitably my atonement would become erotic, but that would not make it any less genuine, more so if anything, as I find it so hard to give myself over to the control of another. That was with Michael. For the moment I would content myself with a ritual before Isaac Foyle's tomb.

Clean and fresh, I climbed out of the sink and dried myself. The day was hot and as still as the night before, the air inside the church heavy and humid. I made up, turning my eyes to dark pits and shading my cheekbones with ash grey. Seven of the black candles, matches and a pot of chrism oil went into my bag. I needed to be naked, as every supplicant should be, but put boots on because of the floor, nothing else. I was confident in my repairs to the corrugated iron blocking the main door, and in Lilitu. She was lying in a patch of sunlight in the nave, eyes closed but one ear pricked up. I spent a moment tickling her under her chin.

I had always wanted to locate the spot where the heart of Father James O'Donnell was buried. As the first priest he would have been the ideal person to make atonement to. His body lay in a village churchyard in Tyrone, but his heart was somewhere beneath the floor in All Angels. I had often wandered the interior, trying to sense the air of sanctity I associated with him, but had never succeeded. Instead I knelt to Isaac Foyle, by his tomb in the little chapel beside the archway to the tower.

Just stepping into it gave me immediate strong feelings, the sense of invention his spirit brought, and apology. Taking the candles, I placed five in a cross among the ornate carving of the tomb lid, each spot already thick with wax, and one to either side of where I would kneel. I lit each, immediately filling the air with the scents of incense and wax, to which that of chrism oil was added as I twisted the lid from the pot. Pushing my finger well in, I pulled up enough to be sure it would show and crossed myself, breast to breast and neck to belly button. I was beginning to tremble a little as I looked down to view the dull gleam of the cross on my chest, and more as I knelt, knees together, my hands crossed in my lap, my head bowed.

The silence was absolute, the scent growing slowly heavier, quickly starting to get into my head. I focussed on the inscription in front of me, Isaac Foyle's name as he had carved it months before his death. The letters held, still and harsh in the stone, cold and unyielding. For one moment I thought I had lost my gift, or been somehow rejected. I drew the scented smoke deep into my lungs, my eyes closed, then open. Slowly, very slowly, it began to happen. The trance state that I am able to bring upon myself by strength of will and meditation. The letters gradually blurred, filling me with hope and then awe as Isaac Foyle came out to me, easing into my head as my gaze rose, swimming, my focus lost as the world closed in around me.

A sense of regret filled me, of a drive to create being broken by death; a bitter-sweet emotion so strong my mouth came wide open and my eyes filled with tears. I let them roll as I completely gave up myself to the spirit, my muscles growing slack, the broken tiles of the floor cold on my hip, my arm, my back as I collapsed. I lay there, broken on the floor, my body wracked with sobs, shivering and jerking, barely aware of reality as he took over my senses.

I heard my own moan and exaltation fill me as my thighs spread, offering myself, open and yielding. No lust came, only a sharp pang of fear, and I was loose, lying on the floor, shivering violently, but on my own. I pushed myself onto one elbow, biting my lip in the hope that the pain would clear my head. Foyle had gone, scared by the lust I'd been unable to hold down. Yet I was still high, and still in need.

Shaking hard, the church spinning around me, I clawed myself to my feet. Bowing, my forehead touched the stone of Foyle's tomb in an apology I knew to be futile. Hot wax spattered my arm and belly as I snatched at a candle, bringing warmth as I struggled to focus on my smeared flesh. I took another, tipping it down my chest and laughing at the sudden, sweet pain as a black line sprang up between my breasts. My head went back, the candle high above my chest to splash hot droplets on the skin of my breasts, between, on one nipple and the other, piling it high.

I panted out my ecstasy as I crossed myself in black wax, laughing and babbling between cries of pain. A second candle in hand and I was back, propped on hard, cold marble, another tomb. My thighs came wide, my neck arched and I was building the balls of the cross, top and bottom, filling the hollow of my throat and my belly button. It hurt so much, every splash sweet pain, and waves of lust were running through me, and more, a spirit eager to fill me from beneath. I cried out once, and he was in.

My body slid down the face of the tomb, onto the hard floor, my knees high and open. The rounded base of the candle pushed at my sex, and in, the tip still lit as I fucked myself, my back arched, my mouth wide. My bottom came off the ground, a gasp of refusal left my lips, too weak, and I was pushing the base of the second candle at my bottom hole. In it went, my own juices easing it, and I was squirming on the floor, doing myself deep and hard, my palm spread on my sex, my back arched tight, writhing in wanton ecstasy to the man in my head.

I came, gasping in pleasure, but it didn't stop, my fingers still pushing the candles in and out of my body as I jerked in my contractions. He was in control, completely, into my pussy and bottom deep and hard, revelling in my naked body, using me. Again I came, utterly helpless, crying louder still and wriggling on the twin shafts inside me, two cocks, his and another man's, a servant, using my bottom as the master fucked me, stripped and marked.

Then I was there, laid out on my back in a great darken space, on a man, his cock up my bottom, another looming over me as he thrust hard between my thighs. Above, the face of a huge goat stared down at me, great curled horns, a lolling tongue and demonic eyes. Black-clad figures stood around, yellow, candle-lit eyes staring out from the shadows of their cowls, drinking in the sight of me. As I tilted my head back to kiss the man beneath me I saw the inverted cross at my head; at the same instant ice-cold sperm erupted into my body.

All of it vanished as quickly as it had come. I was left spread-eagled on the floor, my thighs rolled high, my fingers still easing the candles in and out of myself by instinct, my mind too fuzzy to stop it. It was Lilitu licking my face that finally brought me back to something like normal awareness. I tried to pull myself up, but had to be content with kneeling, my balance completely gone. Lilitu stood looking at me, her great brown eyes radiating concern for her mistress.

Finally I managed to get to my feet, and to pull out the candles. It was impossible not to smile as I limped to the vestry. I had really put myself through it, what was intended to be an atonement through trance and meditation turning into a session of truly wild masturbation. My knees were scraped, my hip bruised, my bottom hole sore, my body aching in a dozen places and hot where I had poured wax on my skin. Yet I was smiling as I picked the hard black spatters away with my nails.

I could remember every detail, the feel of the man's spirit in me, just how rude he'd been with my body, the helpless ecstasy of my response, and the crazy vision at the end. All of it I had experienced before, if never so strong, but not the vision. I had taken myself to a new level, beyond anything I had experienced in communion before, and how. It was disturbing, but still filled me with pride. I had been in a Black Mass, or some similar ritual, really there, or at least I had felt that I was.

Although it had simply been a product of my fevered

imagination, the memory was as clear as that of sex with Stephen the day before. Maybe it was one of those time-slip experiences; glimpses of another reality – of things that actually happened on this very spot. Only as I remembered that the man on top of me had come did I realise that I could check. His sperm had been icy cold, a sure mark of the Devil, for all that I had sensed him as a man possessing me. As my hand stole down to between my legs I had a brief wild vision of myself pregnant with a demonic child, like in some 70s Hammer horror movie, but while I was damp it was only my natural juice, or so it seemed.

I wanted to do it again, but more than anything I wanted to talk about it. Michael was the obvious person. For all his unfocussed beliefs there was a spirituality about him, and he did have an open mind. At the very least he wasn't going to label me as some kind of demented freak. Stephen was a different matter. From the way he behaved it was all too clear that he regarded my Gothicism as nothing more than an immature fancy. So far as he knew it extended to my look and a passion for sex in cemeteries, and that was the way it was going to stay.

It was ironic, really, as he could have gained so much by breaking free of the armour he had built around himself over the years. Yet he didn't even realise that he was repressed, that there was more to personal liberation than a dirty mind and a bit of care and attention to his partner's needs. I had met men before who wanted to release themselves fully but couldn't, clawing at the temple door, as I had once done, but no more than that. Stephen didn't even know the temple was there.

Michael did, only his scepticism keeping him out. I wanted him, and again I considered giving up on Stephen if he didn't get in touch, only for him to turn up on the Thursday evening. We went out, to dinner at a restaurant well off the beaten track and then back to his flat for sex Stephen style, slow and attentive with lots of tongue applied to my pussy.

Friday was little different, except that he cooked for me again, and that after a while on top I let him put me on my knees. He licked me like that, which was wonderful, and left me floating all the way back home. It was so easy to accept his attention, and as I knelt quietly in front of Isaac Foyle's tomb on the Saturday morning I realised that atonement or no atonement, I was Stephen Byrne's lover.

Both nights I made a point of going around the cemetery with Lilitu and a torch, but there were no new pieces or dubs, not so much as a marker pen tag. It had been a while since I'd found any needles or cans either, and I began to hope that the whole tribe of them might finally have decided it was easier to take themselves elsewhere.

When I'd first come to All Angels the cemetery had been a warren of little paths leading to dens, while the walls and a good half of the tombs and stones had been hit with everything from crude scribbles to head-high pieces. Now, for the first time, there was nothing. As I climbed to the roof after my brief atonement I felt that I belonged in a way I had really never done before, that All Angels was mine. There was also the relief that it wasn't about to be torn to pieces by do-gooding local government busybodies.

I stayed for a good hour, just padding over the warm lead of the gutters or peering down at the graveyard beneath me. It was empty, Snaz's hoodie the only evidence of anyone other than me, Lilitu and the dead. I remembered how I'd first seen Michael and my thoughts turned to our relationship. He was due back late that night, and I was to go over in the morning, to model, to talk, to fuck.

It had to happen, or I was going to go nuts. He wanted me, I knew, and if there were sure to be complications with Stephen, that was easy to push from my mind. Stephen was back in Suffolk anyway, with his cold wife, the 'Designer Mannequin' as he called her. Michael and I would be together, alone. Once we'd taken out our passion on each other we would talk, maybe even as he drew me. I would explain my experience, and perhaps he would help me to understand.

I certainly didn't, and ever since had been wondering how much had been in my mind and how much external. Had I had the same experience at the tombs of notable left-hand path devotees, Sir Francis Dashwood, Aleister Crowley or Samuel Mathers, there would have been no doubt at all, but the man who had possessed me was no Satanist, anything but. He was Sir Barnaby Stamforth, a local worthy and landlord whose tomb had never before given me any sensation beyond pomposity and disapproval.

His tomb was the largest of those inside, blocking the side aisle and helping shield the arch to Isaac Foyle's chapel where I liked to kneel. It was a huge thing of smooth grey-black marble with the front face showing a magnificent coat of arms, 64 quarters each picked out in minute details, griffins as supporters, helm and more. Elaborate mantling covered most of the remaining three sides except for the lengthy scrollwork inscription and the lid. On this lay a life-size statue of an improbably well-built man in full armour, his hands clasped to his chest in prayer, his stone face set in blissful repose.

It wasn't real, or at least, it wasn't medieval. Sir Barnaby had been knighted for his services to commerce, and if he had ever worn armour it had not been for any practical purpose. He hadn't been well built either, at least not when he had died in 1874, and probably never. As with all of those burials with which I felt empathy, I had done some research, and in his case there had been plenty to go on. I'd seen several photos in old newspapers, books recording the history of the area and a chapter of biography. The pictures showed a man of less than average height with a whiskery face peering out from under the brim of a stovepipe hat and an impressive belly stretching the front of his waistcoat. He had been in shipping, making a fortune in spice and tea and coffee, and had gained a reputation for self-aggrandisement. That went with the beautiful knight, but his tomb had radiated pompous self-certainty long before I'd known it was his true character. For religion, he seemed to have been a solid member of the congregation and a major benefactor of the church, and I had seen not the slightest hint of depravity, religious or otherwise.

His character had led me to tease him a few times, but I had never sensed anything sexual in response, only angry disapproval. The idea of doing so again was both amusing and arousing, and I climbed back down intent on making the experiment. Reading the lines of the potted life history I'd found in the library, he seemed to have been a bit of a pig with women, intolerant and demanding. Possibly he had been dirty when it suited him; possibly he really had deflowered girls on a Satanic altar, and simply got away with it. If so, his tomb would surely now evoke at least something of what I'd experienced in the rapture of my trance.

I peeled off my dress in the vestry and adjusted my make-up to create a more sultry look. In his day women would have been in long dresses, everything concealed for all the exaggeration of busts and waists and bottoms. To see me in my knickers and boots would fill him with outrage, and hopefully lust, the need to have me and to put me in my place at the same time. I hesitated over a black candle and decided against it. My mind needed to be sharp.

To make it work I needed to see Sir Barnaby in a new light, not as I'd felt him, a crazed Satanist, but neutral, without my preconceptions. He'd died old, wealthy, overweight, respected. Surely he had to have yearned for sexual contact at the least, watching the young women, maybe paying, maybe using his authority to get what he wanted. However it had been, now he would be unable to force me to his will, his power gone, his prestige and his money worthless. He could only take what I gave freely.

I thought of him viewing me as I walked out into the church, his little piggy eyes fixed on my body, his lust rising with his frustration, his impalpable fingers straining to sense my flesh as I came close to his tomb. His sense of outrage rose up as I touched the smooth marble mantling, and I realised that perhaps it was not the reaction of a prig to sexual display, but of a patriarch. Could he be angry that a woman should be free to go naked at her own choice, to pick her lovers, or reject?

My mind turned to how I could do as I pleased, show

off in front of him, maybe have sex in front of him with Michael or Stephen, or not. I could enjoy myself with the beautiful knight he had carved, rejecting him but taking pleasure in the image of himself he had desired. The sense of outrage grew abruptly stronger and I laughed. It was tempting, too tempting, and I reached out to stroke the statue's face. The marble was cool, wonderfully smooth to my touch, and as I explored the contours of the cold, handsome face and thought of what I could do his aura grew stronger still.

The air in the church was deathly still, but my skin was prickling as if to a breeze on my belly and breasts. He was touching me, he had to be, ghostly fingers on my flesh, struggling to force me to comply, perhaps the way he had obliged his wife, his maids, girls from the street, skirts high, drawers spread for access to their pussies, perhaps even to their bottom holes. I wasn't going to. I was going to take my pleasure on the beautiful knight, leaving him to watch and fumble ineffectually at my naked flesh.

I climbed up, straddling the statue's legs, my thighs wide across the cool marble. The codpiece of his armour rose as a smooth, inviting bulge, ideal to rub myself on, which was exactly what I planned to do. I moved forward, mounting up to place the hard lump beneath me, pressed to my sex and bottom through my knickers. The air was musky with attar of roses mingled with pussy. I wondered if he could smell it too, adding to his outraged lust as I began to wriggle myself gently on the knight's crotch.

It felt good, my sensitive flesh and bottom cheeks spreading onto the hard bulge, the marble momentarily cool on my sex lips and bottom hole but quickly warming. I lifted my hands, arching my back to push my breasts out as I took them in hand, feeling my stiff nipples beneath my fingers and stroking away a bead of sweat as it trickled down my skin. Stretching high, I began to wriggle more firmly, revelling in the sheer joy of life and sex as my pleasure rose, purely physical for a brief moment before I turned my thoughts back to Sir Barnaby.

I pictured him paying girls for favours, to strip or suck or fuck, and taking more pleasure the less they liked it. Now in death, he could do nothing, only writhe in an agony of lust as I squirmed on his statue, taunting him with my vitality. I laughed out loud, and suddenly his hands were clawing at me, my skin prickling at legs and buttocks, belly and chest. I closed my eyes, revelling in the sensation, willing him to take me as he had before, to control my body and make me do obscene things to myself, my ecstasy dedicated to Satan as I was drawn in to him . . .

What came was my orgasm, rising up in my head as my sex tightened. I gave in, not as before, but to my own need. Sir Barnaby was denied, I was proud and naked and feminine, full of joy in what I was doing as I came on the knight's crotch, clutching at my breasts as I cried out and my body arched in ecstasy.

It had been fast, unexpectedly fast, my orgasm welling up from nowhere. I was grinning as I came down, panting, my whole body sweaty once more, the marble of the knight's crotch now smeared with my juice. Fury radiated from the tomb, stronger even than Eliza Dobson's, but different. I patted the statue on the head and turned my back, walking away with a deliberate wiggle.

As an experiment it was inconclusive. I had tried to give myself to him, laid myself completely open in the hope of having my body taken over as before. It hadn't happened, but that didn't necessarily prove anything. Possibly I had not been susceptible enough, or my innate defiance of male control too strong to let him in. I'd felt him, I knew that, but as more or less I would have expected beforehand. Obviously I would have to try again with my head full of incense, and maybe a couple of skunk spliffs – a prospect that brought me both pleasure and apprehension.

As an experience it had been fine. I was absolutely buzzing as I washed and dressed, and the urge to talk about it all was stronger than ever. I took Lilitu for a walk to try and take my mind off it, deliberately staying within sight of the tower of All Angels in the half-hope that Snaz would attempt to retrieve his hooded top. He didn't, and it didn't take my mind off possession and Satanic ritual either, so that by the time I got back I knew that I was going to have to go and see Michael that evening.

It would make me seem over-eager, I knew, but I didn't want to play games and I was hoping that after our last meeting he wouldn't either. So I dressed carefully, and my best: black silk pants, fine mesh hold-ups, heeled boots and my longest, tightest dress. Almost an hour spent making up and I was ready. I set off, despite being sure to arrive long before he did.

Sure enough, I was down by the dock before the light had altogether faded from the sky. I found a place from which I could see the window of his flat, but there was no light. There was a trace of wry amusement at my own enthusiasm as I bought myself a take-away – coffee and doughnuts – and went to sit at the base of one of the great black cranes across from him. It was a perfect scene, the evening a touch cool, the water absolutely still, the mass of the cranes etched black against an ultramarine sky shading to deep blue between copper-gold clouds in the west.

I could see Michael's building in perfect reflection in the dock, and watched for the lights to flick on as I sipped my coffee, feeling at once foolish and excited. When it did come it was a surprise, sending a little shock of apprehension through me. I felt aroused, yet also vulnerable, my head clear, the thought of what I wanted from him sending little shivers through my body. This time it had to happen.

A dozen doubts ran through my head as I walked around the dock. He wasn't there at all, but only Chris. Chris would be there too. He would be there, but with another girl. Somehow he would have changed his mind. Anything to destroy the anticipation I seemed to have been building up for ever.

He was in, his voice alone setting me trembling, so badly I fumbled at the buttons in the lift, pushing twice before the doors closed. It seemed to rise forever, and my stomach was tight as I pushed open his door. He was there, standing right in front of me, in black jeans and a black sweatshirt, an open hold-all beside him, smiling.

I pushed the door to behind me. My fingers went to the straps of my dress, pushing one aside, and the other. It fell away, down over my chest and lower. A push and it was off my hips. I was stepping forward, Michael looking surprised and delighted, his eyes flicking over my naked chest, and down, to my legs and the V between them. My mouth came wide, my lips pressed to his and we were kissing, deep and passionate, tongues entwined, my arms around his neck.

He took hold of me, stroking my hair, my back, my

bottom, lifting me. My legs came around him, up on his hips, the bulge of his cock pressing to my mound, my breasts to his chest. His fingers came under me, pulling my knickers aside, holding my bottom wide, brushing my sex, and I didn't mind, eager and ready as he struggled to free his cock.

We went down, Michael sinking beneath me, onto the floor. His zip rasped down, his dick came free, thick and hot between my bottom cheeks. I wriggled as his hands once more clasped my bottom, spreading my cheeks over his cock, his balls between them. He nudged himself at my pussy, growing faster against my wet flesh. I rose, took him in hand, feeling the thick, hard shaft as I put him to my sex, and in.

I sighed as I filled, riding Michael at last, mounted up as I took two handfuls of his hair and begun to fuck. Immediately he was pushing up into me, already urgent, his hands cupping my bottom, holding me, his eyes feasting on my body. Glorious, blissful relief flooded through me. He was in, our bodies joined, and nobody to break the moment. I stretched, pulling at my own hair with my breasts thrust out, seated proud on him just as I had been on the stone knight.

He began to push harder and deeper, jerking into me. I took hold of my breasts, teasing for just a second before the urgency simply became too much. The edge of my panties was rubbing on my clit as I bounced and I was going to come, with just a little more friction, and enough as he went wild. He was coming, and so was I, gasping out his name as I let myself go completely, clutching at my pussy in abandoned bliss, my body tight, my fingers slippery with his come.

Shock after shock of ecstasy went through me as we came together, one to each hard pump of his cock, until

I could hold myself no more and slumped forward on top of him, our mouths opening to each other even as he drained himself into me. His arms came around my back and mine under his shoulders and we were together, held tight in rapture.

We stayed cuddled close together for some time, saying nothing, just kissing occasionally, his cock still inside my body. Before too long our kisses had begun to grow urgent once more, and as I began to wriggle on him, so he once more began to grow hard. Soon my pussy felt nicely full again and he was pushing into me, slowly now, easing himself in and out as I held tight to his chest.

I let my mind wander as we did it again, imagining how he and I would share communion, locked in passion as we were, but on a tomb in the darkened graveyard or by candlelight in the church. Perhaps I could take him with me, into Sir Barnaby's unholy orgy, putting on a display for the delight of the ghosts. Perhaps it would go further still, with the two of them sharing me: Sir Barnaby beneath me, pushing his cock into my straining bottom; Michael on top, fucking to a rhythm. Perhaps not Sir Barnaby ... perhaps the Devil himself, inserted in my bottom hole even as Michael and I fucked, together in supreme ecstasy, sperm pumping into me, hot *and* freezing cold.

Michael was getting more passionate, his strong arms tight around my back, holding me in, his fingers locked in my flesh. My thighs were wide, my bottom spread, so anyone behind could see the thickness of his cock inside me, and my open bottom, ready to be entered, buggered, but not by any man, by the Devil. I snatched back, twisting in Michael's arms, my hand slipping into the crease of my bottom, to touch my hole, push in, one finger, then a second, opening myself.

It was going to happen. My pussy was spread in the coarse tangle of his pubic hair, his cock was filling me right to the head, and I could already feel my muscles contracting as I let my fantasy go. We'd be on a tomb, the tomb of some great Satanic master, fucking, me held tight in Michael's arms with my sex spread on his cock. The master would be in my head, then my mouth, thick and real as I sucked. I'd feel the presence of the Devil, his huge, burning hot cock pressed to my bottom hole before jutting in, shocking me as he jammed it deep, buggering me hard and fast. Three cocks would be working as one in my body, and coming, sperm exploding into mouth, pussy and bottom hole at the same instant as I screamed in the agony of my orgasm.

Just as I did, thrashing on top of Michael as I came, screaming and biting at his shoulder, my fingers working furiously in my bottom hole, my feet kicking on the hard wooden floor, my whole body wrapped in blinding ecstasy for one long, glorious climax.

6

After all my elaborate plans for Michael Merrick, we'd had each other just seconds after I'd walked in the door. From start to finish it had taken maybe three minutes, the first time, but it was as much my fault as his, more really. The second time more than made up for that. It had been one of the best, certainly my best with a man, and I knew it could get better. He was well pleased with himself too, and with me. We went to bed with a bottle of strong red wine and stayed there until close to dawn, kissing and talking and fucking. I lost count of the number of times I came, and the ways. By the time I finally fell into an exhausted sleep I was sore and so was he, while my head was swimming with wine and talk of cultists and devils and bizarre rituals.

My first thought in the morning was that I should be getting back to check up on Lilitu and All Angels. That was staring bleary eyed at Michael's ceiling before the events of the night before began to run through my head. I sat up, wincing slightly, to find Michael down by his art desk. He saw I was awake and went into the kitchen, just as I heard the pop of a kettle. I relaxed, glad that he was playing host properly, and took the steaming mug of coffee as he returned. It was as I like it, black and sweet, strong enough to send a rush through me after the first couple of swallows.

I'd told him about my experiences at Sir Barnaby's

tomb, but not in detail as it had led to another bout of sex before we could really get into it. Like me, he had no knowledge of Sir Barnaby Stamforth being associated with any of the Victorian cults, Satanic or otherwise. He had never even heard of Sir Barnaby, and while I had always thought of myself as widely read, he seemed to know every detail of every religious aberration recorded. I was thinking about it, but it was he who opened the conversation before he was half-way through his coffee.

'So this Satanic ritual. Describe it again.'

'Sure. I was on an altar . . .'

'How do you know it was an altar?'

'I know it was an altar because there was an inverted crucifix just above my head. I mean, it's not a normal piece of household furnishing, is it?'

'No, sorry, but could it have been a table?'

'I suppose, a big heavy one. It was set up in the middle of a room, well, a space, enclosed but large, because the men were standing all around me.'

'You're sure they were men?'

'Yes . . . I mean, I didn't see their bodies or faces, sure, but they had a male feel. I could see their eyes, reflecting candlelight, and light and shadow on the walls and ceiling beyond them. I was on one man, a servant, but I don't know how I knew he was a servant, except that somehow it seemed appropriate that because he was a servant he should be the one in my bottom.'

'Makes sense to me.'

'It does?'

'Sure. Go on.'

'The other one, Sir Barnaby.'

'What makes you so sure it was Sir Barnaby?'

'Well, he was in my head. It was his tomb, that's the way it has always been when I commune with the dead. But yes, his sperm was cold, which means ...'

'The Devil.'

'Maybe. I've never experienced anything like it before, so I don't know. Maybe their sperm is cold anyway?'

'Could be. And this felt completely real?'

'The memory is as clear as ... as what we did last night. I'm not saying that I was physically transported, but it felt that way. I could feel their cocks inside me, I could hear, and I felt the cold of the sperm in my body.'

'That is some experience. You are truly blessed, or perhaps cursed. But come downstairs.'

He'd been sitting on the bed, and rose, the brief glimpse of his hard buttocks beneath his robe bringing back the night before to me as I followed. A piece of artwork was spread out on the drawing desk. He nodded at it.

'The Goat of Mendes, in draft. I was working on it in my hotel room.'

I looked, the rough scene he had sketched out with me as the model now executed in elaborate detail. There was the cabal, in their black robes, faces hidden or indistinct. There was the altar, a heavy table at the centre of a darkened room with a black cloth draped over it and an inverted crucifix at one end. There was the young man, leering eagerly at the prospect of sex with the Priestess, then horrified as he discovered that it was he who was to be penetrated. Next he was on his back on the table, held from beneath by a man in coarse tweeds, the Priestess in him. In some frames the ceiling showed, with a hideous goat's head where the light boss would normally have been. My mouth came open in amazement. Michael chuckled.

'Similar, isn't it?'

'Yes ... but ... but I didn't know ... your story wasn't complete, nothing like.'

'Close enough for your mind to form an image, I think. You are exceptionally sensitive to atmosphere, to suggestion.'

'So ... so you're saying that it was all from inside my head? That everything I've experienced is nothing but elaborate fantasy?'

'No, not necessarily, but I am offering it as an alternative. We can be fairly certain Sir Barnaby Stamforth wasn't a closet Satanist. These things tend to come out over the years, especially if you have a good-sized group. There are always schisms, and people who want to tell the world what they've done, either to gloat or confess. Look at Crowley and the Golden Dawn.'

'True.'

'And even in Victorian times it would have been hard for respectable citizens to go around deflowering virgins, especially on a regular basis. Pimps, blackmailers, relatives ... someone's going to let the cat out of the bag.'

'True, and your scene is very close – only if I was fantasising, I'd be the Priestess.'

'Ah, yes, normally, but you were off your face, and you said you couldn't do it again.'

'Not off my face completely, and no, I couldn't. But what about the cold sperm? I felt it! And the goat's head? You hadn't put that in at all, not even in rough! It was just like that.'

'Exactly like that?'

'Yes! No ... I don't know, I was coming! It was pretty close though, teeth showing, tongue hanging out, staring eyes, great curly horns.'

'Our minds tend to run on the same lines, and we had discussed the whole goat thing. Maybe it stuck in your head?'

'What about the sperm then?'

'If it was the Priestess, with an ejaculating dildo, the cream or whatever would be cold. You would know that subconsciously.'

'I'm not convinced. So how do I pick up on atmosphere from places and people I know nothing about?'

'Hard to say. It could be a little thing, evident only to your subconscious mind, like with the sperm. In France you would have been aware of the great war cemeteries even if you hadn't focussed on them. The tombs at All Angels are very personal, each reflecting something of the personality of their occupant ...'

'No, the tombs convey the essence of how their occupants really were – not the personas they created in life, but only how they saw themselves. Sir Barnaby's tomb is grand and fine; he may have thought of himself that way, but he was pompous and stuffy. The same with Eliza Dobson. Her inscription makes her out to have been the next thing to a saint, and I'm sure she thought of herself that way, yet the tomb radiates outrage and bigotry.'

'What was saintly to her is bigoted to you. What was grand to him is pompous to you. Or, there could be something spiritual there ... perhaps a lingering aura related to the dead individual, without their spirit being cognisant in any way. Perhaps a bit of both, what you experienced being a combination of influences –

my story and a spiritual dimension. Or maybe you're right. Maybe you had a vision of another time. Maybe you fell through some kind of portal; a quantum leap across dimensions.'

I nodded, my mind whirling with ideas, wanting to believe I had some special power. What he said made sense, at least some sense, but I didn't want to accept it. It felt as if he was trying to be kind by extending his ideas to admit the possibility of mine. Kind, yes, but it was hard not to see it as condescension. I didn't answer him, but stood there looking at the illustration and trying not to look sulky. After a while he went on.

'The servant thing is funny though, and hard to explain. I hadn't put him in my draft at all, had I?'

'No.'

'So you couldn't have seen him, yet you came up with the same image, allowing only for the difference in sex between you and Dave there.'

'Dave?'

'Dave. Guys who have awful things happen to them in my drawings are generally called Dave. I'm hoping it will become an accepted noun for a hapless male, "a Dave".'

I smiled despite myself.

'You're right. How do you explain it?'

'I can't, but I know where the servant thing came from in my head. It was in a graphic novel I saw when I was a kid. A naked woman, sexy in an upper-class sort of way, with a tattoo on her belly saying "servants' entrance around the back". I thought it was funny at the time, but it left me with this vivid image of upper-class women inviting their servants to have anal sex. So, yes, when a servant fucks any woman but another servant, it's up her bottom.'

'I swear I never saw that comic.'

'No? So why did you feel it was appropriate? Something from Sir Barnaby? Some bizarre genetic memory? Some memory buried in your subconscious?'

'You'd say the last option, wouldn't you?'

'I'd say most probably the last option. After all, you might have been, say, on a bus, and have heard the joke told. You don't remember. Maybe you didn't even hear it consciously, but it still fixed in your head.'

Again I nodded. There was a cold logic to everything he said, impossible to refute, but irritating, and it was impossible not to feel mocked. My sense of defiance started to rise but I bit down the comment that came to my lips. We'd made love, and it had been wonderful, strong and spontaneous and uninhibited. To spoil it because we didn't see eye to eye on just one point would have been stupid. Besides, he was keeping an open mind, or at least he said he was. I allowed my defiance to switch to a determination to prove myself right as I made my excuses.

'I must go. Lilitu needs feeding, and I've been having problems with writers.'

'Problems with writers?'

'Graffiti artists, taggers. They call themselves writers.'

'Oh. I used to do a bit of that as a kid.'

'So did I, well, as a teenager.'

'I found it too crude a medium, but some of it can genuinely be called art.'

'Sure, but not in my graveyard.'

'Absolutely.'

I moved close to kiss him, then made for the bathroom. No way was I going back in my dress and boots and tourmalines without my face right, so I took a while making up. It was gone noon when I left, the sky leaden with clouds, the air warm and sticky. I took a bus back, not really feeling up to the walk in my heels with my body still tired from the night's sex.

Michael had fixed me toast, but I was still starving, and got off a couple of blocks from the church, just as soon as I'd seen that Snaz's top was still safely in place. I bought milk, dog food and a packet of Crunchy Nut Cornflakes, just right to see Lilitu and myself through the day, and set off alongside the railway arches. I hadn't gone fifty metres when I saw it, a huge double piece, painted on the old dark brick of the railway – Snaz and Biggy.

I couldn't help but smile. They were still up, out but not down as it were, painting for all they were worth but not in All Angels. That was just fine by me, British Transport Police can take care of themselves, and while it was desecration to bomb the church, on the drab arches it was a definite improvement. It was a great piece too, far beyond anything I could have done.

The letters were taller than me, and had real style, both pieces. Biggy's were balloon fat, as if each were about to burst, in brilliant purple with silver highlights fading in through mauve and black low lights through indigo. The background was silver, and ended in a dead straight diagonal where the roof of some long vanished building had once been cemented to the bricks, creating a perfect boundary for the vivid pink background of Snaz's piece. His letters were a riot of colour, crazy interlocking snakes of violent electric blue, sky blue, his trademark green and a rich leaf green, each picked out with darker lowlights to bring the whole thing into relief.

To do it they had had to climb onto the roof of a

garage and in some cases up on the big hooks supporting the cables for the railway, risky stuff, and I knew.
Even when I'd taken in the letters I was still trying to
figure out how they'd reached some parts. It was
signed 'TST', obviously their crew name but not something they'd ever used at All Angels.

I only walked on when my arms started to tire from
the weight of my shopping. At the end of the alley I
put it down briefly to rest and glanced back for one
more look at the piece, knowing it might well not last
long. It looked even better from a distance, the blend
of colours finer, and with a train on the railway above.
I wasn't the only admirer either. There was a girl
taking a photograph. I'd have done the same if I'd had
a camera, but it made me pause for thought.

She was my age or a bit less, pink hair, crop top,
bare midriff, low-rise jeans, Timberland's. As she
turned to get a different angle I saw that the top of a
pink thong showed over the waistband of her jeans,
cutesy, very cutesy. She might have been an art student, someone wanting to be a photographer or a
reporter, just someone who got a kick out of graff,
except for the Timberland's. Everything else she had on
was made for showing out, the boots were not.

I watched her, wondering if she could just possibly
be Snaz. There was something girlie about the style,
and while one of the people I'd heard in the graveyard
had undoubtedly been male, the other had just hissed.
I hadn't seen anything more than the outline of a
hoodie, but her height seemed right, her build reason-
able. She was certainly taking an interest in the piece,
photographing it repeatedly, and she seemed well
pleased with herself.

She hadn't seen me, I was sure, a thick overhang of

sycamore on the railway plunging the turn of the alley into deep shadow. So I watched for a while, wondering if I should pass her and see if she recognised me. If she did, she had to be Snaz, but she was hardly likely to be friendly. I was going to do it anyway when the question was answered.

A man stepped out from the café at the far end of the alley – young, black, pushing six foot and hefty, a sandwich in one hand. He came towards the girl, grinning, turned to look up at the piece, slapped hands with her and walked on. She slipped the camera into her pocket and quickly caught up with him. He had to be Biggy, and that made her Snaz. I melted into the shadows.

As on the nights before, All Angels was untouched, Lilitu undisturbed. I double-checked, walking her right round the outside wall, even under the sycamores that were rapidly forming a copse at the bottom. There was nothing, not so much as a beer can or a fag end, and I went in certain that I really had succeeded. Snaz and Biggy had moved onto other things, the others like-wise. I was secure in All Angels, and if I had to confess to a faint sense of disappointment as I lay thinking on the roof that afternoon, it was a minor thing.

The major thing was Michael Merrick. I had to go back for my modelling session later, once he'd caught up on sleep. We'd fuck, and I wanted to, but our conversation that morning had spoilt something of the intimacy I'd felt for him. In telling him about commun-ion I had revealed my most private secret, and while he had accepted it, he hadn't believed. I wanted to prove it to him, to make him just a little less certain, just a little less smug. Only then would I be able to let myself go completely the way I had the night before.

Just a suspicion, right at the back of my mind, suggested he'd done it on purpose, to make me more determined. If it was true, then he'd succeeded.

How to go about it was a very different matter. First I needed to prove it to myself, because Michael had sowed the seeds of doubt in my mind, which was not good. When I had the time, and was a little less sore, I was going to have to select an important tomb, probably in another cemetery, indulge in communion, see what happened and then find out about the person. Ideally I would be led there blindfolded, but that raised the complication of having someone else to help me, someone I could trust. It could hardly be Michael, and Stephen only if he was then prepared to go away and leave me in peace. He could hardly be expected to be happy about that.

The situation with Stephen was another problem. After the way Michael and I had been it was impossible to tell him about Stephen. We were lovers, but we hadn't set out the dos and don'ts of our relationship. Generally I don't bother, and it puts me off when men do, as it might well put Michael off if I did. Stephen was a different matter. I was sure he was only waiting his moment to make it clear that he was only in it for the sex. That was fine, and would give me an excuse to tell him about Michael. If he didn't like it that was just too bad.

Had it not been for Michael's condescension I would have been ready to drop Stephen. As it was I didn't see why I shouldn't have both, at least for the time being. In bed Michael had been uninhibited but very male. Everything centred on his cock and where he could stick it. That was great, so far as it went, and he had licked and kissed plenty, but not in the way Stephen did it. With Michael it was raw passion, with Stephen it was ... almost worship.

I climbed down from the roof with the sun already turning the lead dull gold. Michael would be waiting, I knew, but I felt only a little of the urgency I had the night before. Not that he seemed to notice one way or the other, greeting me with a friendly kiss that quickly turned into an open-mouthed snog. He was hard to resist, and I'd have gone for it if he'd pushed, but he broke away, turning back to the art desk.

'OK, I need some expression here. This is the second spread. You're with the cabal, you're talking, discussing the import of the ritual deflowering and why it didn't work.'

'It didn't?'

'No. The idea is that an act of extreme debauchery will draw in the spirit of the Goat of Mendes, the Regency cabal leader, yeah?'

'Yeah.'

'It didn't happen and you're taking it over. Most of the cabal are just background, but there's the founder, Albrecht Dawes.'

He pointed to the page, where he'd drawn a face that radiated confidence and strength, also evil. It took me a moment to realise he'd modelled it on his brother Chris.

'He's been something of a Svengali figure to you, Bernadette ...'

'Why Bernadette?'

'A strong name but a pretty one, I thought. It's hard with female names. You don't want to be too corny, or too soft, or too harsh. Not only that, but Bernadette's a name I can use equally well for both the British version and the French one.'

'Right.'

'So think Bernadette. You started out much as you really are, and you've been drawn into Albrecht Dawes's cabal. You're no innocent though. In fact you're already starting to break away from his influence. He thinks the details of the summoning were wrong. You think sodomising Dave simply wasn't debauched enough. It's getting quite heated.'

'I'm with you.'

I sat down on a chair he'd set out in the middle of the floor and waited while he set up a big spotlight just a few feet from my face. The bulb was deep yellow, and not all that powerful, but I could feel the heat. I tried to think of myself as Bernadette, myself but older, with more knowledge. Could I have lulled a young man into a false sense of security with the promise of sex and then sodomised him on an altar?

The answer had to be yes. He'd wanted sex, and he'd got it, perhaps not quite the way he'd expected, but then who does? Perhaps he'd been pushy, cocksure, laddish, the sort of man who thinks it's funny to come in a girl's face. I'd met them, like Johnnie Moore, 'RJ', who I'd been on a date with shortly after I'd left school. He'd been the best-looking boy around, the dream date for just about every girl I knew, and a complete bastard. Yes, I could have buggered him as he writhed on an altar, happily . . .

Michael broke into my thoughts.

'Perfect, that look I have to capture.'

He'd already done it, penning the expression on my face as I had considered how RJ would have looked with eight inches of rubber dildo stuck up his bottom. I looked evil.

Michael continued.

'Now you're talking to Albrecht Dawes. You know the ritual of summoning was right. You went over every detail yourself. You don't like to be doubted.'

I focussed on being Bernadette, skilled and methodical. Like me she would read avidly, taking in every detail to feed her craving for knowledge, my craving. I would know I'd surpassed my mentor, and that he knew it too, his doubt driven more by envy than anything rational. I'd have said from the first that it was no good merely sodomising Dave. Dave needed to be corrupted, to be brought to the point where he revelled in the act, crawling naked on the floor with his anus lubricated, on my chain, begging me to have him, whip him and fuck him ...

'Great, beautiful. Now you're trying to persuade him that it would be better to corrupt Dave.'

'That's exactly what I was thinking.'

'We think alike, you and I, Dusk, we really do. Go for it.'

It was right. Debauchery needs compliance. Albrecht could see it only as something to be imposed on another individual, a typically male view, and wrong. Dave had to be shown how to take full pleasure in his body, to throw off everything society had taught him, to delight in the penetration of his anus, in licking my pussy and bottom, in sucking other men's cocks, their balls, defiling himself on the floor for my amusement.

'Wrong frame, but good. More aggression, less lust.'

He'd filled in the last frame, showing my face in gleeful triumph and not a little lust. It made me laugh, and he was grinning as I once more tried to focus, this time without getting carried away.

I, Bernadette, understood the concept of debauchery. I had more flexibility than Albrecht Dawes, taking in broad ideas from the full width of human experience while he concentrated on the handful of men he respected as Masters, all long dead, all dedicated to Satan. The most he could ever hope for was to equal them, never to move on, and it was his hidebound view that was holding us back, fiddling with symbols and arcane detail instead of celebrating his Master with lewd acts...

'Perfection, so intense, so determined. I couldn't do this with a professional model, not ever. Registering is all very well, but you understand what I need in a way they never could.'

'You use models a lot then?'

'Only recently, now that there's some cash coming in.'

He was amazingly fast, sketching three ovals to create an approximate head shape and adding lines in sudden, precise strokes, so that even as I watched my face grew from the page, rough but recognisable, with the expression he wanted painted clear. Even as he spoke he still drew, filling in details apparently at random, shapes, shade, borders, always gently. The heat from the lamp was beginning to become uncomfortable and my muscles were starting to stiffen, so I was glad when he finally stopped and declared himself satisfied.

'Enough for now, I think. That's coming on nicely.'

'Great.'

I gave him my most wicked smile and stretched, wincing as the blood flowed back into my limbs. We'd been at it for an hour, although other than my aches and pains it felt less, and I was in need of coffee, and more.

'Chinese?'

'Bed?'

'Why bother with the bed?'

'Suits me. I don't suppose you've invested in one of those strap-on things?'

It was a shame he hadn't had a strap-on, or he would have got it where it did the most good. After that I wouldn't have felt he was being condescending to me, whatever he'd said. We went to bed anyway, for another night of unbridled passion, although not quite so unbridled as the first. Again I rose late and took the bus back to All Angels, with the promise of seeing more of him during the week and another modelling session at the weekend.

He'd paid me too, pointing out that he paid other people and could claim it back off his tax in any case when I'd tried to refuse. At that I'd given in, reasoning that had I sat as a model for an art class I'd have expected to be paid, so why not for Michael? After all, he stood to make plenty out of the story.

I wanted to see Snaz and Biggy's piece again, and took the railway alley. It was actually being buffed, two men painting it over with white masonry paint to create an eyesore where the piece had provided colour and life. I watched for a while, feeling more than a little down. The one problem with looking after All Angels was that it set me against people I might normally have got on with. Snaz seemed to be the sort of girl I'd been friends with at school, and since moving I'd hooked up with very few other people.

Not that there was anything I could do about it. She was going to think of me in much the same way as the transport police and council workmen, only weird. It was true, from her viewpoint, but as I walked back I was wishing I'd known that she was a she earlier. That way I might have played things differently.

At the least I could stop being actively antagonistic, and I climbed the tower to take the hooded top down from the flagpole. I could see the railway, and part of the alley with the garage roofs, if not the actual piece. They'd almost certainly worked at night, but had I been on the tower I would have seen them. It was an intriguing thought, and carried an edge of excitement, although they were hardly likely to hit the same place again, at least not for weeks. I stayed for a while anyway, scanning the buildings alongside the railway and trying to read the distant dubs and pieces, those few which hadn't been buffed with white paint.

It brought back memories of the guilty thrill of tagging windows in buses, and later, moving from shadow to shadow alongside deserted railway lines, my stomach tight with apprehension. I'd always liked the night and the thrill of fear, and had never once gone back before completing at least something. Nor had I ever been caught. There had been bad moments, like when I was standing in the shadows admiring the big black and gold dub I'd put on a transformer box and all Hell had broken loose just metres down the tracks.

The local crew had been caught by the BTP, because some idiot hadn't switched his mobile off and it had rung as a patrol was passing their hiding place. Two of them had been caught and made to clean up, my dub included. They'd blamed me, which was hardly fair, and it had ended up with them tagging my bare chest. I'd fought like mad at the time, and not one of them had come away without scratches, but now the memory brought a bitter smile to my lips.

It had only made me worse, up every spare moment, trackside and anywhere else I could find blank space. I'd even got my job with the cleaning firm to pay for my paint. Then there had been my first piece, up painting on a switchgear shed all night, drinking Tennants until I was so off my face I didn't care if I was caught or not. It hadn't been that wonderful, and they'd still called me a toy, leading to my last piece, the grand climacteric of my writing, halfway up Solomon Brothers office block from a cleaning gondola, sober. Then they'd stopped calling me a toy. Some had gone for 'mad bitch' instead, but there had been envy in their voices. It had been a wonderful feeling, but pale beside what I had discovered during my nighttime escapades. I had experienced my first communion.

My idea had been to go trackside in the big international depot by Scrubs Lane in the hope of hitting a Eurostar. I'd been trying to figure out the CCTV coverage from the bridge when a security guard had challenged me. As I'd had a bag of paints with me I'd made myself scarce, taking to St Mary's cemetery for safety. It was the sensible place to go. Most men don't think a girl would hide in a cemetery, and fewer still will search one. I never did know if he followed, but I hid for a good half-hour, in the shadow of a huge granite tomb.

It was not my first time in a cemetery at night, by any means. I'd often wandered in the moonlight between the stones and tombs, letting my senses fill with every emotion that came. This time it was different, my overriding sense not melancholy, or peace, or regret, but a strange, malign humour, frightening and arousing too. As my heart had gradually slowed and my fear of being caught died away it had been replaced with an urge to be naked, and more than that, naked in rude, blatantly sexual positions. I'd fought it, scared but too curious and too bloody minded to flee. Before I'd really known what I was doing my top had been up and my hand down the front of my panties to give myself an orgasm immeasurably stronger than anything I had experienced before. Only later did I discover who was buried in the tomb: Jean-Jacques Lamarche, a man who boasted he had enjoyed over a thousand women.

So after the office block hit I'd given up writing. It was fun, but it could never approach the blinding exhilaration of communion. Besides, anyone with a marker pen could tag and there was endless beef. Communion was mine alone, wonderful and absolutely secret until I had shared it with Michael. Who had promptly cast doubt on my experience . . .

I was still on the roof when a voice called up to me from the street – the postman. He was used to me, and a friend of sorts since I'd persuaded Lilitu that he was not fair game. I called back, climbing down to find that he had a parcel which I was supposed to sign for. Intrigued, I took it into the vestry and quickly pulled the wrappings off, to find a mobile phone within. There was a single number in the memory: Stephen's.

7

In a way, accepting the phone from Stephen was one more step towards being in his control. I soothed my pride by calling him during the day in the hope of catching him in the middle of some frightfully important meeting and starting to talk dirty the moment he answered. From the formality of his voice when he responded I knew I'd done it, and he was not best pleased when he rang back later. It didn't stop him wanting a date though, and I agreed to have dinner at his flat on the Friday.

That left the rest of the week to myself, and Michael. I went down most days, to fuck and model and fuck some more. The Goat of Mendes quickly grew to a full story, and I grew so used to being Bernadette that I had begun to think like her even when I wasn't posing. Michael lapped it up, quite happy to be pushed on the ground and mounted, but always taking his turn on top.

It was great sex, but I knew I couldn't take it further and invite him to commune with me, not when he didn't believe. That I set aside for when I could convince him I was drawing on something other than my subconscious. I didn't bring it up in conversation either, although we frequently skirted around it. Another thing that didn't come up in conversation was Stephen Byrne. I knew I should say something, and with each time we had sex I grew a little more guilty, but I just couldn't bring myself to speak out.

Making my excuses for the Friday evening made me more guilty still, especially when Michael accepted them with his normal casual style. I was feeling a complete bitch on the bus, and not a lot better as Stephen drove me across town, although he was in the brightest mood I'd seen him, full of nervous energy and wit. I knew I could at least tell him, and that it would make me feel a little better. I let him have it as soon as we were in his flat, straight out.

'I um . . . I think you should know that I have another lover.'

'You do? Great.'

'Great?'

'Well, yes. Don't take this the wrong way, Angela, but I need discretion and common sense in a woman. After all, however much the rest of the populace may screw around, a politician is expected to set an example.'

There was more than a little bitterness in his voice as he went on.

'I wouldn't mind so much, only I've never spoken up for family values and all that rubbish in my life, so I can't very well be accused of hypocrisy, but they'd still come down on me like a ton of bricks. Still, things are getting better, slowly. An MP can be openly gay and get away with it, more or less, which is a step in the right direction. Anything less politically correct though, let alone . . .'

He stopped, pursing his lips and for a moment I wondered what he'd been going to say, but he went on.

'Risky business, affairs.'

'Why do you do it then? I mean, I take it I'm not the first?'

'Why do I do it? How can I not do it? Do you know how long ago I last had sex with my wife? Guess.'

'I don't know. A month? A year?'

'Fourteen years. OK so we married for expediency's sake, but I did try. We had separate bedrooms from the first. Damn it, she cares ten times as much for her precious job as she does for me, and her bloody horses, even the dog! I can't handle the idea of paying for sex either. It turns me right off, and it's risky too. A woman who's prepared to sell her body is quite likely to be prepared to go in for a bit of blackmail, or at the least to cash in by selling her story to the papers.'

'Isn't that a risk anyway?'

'Yes, but I choose carefully.'

'I'm flattered.'

'So you should be. Normally I spend quite a while getting to know a woman before I make my intentions obvious. I need to be sure she's honourable, safe if you prefer. With you I took a bit of a risk, I'll admit. Then again I've had a great deal of practice at judging people and I've not come unstuck so far.'

'Why take a risk on me, some ditzy skater-girl with a beef?'

'You really have no idea, do you? No. Young women never do.'

'How do you mean?'

He laughed and shook his head.

'Seriously, how do you mean?'

'You really have no idea how beautiful you are, do you, how alluring?'

'Yeah, I turn heads, but I never know if they're thinking "she's cute" or "what a weirdo". I don't really care either.'

'You see. You wear your beauty like a paper crown.'

'No. I spend hours on make-up, and most of my money.'

'You're equally lovely naked. You'd be equally lovely in an old sack with bits of straw in your hair.'

'Sure!'

'The first time we met, when you came into the hall, just to be near you made me ache, everything about you, the way you move, your elfin face, those huge eyes, full of innocence and determination, your little round bottom...'

'Which I fell on?'

He laughed.

'Have you any idea, the least inkling of how fresh, how delightfully, deliciously free that made you seem, sweet and lovely and naïve and...'

He finished with a sigh. I had known, sort of, but I'd had no idea the effect had been so strong. He went on, wistful and earnest.

'All the women I meet are impossibly sophisticated – a word with a Greek root by the way, meaning "false wisdom", which just about sums it up. They know how beautiful they are, to the last penny of their manicures or in some cases their last Botox shot. The irony is that by the time they learn it's usually too late, you see. Anyway, I have a special treat for tonight, lobster, fresh down from the Suffolk coast, the wine, a Clare Valley Riesling, but first oysters and champagne.'

He gave a sweeping bow and walked into the kitchen. I composed myself on the settee, quite ready for another session of being pampered with fine food and attentive sex. Having admitted to being with Michael had made me feel better, a lot better. I couldn't help but wonder if Michael would take the news equally well. He hadn't staked any particular claim to me, but then men generally don't, not at first, they just assume.

I was determined not to let my bad feelings spoil the evening in any case, and hit the champagne pretty hard. The oysters I couldn't eat, horrible slimy things that were still alive. It was like swallowing come, but without the kick from knowing what you're doing. The lobster was delicious though, as was the sticky chocolate cake that came afterwards, leaving me feeling stuffed to the brim, pleasantly drowsy and also naughty.

Stephen was different. Before he had always been pretty sure of himself, except when I'd first suggested sex in the graveyard. Now he was anything but, and getting rapidly worse, still full of nervous energy, but with more of the nervous. Once we'd finished the cake and the sweet, heavy wine he'd served with it he rose, crossed to the drinks cabinet and took out two brandy glasses and a bottle. He poured a generous measure into one glass and a smaller one into a second, only to suddenly change his mind and fill it properly. One he gave to me, the other he put to his lips, swallowing about half the contents in one gulp, then spoke.

'Lie down a while, let your food settle.'

As he moved towards the bedroom door I followed. Something was going on, and I was expecting it to be dramatic, maybe his bedroom transformed into a full-on Gothic dungeon, complete with rack and iron maiden. There was nothing of the sort, not so much as a whip or chain. Feeling slightly disappointed I laid myself down on the bed, flat on my back, once again too drunk and too full to pose. He went to the TV, turned it on and pushed a video into the slot. I smiled to myself, wondering if it was a porno and if that was what all the fuss was about.

'Do you like Westerns?'

'Well ... er ... not particularly.'

'Indulge me. This is *McLintock*, with John Wayne and Maureen O'Hara.'

I propped myself up, completely puzzled but quite happy to watch old movies with him if that was what he wanted, so long as we got down to business eventually. It was actually quite funny, especially because I was so drunk, well over the top, and before long I had my head on his shoulder and we were laughing together. His arm was around me, his fingers just inches from the curve of my breast, and I kept expecting him to touch me, or to kiss me, start stroking my legs, anything.

He didn't, but I could feel his body trembling against mine, and as I recovered from the meal my arousal grew steadily, with his warmth and scent slowly working their way into my head. We had to be waiting for something, but I had no idea what, and as the film moved on I determined that the instant it was over his cock was coming out and that was that. Meanwhile I could at least tease.

My hand was resting on his stomach, and I slid it further down, to where I would find the fun zone. There was a satisfying bulge in the front of his trousers. He gave a pleased sigh as I squeezed gently. I made to kiss him, only for him to turn away and take hold of my questing hand at the same moment.

'Hang on, this is the best bit.'

I turned towards the screen, feeling pretty irritated, to see Maureen O'Hara climbing out of a window in nothing but a black and white corset and some fancy Victorian underwear. It was funny, and I promised myself I'd watch and then get my own back by teasing Stephen later. Then everything became very, very clear as the on-screen chase reached its climax, with John Wayne turning an outraged O'Hara across his knee and spanking her with a coal shovel. Stephen was absolutely silent. Not me.

'So that's what you want to do is it, you dirty old sod!'

He went purple, real beetroot, and began stammering denials. I just laughed and put my hand over his mouth as I climbed on top of him, to sit right on his cock. Seeing I wasn't angry, he shut up, biting his lip as I took my hand away. I really didn't know what to say, or do, but I was enjoying his embarrassment even as I was genuinely put out by the idea that I should let him spank my bottom. My hands went to my hips and I looked down on him in outrage that was only partly fake.

'You have got a cheek, Stephen Byrne. What, you want to show me where a woman belongs, do you?'

'No, I just . . .'

'Oh yes you do, and don't give me any of your bullshit. You'd love it, wouldn't you? What would you do, spank my little bottom all pink and then make me go down on you?'

He went red again and swallowed. His cock was getting hard under my pussy, so I gave him an encouraging wiggle and laughed at his sudden intake of breath. I wiggled again, rubbing myself on him to send a jolt of pleasure right through me. He reached out to take my hips, still a little doubtful but well turned on. I shook my head.

'That's what you've been after all evening, isn't it?

All that trouble getting me drunk and mellowed out, then the funny film which just happens to have a girl being spanked in it. You were going to suggest it might be fun to do the same, weren't you? Yes you were, just as if you'd thought of it on the spur of the moment. And then you were going to put me across your knee, weren't you? You were going to pull up my dress, and take down my knickers, and spank my bottom, weren't you, Mr Stephen Byrne, MP. Admit it!'

He nodded, his face still beetroot and his penis a rigid bar in his trousers. Much more and he would come, I was sure, and if it hadn't risked missing out on my own fun I'd have made him. As it was I gave him another little wriggle and climbed off, sticking my nose in the air in mock disapproval. If he'd had any sense he'd just have done it to me, because now he was in real trouble. He was so repressed, for all his dirty mind. It was just too tempting to make him suffer for it.

'Well you're not going to, at least not . . .'

'Anything, just say how much you . . .'

'Uh, uh, don't be sordid, Stephen.'

'Clothes then. Any designer you name. Or high boots. Or a corset. Do you like corsets?'

'Yes, but you're missing the point. The reason I'm not going to let you spank me is because it would make me feel that I was the lesser person.'

'No, not at all, I would respect you more if anything, I . . .'

'Shh . . . that's how I feel, Stephen, but then, maybe I would quite like to do it to you, or something similar.'

'To me?'

'Yes. Why not, if you can do it to me?'

'Well . . . no reason, I suppose. It's just that . . . dammit, I'm a man! And how do you mean something similar?'

'So what if you're a man? Similar means similar, something a good girl, a nice girl, wouldn't even think about.'

'So, so don't you think a man should take ... No, I don't suppose you do. So what you're saying is that I can spank you if we do something you want in return?'

'No, I don't, if you were going to ask if you think a man should be in charge in bed. I suppose that sort of attitude's acceptable for your generation, just about, but it won't do with me. As for taking turn and turn about, maybe, but I have a better idea. If you want to indulge your dirty little perversion with me, you have to win the right.'

'How do you mean? By proving my respect for you?'

'No, nothing so soap-opera. In a game.'

Suddenly the wicked glint was back in his eye.

'Fine. Backgammon? Chess?'

'No. I bet you're ace at both, and I don't play either.'

'Let's toss a coin then.'

'No, too quick, and I think I should choose, that's only fair.'

'Cards? Poker maybe?'

'No. Pinball.'

'Pinball!? What, you want us to go out to an arcade?'

He was fit to burst, and didn't look too pleased. I laughed.

'No, silly, on your computer.'

'I don't have it. I don't have any computer games.'

'Yes you do. I'll show you.'

He had a PC, so he had pinball, which was one game I was absolutely sure I could win. Every time I visited home I spent hours on it, usually with my parents shouting at each other downstairs. Stephen didn't have a prayer. He knew it too, and was complaining the moment I'd got it on screen.

'But I've never played this!'

'Good.'

'That's hardly fair!'

'You're starting to whine, Stephen. Do you want to smack my botty or not?'

I stuck it out and wiggled for him. He immediately tried to slap me and I danced away, laughing. He was red-faced with a hard bulge in his trousers. I sat down on the computer chair to protect my rear.

'Well, are you going to play?'

He sighed.

'OK. My side of the bargain is what you suggested, a spanking for you and then you suck me.'

I nodded.

'And yours?'

I hesitated, not really sure what I wanted. I could whip him, and probably enjoy it, but it wasn't really me. What I need is a setting, somewhere special, and his flat was just too mundane, too domestic. I did want something from him though, something I'd been sure he would be reluctant to do.

'I know. You have to take me to a cemetery, Highgate or maybe Abney, and do just as I say.'

'Just that?'

'Just that.'

'OK, if you're sure, so long as you realise that I can't afford to take risks.'

'No more risk than shagging on Eliza Dobson's tomb.'

'OK ... that's if you're sure. Isn't there anything you'd like to do, some fantasy you need to express?'

'Not that I couldn't ask you for anytime.'

'Fair enough.'

I put my fingers to the keyboard, feeling thoroughly pleased with myself as I cued up a ball. It was good to see him in such a state, and more than I could resist not to draw out the agony. He was watching as I began to play, and I could feel his growing frustration as my score started to mount up. It just made me worse, and I began to bat the ball on the flippers, pretending to let it fall only to send it up again. Unfortunately I was just a bit too clever for my own good and dropped it the fourth time. I had nearly two million and two balls left, so I wasn't worried, laughing and patting his bottom for him as we swapped seats.

He made a big show of it, reading the rules, testing the sensitivity of the keys and trying different positions for control of the nudges, then flexing his arms and fingers before he started. The first ball fell without scoring, allowing him to replay but leaving me laughing so hard I could barely stand up. He cued up again, and this time managed to hit the ball, driving it straight up the launch ramp with a lucky shot. As it came down he caught it on a flipper, tapped it to try and get himself a mission, and missed.

I was trying not to laugh as I watched his desperate attempts to control the ball. He was not doing well, and it showed, mumbling and cursing under his breath every time something didn't work as he wanted it to and slamming his fist down on the desk when he fell, at under the half-million.

'Not bad . . . for a beginner.'

All I got was a grunt. I took his place, fully confident that he couldn't even match my first ball, never mind all three. I was on a roll too, making up to Ensign just before I fell to an unlucky rebound. My score stood at well over three million.

He took over, and was soon swearing again, but he'd hit a lucky streak and again and again missed falling by a whisker. Not that I was worried, but I gave him an encouraging little clap when his score topped the million. He'd stopped grumbling by then, and was playing with a quiet intensity, sometimes even making the ball go where he wanted it to. It wasn't enough, and he fell short of the two million mark.

As I sat down I was already planning out my blind communion in my head. Stephen was the right person, because he'd do as he was told without interfering, and if I dangled the carrot of his little perversion in front of him I could count on immaculate service. I should have been concentrating on the game, because I fell before I'd completed my first mission, to leave the score just over three and a half.

He had to double his score to win, and he'd been lucky so far. He was getting better though, and I watched with interest as he played, amused by the expression of tight-lipped determination on his face. He made two million, getting a fluky mission to reach Ensign. It took him past two and a half, and I started to get a bit worried. He began to whistle, some old tune from the 70s, now playing with easy skill. I was getting very worried as he passed three, three-one, three-two, now playing with cool certainty and real flair. I was biting my lip as he got a mission that was going to take him clean over my score if he completed it. My bottom cheeks had began to twitch in trepidation as he passed three-three and I realised I might actually be going to get a spanking, and my mouth came open in shock as the mission came in and his score shot up over four.

'Shit! You bastard!'

'Got you! The old touch hasn't deserted me after all.'

'What old touch? You said you'd never played!'

'I haven't, not on a computer. On the front in Yarmouth I was the best, the original pinball wizard. Those were real machines, of course, back in the 70s – Blue Note, Foxy Lady, Wild West, I could take any of my friends on any one of them.'

'Oh, shut up!'

'Temper, temper!'

'You might have told me, bastard.'

'Now, now, that's no language for a young lady, not when she's about to have her bottom warmed. Come along then.'

He let his last ball fall and reached out for my hand. I let him take it, feeling numb and seriously resentful as I trailed after him into the main room. My brandy glass was there, and I poured myself a hefty shot, downing it in one. I was going to take it, I felt I had to, but it was not going to be easy, and I was trembling badly. Stephen looked well pleased with himself, leering and rubbing his hands together in anticipation, then steering me into the bedroom with a firm swat to my bottom. That touch really brought the shame of what I'd let myself in for home and I found myself babbling.

'Look, could we ... could ...'

'Not backing out, are we?'

'No! It's just ... just ... I don't know. I've never been spanked, and ...'

'Well, you must at least admit you deserve it, after that phone call.'

'No!'

'No? I was in a meeting, Angel, with the chair of my constituency party and half a dozen bluestockings!'

'Whoops.'

'Whoops is about right. Now come across my knee, young lady, and no more nonsense.'

He sat down on the edge of the bed and patted his lap. I swallowed, desperately telling myself that it was just a game, that I could take it, that it was not a total surrender of my dignity. For a moment I just couldn't make myself do it, until I told myself I was being pathetic. Still I was burning with embarrassment as I laid myself down across his knees. I was also fervently wishing I'd taken him up on his suggestion of swapping kinks. That way at least I'd have been able to do something horrible to him in return, maybe bugger him like Dave in 'The Goat of Mendes', whip his backside so he knew how it felt or piss all over him.

'You do realise that your knickers are going to have to come down, don't you?'

'Yes. I'd guessed.'

I had tried to keep the sulky tone out of my voice, but it hadn't worked. He gave a dirty little chuckle and cocked one knee up, lifting my hips, and it had begun.

He was a real pig about it, fondling and patting my bottom through my dress for ages before he pulled it up. When he finally did, he tucked it high and began to explore my bum again, making me giggle by tickling the tuck of my cheeks and the flesh between them and my hold-ups, stroking the seat of my panties, and patting me, more firmly now. I didn't want to admit I liked it, but I couldn't help but react. There was no real pain, which I'd expected, but for all the indignity of my position it was making me warm and ready. Before long I was starting to push my bottom up and wish he'd take my knickers down.

Eventually he obliged, pushing a thumb down the back of my waistband and peeling them down around my thighs. Then it was back to feeling me, patting and stroking my cheeks, pulling them open to show me off behind, teasing my thighs, my bottom crease, my pussy. When his thumb slid into my body I could no longer hold back my reaction and let out the sigh that had been building in me since the beginning. He cupped my pussy, probing me and rubbing while he smacked my bottom with his other hand, more firmly than before.

I was being spanked, and it was not at all what I'd expected. In the occasional darker moment I had imagined punishment, not being spanked, but whipped in some dungeon or crypt, with evil men revelling in my pain. I had thought spanking would be a lesser version of the same, my pain for Stephen's pleasure, not the gradual bottom warming he was giving me, dirty, but closer to worship than punishment.

He finished playing with my clit and turned his full attention to my bottom, holding me around the waist and slapping my cheeks with his fingertips, just hard enough to make my skin sting. Soon I was in a rosy haze of pleasure, not so very far from orgasm, with my whole bottom warm and open and sensitive, my sex aching to be filled, my clit badly in need of some more attention. He was going to make me come, I was sure of it, but in his own good time, at once enjoying my body and taking his revenge for me tormenting him. Until then all I could do was lie there and let myself be brought slowly, slowly higher, my dignity forgotten as I surrendered to the delicious thrill of my first spanking.

Then he laid in.

It was completely unexpected. One moment I was lying across his lap with a silly smile on my face and my bottom pushed up for his attention, in bliss and completely accepting what he was doing. The next his hand had landed across my bottom with the full force of his arm, his grip on my waist had locked and I was screaming blue murder and thrashing crazily. He didn't stop, but just kept right on going, holding me hard to prevent my escape as he spanked me, his arm moving up and down like a piston, my body bucking wildly, my bottom burning with hot pain. I kept on screaming, begging, whining, anything to make it stop, until I was mad with pain and frustration. When finally I managed to fight my way free I slipped from his lap and sat down hard on the floor.

For a moment I couldn't speak, but only sit there, rubbing my blazing bottom cheeks with my mouth hanging open. My smacked skin felt thick and glowing hot, and I was shaking hard with reaction, some of it anger. It had hurt, a lot, and I was not pleased with him, but I couldn't deny the urgent need in myself. The spanking had put me on heat, there was no other way to describe it, with my hot bottom the focus of my body, my pussy at the heart, desperately needing to be filled. I wanted to be fucked. I wanted to suck his cock. I had never realised it was possible to resent my own desires. He'd taught me otherwise. At last I found my voice.

'You bastard!'

He just chuckled, and very casually pulled down his fly. I swallowed.

'Are you really going to make me do it?'

'Not if you don't want to.'

He knew I did.

'You really are a bastard, aren't you?'

I shuffled forward, to between his knees, taking in the rich male scent of his penis a moment before I'd opened my mouth around it. He sighed as I began to suck, his half-stiff shaft immediately starting to swell in my mouth, soon erect, and in my hand. I knew what I wanted to do, and I couldn't stop myself. My other hand went down, between my thighs, to stroke the swollen, sensitive lips of my pussy, and between. As I started to rub I set up a rhythm on his cock, my lips working up and down his thick shaft. He took my hair, twisting his hand in to it, to pull himself deeper into my throat, and back, leaving a ring of black lipstick just an inch from the base of his erection.

My thoughts turned to my hot bottom and the way he'd treated me, stroking me, tickling me, spanking me, taking more time over me than any other man I had known. It had hurt, at the end, but that was a small price to pay for the pleasure he'd given me, seeing to my bottom just as I was seeing to his cock, slow and attentive, unhurried, the way good sex should be.

He came unexpectedly fast, suddenly grabbing the base of the shaft to milk hot, salty come into my mouth. I struggled to take it, so close to the edge, then over, swallowing over and over with the waves of ecstasy washing over me, my body tight in orgasm, the warmth of my bottom a thrilling, delicious thing. For a long moment it was pure bliss, all the chagrin of letting him spank me gone, and then it was back as I sank down. Before I'd caught my breath I was thinking of revenge.

8

'Revenge' was a bit strong. Return match was more like it. He had upped the stakes, taking me somewhere I had never been before, and it had left me feeling out of balance. I needed to get that back, restore a bit of pride. It was tempting to demand a return match, but I had a nasty suspicion I'd just end up getting turned over his knee again. Deep down I knew I wanted exactly that, which made it worse.

I could have slept with him, but I went back, trying not to sulk and not to play with myself as I lay in the darkness of the vestry. As I'd passed down the yew alley I'd felt the Major sniggering. Somehow he knew, and it had made me blush, for all that Michael would have said it was just in my head or the wind in the trees.

The weekend was mine: Stephen was in Suffolk and Michael off at some convention in Birmingham. I felt I needed it, to get my head together, not only because I'd managed to involve two men in my life, but because each was fucking with my head in his own way. It needed resolution, but first something to think about, just to clear my head.

Research seemed the best bet, something to concentrate on and also productive. After taking Lilitu for her walk and making my round of the graveyard I headed up west, to the British Library. If there was any evidence at all of Sir Barnaby Stamforth being involved with Satanism, then it had to be there.

I searched all afternoon, buried in tome after tome, on the computer and in the microfiche. There was plenty about him, but all of it marked with exactly the blend of pomposity and fantastical self-aggrandisement I had come to associate with him. He'd had statues put up to him. He'd had streets and buildings and charities and ships named after him. He'd even had a brand of Christmas pudding named after him. He'd also travelled the world, made a huge fortune, had eight children, done all sorts of arcane industrial things and been an MP. The only thing he hadn't done was indulge in Satanic sex rituals.

The more I read, the more I became convinced that I had manufactured the entire experience in my own head. I didn't want to accept it, because if I did, communion was never going to be the same again, maybe not even possible. That was enough to bring me to the edge of tears as I left the library, and I was cursing Michael. Yet the experience had been so powerful, and so real.

It was going to be a bad night. My head was full of ideas and images, doubts and yearnings, senses of stupidity and shame, defiance, arousal, me as Bernadette, me bum-up across a man's knee. I knew that the moment I tried to sleep they would all come crowding in. I had to get out of myself, somehow, and it was no use just getting blasted, because it might well not help and would only make matters worse in the morning. As a final straw I could feel my period coming on, adding PMT to my troubles just when I did not need it.

Yet there was nothing I could do. Taking a bus the other way and heading back to old haunts, did occur to me, even going home. It was not going to help, or not much. There really was nobody I could talk to the way I needed to. I couldn't commune, it was impossible, not with the doubt Michael had planted in my head nagging at me. I could go out, walk the streets with Lilitu to keep me safe until I was simply so exhausted that I slept regardless of what was going on in my head.

There was nothing else for it. I'd dressed casual so that I didn't get any stress at the library, and stayed that way: black jeans, black top and, on sudden impulse, Snaz's hooded top. That made me think. I had her cans too. I could go and hit somewhere, give myself a rush that had nothing to do with men, or sex, and keep myself focussed for hours. It was pretty retrogressive behaviour, to use one of Stephen's expressions, but I didn't care. I wanted the hit, and the feeling that it was me against everybody else, that I was alone, laughing at them all.

I got the bag and checked through its contents. Snaz's colours were just not me, but Biggy's were better: purple, silver and a green not too far from tourmaline. There was a black needle-cap too, and I fed the four into my pockets, not wanting the added risk of carrying a bag. Nor did I want to be identified, and put down my mobile. Lilitu was eager, sensing my mood, her tongue lolling out and her tail wagging furiously.

It felt good, my worries already pushed down as I made my way down the yew alley and into the road. I stopped at the corner shop and used some of my modelling money to buy a four pack of strong lager, always a help. Just a few hundred yards away was the huge expanse of white paint where the big twin piece had been buffed over. To hit it would have been madness, with everyone who had anything to do with the place on the look out. On the other hand it was oh so tempting. It would also have been a tribute to Snaz, which was silly, but what I wanted to do. Not that she'd know.

I went down the alley, but the café was still open and there were far too many people about. There was no harm in scouting it, and I hadn't eaten, so I bought coffee and a bacon butty for myself, a saveloy for Lilitu and went to sit outside. There was a great sense of wickedness building up as I considered how it could be done, all my problems pushed away into the back of my mind, just as I had wanted.

Getting on the roof seemed easy enough, with several cars and a breakdown truck parked tight up against the garage doors. The high bits they'd done, and the bit beyond the end of the garage was out of the question, and I could only imagine that she had sat on his shoulders to do it. A big piece was foolish anyway. I was out of practice and I was very unlikely to be given the time. Dubs were better, far quicker, and if it came down to it I was sure I could scramble up the cables onto the viaduct above.

There were still way too many people about when I'd finished, so I went down under the bridge and into the park, sipping beer and trying to remember how the lines looked from the top of the tower. About a half-mile east there was a junction, which always meant plenty of transformer boxes and stuff, but it was very open, better for bombing than anything else.

Then it hit me. The hideous concrete box of a community centre in which I'd first met Stephen was perfect. Its long, featureless walls just cried out for some colour, and it was sure to come to his attention.

He knew nothing about my graff exploits, and although I had told him I liked to be called Dusk, he never used it. I could do letters so crazy he couldn't even be sure, but he would surely suspect. That would give him a reason to spank me ... no, that would teach him a lesson for doing it.

I doubled back on my tracks, deliberately walking slowly. The centre would be shut, I knew, but it was foolish to risk anything before midnight. I drank my second beer on a bench at the edge of the park, feeling gradually more detached from the people around me as the alcohol kicked in. Only when the pubs had chucked out did I move on, my stomach tightening as I grew close to my target.

Two rich yellow streetlights illuminated the front, with an alley at one side a black mouth overhung by creeper to make the side wall an easy target. That was not for me. Nor was the front, with its tattered posters and shuttered windows. I moved to the corner, peeping into the car park. A CCTV mast stood against the near wall, fixed camera, set to cover the parking spaces. That was just fine.

Keeping a close hold on Lilitu's lead, I worked my way along the wall, my back against the brick, under the camera mast and on. The back was perfect, no camera, two huge bins to shield me from the car park and a high, creeper-hung fence behind. A plain concrete wall stretched from the bins to the rear door – my canvas.

I spent a moment listening, my throat and stomach tight, my hands trembling slightly. It felt good to be back, a street urchin once more, and I was grinning as I popped another beer and set out my cans. I'd come this far, so I should do it properly, a piece. Already I was buzzing, and I could just imagine Stephen looking at it with his face of concern and disapproval, the one he kept for just such occasions. He would speak with regret about fund allocation for youth services and the need for channelling creative energy, complete bollocks, and all the time thinking of how much he'd like to spank my bottom for me.

Michael would be less fun, accepting of the act but critical of my abilities. That was what determined me to make it as good as I possibly could, and I paused with the black needle cap in hand. The old black letter 'Dusk' was not enough. I wanted full-on Gothic, illuminated capitals, as if it had been done by some berserk medieval monk. I could do it too – I'd spent enough time looking at them and writing them.

I began to work, a can in each hand – one beer, one paint – focussing on the way a raven's quill runs on paper as I put down a bold, sweeping D. It was right, straight out of the Book of Kells, and I knew I was on a roll. My u followed, s and k, all perfect lower-case black letter. I drained my beer and opened the last, wishing I'd bought six instead of four. Taking up the rich purple, I filled the upper part of the D, faded and filled the lower with green. The others followed, and more black, thickening the outlines and adding serifs. Then the silver, to create a pattern of Celtic scrollwork around each letter, crossing over and under to bring it all up into three dimensions and ending in beaked birdheads like the prows of Viking longships.

It glowed. Only a neat 1 to sign it and I was done, my piece perfect, Goth graff art at its best. I was laughing and grinning as I stood back to finish my beer and let the image soak in, and wishing I had a camera.

It would be gone in days, I knew, buffed or gone over by some toy bombing crew. I didn't want to go. It was a work of art, my best, not like Michael's, but an infinite improvement to the dreary concrete wall of the centre. The council were not going to see it that way.

I was still standing there maybe half an hour later when Lilitu alerted me with a deep growl. She had lain quietly as I worked, used to being patient while I did strange, human things she couldn't understand. Now she was anything but, standing stiff with her legs braced and her ears pricked up, her teeth showing in ready snarl. I melted back into the shadow of the bins, absolutely still, my heart hammering, my hand clamped tight over Lilitu's muzzle.

Police come in cars, or noisily, and all I could hear was the dull hum of London's traffic, which never goes. There are worse things than the police out at night, and I was as glad of Lilitu as I had ever been, and more, as I heard the stealthy pad of footsteps from the car park, and a female whisper. There were two people, probably a couple looking for somewhere to shag. Confident once more, and not wanting to totally wreck their fun by unexpectedly finding themselves looking down the muzzle of a Doberman, I rose.

To find myself face to face with Biggy and Snaz.

What do you say? What can you say? I'd had an embarrassed apology on my lips, expecting a pair of lovers eager for privacy. What I got was two people I'd been more or less at war with for months, and the shock of fear that hit me was anything but pleasant. It was nothing to theirs – Biggy's face a mask of utter terror as Lilitu reared, clawing at his chest, her jaws snapping at his face. He ran, and so did Snaz, smack into the giant wheelie bin, her forehead on the handle, and she was down, clutching at her face and begging not to be hurt as Lilitu lurched forward.

I pulled on the lead with all my strength, yelling at Lilitu to back off. She did, reluctantly, growling, her front legs braced to attack. I knelt, put my arm around her, stroking her behind the ear, and slowly her muscles began to relax. Snaz did not look good, her face creased up in misery, her hand clutching her bloodied forehead. The moment Lilitu was calm I went to her, reaching out, only to have my hand smacked away as she found her voice.

'Fuck off, you psycho bitch! What are you doing here? This isn't your ground! I'm not fucking doing anything to you, am I?'

She burst into tears, still swearing at me, but brokenly, then just sobbing as she tried to pull her hair away from the cut on her head with one trembling hand. Biggy was nowhere to be seen, and as Snaz tried to stand her legs gave way under her. I swore under my breath, feeling out of my depth and wishing my head wasn't spinning so badly. I reached out to her again, because it was the only thing I could think of to do, and she was crying really bitterly.

This time she let me touch her, and I helped her to her feet. It was only then that she saw my piece. A flicker of surprise crossed her face but quickly changed to pain. Her cut was bleeding quite badly, and even in my drunken state I could see she needed help. It was more than I could give except to get her somewhere she wasn't likely to be accused of vandalism, or me.

I had the sense to keep close to the wall as I helped her to the road. She let me, leaning quite heavily on my shoulder, but tried to push me away as we reached the street. I let go and she staggered a bit, sitting down heavily on a low wall. Biggy was still nowhere to be seen, or anyone else. Snaz looked as if she was about to keel over.

'Look, have you got a mobile?'

'No!'

'A number? I could call your parents ... or someone.'

'No! Dad'd fucking kill me!'

'I ... I'd say you fell or something ... I don't know ...'

'Look, just fuck off, leave me alone ...'

'No, I can't! Do ... do you want your hoodie?'

She looked up, out of tear-stained eyes, as if I was completely mad. I shrugged and pulled off the hoodie, wrapping it around her shoulders. She was right, when I'd been up all the time myself the last thing I'd have wanted was my parents to know. There was nothing for it but to get her to an A and E as fast as I could.

'Come on, I'm taking you to casualty.'

'No. Fuck off!'

I ignored her, helping her back to her feet. For a moment she tried to resist, then gave up abruptly, leaning her weight on my shoulder. It was all I could do to walk, but I couldn't just dump her, and I didn't dare go into a house for help so close to my piece, and stinking of beer and paint fumes. I made the end of the street, onto a busier road, and suddenly there were people about, looking at us, but not one offering to help. There were cabs, coming out from the city. I tried to flag one down, and a second, both driving straight past. The third stopped, a sullen-faced man who muttered under his breath about drunken sluts and dogs in the cab, but took us there.

Casualty was packed, thick with the smells of vomit and disinfectant, people shouting, a hard-faced woman blocking the desk as she demanded that her son be seen immediately. There were different desks, signs everywhere, everybody hurrying about or busy. I stuck Snaz in a seat and joined a queue, took a number, got told sharply to take Lilitu outside by one person and to stay with Snaz by another. It was not how I'd planned my night.

What it did do was keep my mind off Michael and Stephen. By the time casualty had patched Snaz's head up and we'd got out of the hospital I was so tired I could barely stand up. She left me with a grudging thank you and I made my way back to All Angels to collapse onto my bed. I was asleep in moments, and didn't wake up until well into the afternoon.

The events of the night before came back slowly: walking the streets getting drunk, painting my piece, Snaz and Biggy, the hospital. All of it seemed unreal, a good deal less real than my memory of the Satanic ritual, that was for sure. It had happened though. My fingers were still stained with paint and my head ached slightly. I remembered that I'd left the cans and wondered if I should go back, only to decide against it. The centre would be busy, or at least as busy as it ever was, and with the caretaker there it was quite possible my piece had already been buffed.

It was worth it, the whole experience, and the more so if Stephen found out. The only shame was that I didn't have a photograph. There was some money left from my modelling sessions, not much, but enough for a basic camera. I'd meant to treat myself, too, but so far I'd spent it on drink and cab fares. A camera was a good idea, and yet it was always possible that my piece would be left.

I needed to do something anyway, because I knew

I'd be brooding again in minutes if I didn't keep my mind occupied. So it was down to my local retail estate for a ten-pound disposable camera, then to the centre. This time I approached casually, excuse ready to hand as I walked in at the front door. The business with redeveloping All Angels was still going on, in theory, although with inside knowledge from Stephen I didn't need to do anything about it. I could pretend, and spent a while harassing the caretaker until he let me use his computer and printer to make a petition.

He was not in a good mood, on the phone to some-body as I stapled my sheets together, pointing out that he couldn't be there 24 hours a day. I asked innocently what the matter was and got a brief but heartfelt spiel on the problems of his job and his opinion of graffiti artists, especially the one who had defaced the entire back wall. It was exactly the excuse I needed. After making a few sympathetic noises I pinned my Save All Angels petition to the board with both my signature and his to start it off and walked around the back.

My piece was still there, perhaps not quite so perfect in the cold light of day and without the benefit of several cans of strong beer, but still pretty good. The caretaker hadn't followed me out, so I used the whole film up on it. I could understand the caretaker's point of view, when someone else made the decisions but he had to do the dirty work, but there was no question in my mind that to have my piece removed was the act of a Philistine.

I had it on camera, at least, and there was a website or two I could stick it on, just to make sure that it was seen by people who would appreciate it. Michael would, I was sure, and I wondered if it would be possible to bring him up before the piece got buffed.

The answer was no, as I discovered when I went back in to get a coffee. The caretaker was mixing up a bucket of cleaning fluid. I had to at least try.

'Why bother?'

'I bother 'cause I'm told to bother.'

'They'll only do it again.'

'Yeah, sure they'll do it again. It's not the first time either, but Mrs Goulding says it's got to be done by this evening, so it's got to be done by this evening.'

'Mrs Goulding?'

'Mrs Councillor Goulding. She's coming here this evening, for one of her meetings. Street crime, it is, and it won't do to have that dirty great thing on the wall.'

'I doubt they'll even notice it.'

'They already have. You can see it plain from all the end spaces. There's Byrne coming and all.'

'Oh, right.'

'Don't suppose you fancy giving us a hand?'

'Er . . . no, sorry. I'm not really dressed for it.'

He gave a chuckle, sarcastic and dirty too, his eyes flicking briefly to the hem of my skirt as he squeezed out the last of the bottle of cleaning fluid. I turned away, wondering if I should wait for Stephen. With luck he might turn up before the piece was completely buffed, and it would be so funny to tease him.

The Jaguar pulled up no more than five minutes later, while I was still sitting outside sipping coffee. For a moment I caught Stephen's face as he passed, and he saw me, but didn't give so much as a flicker of recognition. I soon discovered why. There was somebody with him, a middle-aged woman with a face like a hatchet and an expression of cold severity. For a moment I wondered if it was his wife, but I'd seen her before, probably at the All Angels meeting. Sure enough, when he appeared from the back the caretaker addressed her as Councillor Goulding.

She walked straight for him, brisk and purposeful, Stephen made to follow, then turned as he saw that I was approaching, looking shifty for an instant before he turned his politician's smile on. Councillor Goulding had stopped to talk to the caretaker and was in easy hearing range, just adding to my sense of mischief as Stephen addressed me.

'Ah, Miss McKie. Have you come to give your opinion at the meeting this evening?'

'No. I came to put up a petition to stop the All Angels development.'

'A pity. I'm sure with your experience with the church you would have been able to make a valuable contribution. We will be considering a major new initiative to combat street crime with a zero tolerance policy, in particular the recent spate of graffiti attacks. In fact I understand that there was an incident here last night.'

Councillor Goulding had turned and was looking at me with an air of disapproval that would have done Eliza Dobson credit, her eyes fixed to my crucifix of long tourmaline crystals set in silver, and doubtless wondering if it was hung upside down on purpose. There was more than a little doubt in her voice when she spoke.

'Miss McKie is involved with the church?'

Stephen stepped in before I could claim to be with the Reformed Satanists.

'I was unclear perhaps. Miss McKie is the caretaker at All Angels on Coburg Road. She has, I believe, enjoyed considerable success in deterring vandals and er ... other anti-social elements. Miss McKie, meet

Councillor Goulding, who is chair of the committee on urban regeneration.'

The Councillor gave me a marginally less frosty look.

'How did you go about this, Miss McKie?'

'I set my dog on them.'

The look became frostier again. Stephen went on, now walking towards the rear of the building.

'A great shame you are unable to attend the meeting, Miss McKie. Hmm ... yes, I see. I always wonder what these things say.'

We had come in view of my piece, at which the caretaker was working methodically but not with very much success. It was still perfectly legible, or at least more so than the majority of wild-style pieces.

'That's a D first, or maybe an O. No, D, and u, and z ... no, s, and k. Dusk. Dusk.'

He shot me a glance. I returned a bland smile. He knew, and there was worry on his face as he turned to the Councillor.

'Did we capture anything on the CCTV camera in the car park?'

The caretaker answered.

'They were sneaky, came in along the wall. Got some feet. Three of them, there were, and a dog. Left their cans behind too, they did. Get some good fingerprints, I reckon.'

Stephen spoke quickly.

'I doubt the police would consider that an effective use of resources, and besides, with young offenders of this type it is not particularly likely that their fingerprints will be on the record. Nor am I certain that applying the full weight of the law is necessarily the answer. Yes, it is destructive, of course, and certainly we must do everything we reasonably can to prevent it, or at the least implement some form of damage limitation policy, yet I cannot help but think that the root of the problem lies in time management. If only we were able to increase fund allocation for youth services we might be able to somehow channel the undoubted creative energy that is expressed here.'

Councillor Goulding was unimpressed.

'Nonsense. Our policy must centre on deterrence. What is needed are heavier fines, increased CCTV surveillance.'

'Perhaps, but again we run up against budgetary constraints. If I may address you, Miss McKie, as – dare I say it – a typical young person of the borough, what do you think?'

It was just too good to miss.

'I think they should bring back the birch, that's what I think, so just give them a good old-fashioned spanking.'

Councillor Goulding shot me a filthy look, which was just as well as Stephen's face had gone crimson. I smiled sweetly and made my excuses before he could say anything else, struggling not to grin as I walked away.

Our little exchange had made me feel a great deal better about taking the spanking. I had turned it neatly round to my advantage, making it something that made me the stronger partner, not him. He would be round later too, unless I was very much mistaken.

Other than a mouthful of Crunchy Nut Cornflakes I'd had nothing to eat since my snack at the café, and I stopped for chips on the way, eating them in the park and wishing I'd had the sense to retrieve the cans. Not that it was likely to be a problem, but I do like to be careful. After all, the whole idea of taking risks is to come out on the up side.

By the time I got back the evening was already beginning to draw in, with a slight chill in the air, bringing the first hint of autumn to the graveyard. After feeding Lilitu I went to sit on the wall, drinking the atmosphere in as the light slowly faded. Whatever Michael said, I could sense the presence of the dead around me, and I knew it would not have been the same anywhere else but there. He was wrong, and I would prove him wrong.

My emotions were still a little raw, but I was nervy rather than down. I considered communion, perhaps another attempt at Sir Barnaby Stamforth, but I knew that part of my mind would be detached. The experiment needed to be made, but in the right way. Only then would I be able to retrieve the exquisite pleasure I'd grown used to. Until then . . .

Until then I could content myself with Stephen, who was sure to be along presently. I still felt tired after the night before, and relaxed back against the gatepost, drinking Coke and scratching Lilitu behind the ear. I could see the full length of Coburg Road, and made sure to keep up a pose of languid elegance with just a touch of the naïve and just a touch of the urchin.

His extravagant praise had been flattering, even if it had been designed to get me across his knee, and he had said it with real feeling. It was strange, because for all the effort I'd put into my look, it wasn't Gothicism that attracted him at all, but his perception of Gothicism as charmingly naïve, as a childish conceit. Really I should have felt resentment, but I couldn't find it in myself, preferring to feed his image of me.

Undoubtedly he would want to spank me after I'd cheeked him so badly, but I wasn't going to let him. Instead I would tease to make him more eager, suggest playing a game as before, but this time win, or lose, and rely on his sense of obligation to make him help me with my blindfold communion. I adjusted my dress a little, 'accidentally' showing off a little more thigh.

'Don't move. I have to catch you like that.'

I nearly fell off the wall, catching myself only just in time, and turning to find Michael standing at the gates, sketch pad in hand. Lilitu was snuffling at his foot.

'Hi, you made me jump. I thought you were in Birmingham?'

'I was. No, no, stay there.'

'OK . . .'

I let him capture the sketch he wanted, then hopped down from the wall. It was more than a little awkward, with Stephen likely to turn up at any moment, and the sensible thing to do was obviously to make for Michael's flat. I kissed him and gave his cock a cheeky squeeze.

'Your place then?'

'Out of service, I'm afraid. You know that couple Chris was showing round the flat? Well, they're going to buy, almost certainly. They're round there now. I need a new place. Anyway, this is a great light, how about a few poses for me and then I'll buy you dinner?'

'I've eaten, thanks, but yes . . . some sketching . . . good idea. The light is beautiful, isn't it? I tell you what, how about something a bit more industrial, like . . . like cranes or something?'

'Industrial? Cranes?'

'Yeah, sure . . .'

A big, shiny black Jaguar had turned in at the far end of the road.

'Well, it's an idea, but I really wanted some more background material for the Goat of Mendes project.'

'Yeah, OK, or ... oh never mind. There's somebody I'd like you to meet anyway.'

The Jaguar drew to a stop directly across the gates. Stephen climbed out, his face bland and official as he extended a hand to Michael. I drew a sigh.

'Stephen, hi, this is my friend Michael. Michael, meet Stephen Byrne MP.'

9

I suppose it was bound to happen, sooner or later. Stephen knew, of course, and behaved like the experienced adulterer he was. First he created his excuse for being there, stating that he 'intended to ensure that my petition was given due consideration at the next consultative committee meeting'. Next we chatted politely, discussing the one thing we had in common, All Angels, Michael and I pointing out various features of the architecture while Stephen made polite comments. Finally he excused himself, saying that he had a lot of paperwork to catch up on. I had never seen an exhibition so studiously dull in my life.

Michael remarked on it, making a joke about greyness and politicians. I laughed, if not for the right reason, but I was feeling more than a little guilty underneath. I did my best to make up for it, sucking his cock and going down on all fours on the vestry floor for him, but my heart wasn't really in it. I kept thinking about Sir Barnaby, and how Michael and I should have been at that moment in ecstatic communion on some appropriate tomb.

He stayed, and for the first time I slept with a man in All Angels. It was strange, after so many nights alone with the ghosts, and I could feel them crowding around as I lay there long after he'd fallen asleep, some disapproving, some filled with lust and envy, some merely curious. If it was no more than my mind playing tricks on me then it seemed very, very real.

It was raining in the morning and we spent it inside, Michael sketching the tombs of Isaac Foyle, Sir Barnaby and the poet Nathaniel Gold. I sipped hot sweet coffee and watched, as entranced as ever by his art but unable to stop myself from brooding. He didn't seem to pick up on it, as cool as ever, and when the rain had stopped asked if I'd like to go flat hunting with him. I declined, telling him I was busy, which again he accepted with absolute nonchalance.

Once he'd gone I took Lilitu for a walk and handed my camera in to get the film developed. The streets were wet with rain, and the smell of autumn was in the air, something that always brings back the beginning of school terms, making everything seem new and uncertain. Now it served to bring home my ill feelings with a vengeance, and I found my mood growing blacker by the minute.

Nothing appealed, not communion, not reading, not tagging. When I got back to All Angels I went to sit on the wall at the bottom of the graveyard, staring out over the rank grass, bramble and sycamore growing between the gravestones. I knew my mood would lighten, but that didn't mean I could break it, anymore than I could push the smell of dank earth and wet leaves from my head.

I was still sitting there when I heard a voice from near the church. That I could handle, and there was a savage determination in my heart as I whistled up Lilitu, only to realise that it was somebody calling my name. I walked over, wondering if one of my old friends had decided to drag herself across London, to find Snaz standing between the gates. She looked as sulky as I felt, with her hands pushed deep into her pockets and her face half-hidden. I grabbed Lilitu's collar, struggling to hold her back. Snaz retreated and I quickly called after her.

'It's all right, she won't hurt you. Are you OK? How's your head?'

She stopped and turned around, still eyeing Lilitu as she spoke.

'Good. OK. I . . . I just wanted to say thanks, yeah? For helping and that.'

I shrugged and smiled. She stayed put, not looking at me, but at a car across the road. Something inside me badly wanted her company, and I was going to ask her if she'd like coffee when she spoke again.

'The big piece down the centre. Yours, yeah?'

'Mine, yeah.'

'You're no toy, you.'

'Nor are you, you're good. Biggy too.'

For the first time she smiled.

'That prat. He ran. He's a good writer but he's chicken.'

'Bigger boys than him have run from Lilitu.'

'That's your dog?'

'Yeah, but she's all right once you get to know her. Aren't you girl?'

I'd squatted down to scratch Lilitu's chin. She returned a quizzical look, doubtless wondering why a prey beast was suddenly one of the pack. Snaz didn't move, but pushed back her hood. I hadn't really focussed on her dressing before, but it looked awful.

'That had to hurt!'

'It did. I didn't know what day it was.'

'I bet. So, do you want a coffee or something? Ever been inside the church?'

'Yeah, plenty, before you moved in. So what's the deal?'

'I get to live here so long as I look after it. It's not official, but my uncle's a Commissioner.'

'Right. I couldn't figure how come you're a writer but you buff all our shit?'

'I'd be out if I didn't, and this is my ground.'

'You into all that Goth stuff then?'

'Yeah. Did you like my letters?'

'Yeah, real style. D'you bite them from someone old school?'

'No. They're like the way the old monks used to write, only with a bit of my own style. It's already been buffed.'

'Yeah, I know. I went down the centre.'

'I've got flicks. We can get them now, if you like? We'll have coffee down the café where you and Biggy did your piece. You're up plenty, you two.'

That was it. We kept talking as we walked, first to the photo shop, then to the café, giggling over the pictures and my piece and swapping stories. My black mood had gone by the time we left, so completely I couldn't even understand why I'd felt there was a problem. I wasn't married, I could fuck with who I pleased, and Michael was sure to be open minded, which was really all he was being about communion.

We bought a pack of beers each and walked east alongside the tracks, first through the park and then along an alley, way beyond anywhere I had explored before. She lived high up in a block with a prime view over Coburg Road and All Angels, also the railway. She had caught the writing bug watching crews at work trackside, far beneath her. She was worse than me, tagging buses at twelve and trackside before she was sixteen. Like me she'd found it difficult to be accepted as a female artist, being called a toy and having her work dissed by people without a fraction of the skill.

I could sympathise, and did, telling her about my hit on the tower block, and more. She gave back as easily, explaining how she and Biggy had been determined to stay up at All Angels, which now just made me laugh. She'd been scared by Lilitu, but he'd been terrified, and it had been his decision to back off. I just laughed, our previous enmity now something to be shared.

We got thoroughly drunk, and while I held short of trying to explain communion to her, just about every-thing else came out. I told her about Michael and Stephen, her advice being to keep shagging both of them as long as I could. She thought the idea of having an affair with an MP was hilarious, and like me had thought of him as a cold fish, in so far as she had ever thought of him at all.

Back at All Angels with pies, bags of chips and more beer it grew better still. She was no Goth, but she was well into colour and design, and loved my jewellery, swapping a silver goat's skull with garnet eyes for the aquamarine tipped peg from her belly button. That got us comparing piercings, then swapping clothes. She was much my size, a touch shorter and with another couple of inches of tit, but just about everything fitted. By the time we'd dressed her up in full Goth gear of fishnets, short black dress with nothing underneath and about half my jewellery collection I was down to my panties and laughing so hard I could barely stand. I'd been a Goth since before low-rise jeans came in, and tried hers on, only to find I couldn't get them far enough up to cover the crease of my bottom, which we found absolutely hilarious.

We started making up, borrowing each other's gear to swap looks. She went first, her face pale, black lipstick fading to purple, heavy mascara under deep-purple eyelids, an inverted cross painted on her cheek. I was just trying to put on her vivid red lipstick without making a complete mess of it when my phone rang. It had to be either Stephen or Michael, and I was trying to repress my giggles and shush her with my hand as I answered. It was Stephen, and he was parked outside.

I let him in, too drunk to care what he thought, and making a point of walking ahead of him to show off the way my bum looked. Snaz wasn't much better, sprawled on my bed with the dress tight over her chest and her nipples poking up and a good deal of thigh showing too. It immediately got him flustered, tripping over his own tongue as he tried to make small talk, which had us in fits. He was grinning though, embarrassed but enjoying the view, and I just had to take it further.

'He spanks me, you know. Pervert.'

Stephen went bright red. Snaz dissolved into giggles. There's nothing like a bit of encouragement.

'He does, really, over his knee with my knickers down. I suppose it's because he went to public school. They're all very repressed, naturally, but oh girl, does he get up to some mischief!'

I'd gone up to him, and kissed his cheek as I pulled close, raising one leg to brush the front of his crotch. He was going to explode, his face beetroot coloured, his mouth working between a silly grin and tight-lipped annoyance. His cock was more than a little hard though, and I gave him a squeeze as I stepped away. Snaz put in her pennyworth.

'Dirty little boy. You should spank him, not the other way around.'

'Perhaps I will.'

'You should. I bet he'd love it.'

'He would. I bet he would. Well, Stephen old chap, how about it? Six of the best, that's what it used to be at the good old school, didn't it? Still, never did you any harm, eh? Frightfully good for you. Character building and all that!'

I had suited actions to words, imitating his voice as I marched stiffly across the room, bent over the table and stuck my bottom out, my face set in a mask of overdone pomposity. Stephen was gaping like a cod fish, completely unable to cope, Snaz in a great gale of laughter, clutching at her tummy and mouth. I went on, thinking back to when he'd done me.

'Nah, he prefers to dish it out, he does. You should have heard him – "You do realise that your knickers are going to have to come down, don't you" – "Now come across my knee, young lady, and no more nonsense".'

I was doing his accent in wild exaggeration, and he seemed to be getting to the point of apoplexy, Snaz too. Finally Stephen found his voice.

'I'm quite capable of doing it, Angel, here and now, whether your friend's watching or not, and yes, I will take your knickers down.'

It was my turn to blush as Snaz went into a fresh fit of giggles. I laughed too, then stopped abruptly as I realised he was serious.

'No, Stephen, that's not funny . . . it's not, really!'

It didn't stop him. He came on, grinning. I was wagging my finger at him as I backed away, protesting but simply unable to keep the laughter from my voice.

Snaz was still giggling, and obviously just thought it was funny. I turned to speak to her, and suddenly he had me and I'd been lifted clear of the ground, around my waist, as if I weighed nothing. I gave a frantic squeal of protest, but too late as my jeans were hauled down, panties and all. My bare bum was showing to Snaz, and my mouth came wide in outrage, then screams as he laid in, spanking me furiously hard. She was laughing crazily as I went into a frenzy of kicking and scratching, for one awful moment I realised that she could see every detail of my pussy from behind, and then he'd dropped me.

I sprawled on the floor, bum up, gasping and swearing at him, struggling to sound serious, but I still couldn't keep the laughter out of my voice. Snaz just laughed all the louder and, as I struggled to pull my jeans and panties back up, I didn't know whether to be angry, or turned on, or hurt or what. Stephen had stood back, and was looking unsure of himself as I got up, unsteady, clutching my hot bottom, my head spinning with drink.

'Bastard!'

It was the best I could manage, and for just a moment Stephen really did look worried. Snaz did not help.

'Fucking priceless! You should have seen yourself, Dusk, what a fucking hoot!'

'I'll give you the same in a minute!'

It was the best I could do, my cheeks burning with embarrassment for all the irrepressible urge to laugh. She got up, as unsteady as me.

'Don't even think about it girl ... I've got to go, I've really got to go. I've wet my pants laughing. I'll leave you two lovebirds at it.'

She was still laughing as she staggered across to the door. I let her go, too far gone to worry about the fact that she was wearing my clothes, or anything else. My bottom felt warm, my pussy ready. Stephen mumbled some stupid apology for some reason and was biting his lip as the door closed behind Snaz.

'Are ... are you all right, Angel? I ... I didn't mean to.'

'Oh shut up, Stephen ... stop worrying about it and fuck me.'

I flopped down on the bed, pushing my jeans and knickers back down the moment I hit. Stephen just stood there, trying to make sense of what was happening.

'I think you're rather drunk, Angel.'

'Just fuck me!'

I rolled over, sticking my bottom up to let him see my red cheeks.

'That's what you like, isn't it? Just put it in, you dirty bastard!'

He swallowed hard, but it was too much. As I stuck my bottom higher to let him see my pussy he was struggling with his fly, wrenching the zip down, snatching his dick free, the shaft already swollen with blood. I moaned as he climbed on top, his cock was probing at me, between my cheeks, right on my bottom hole and then in me, deep up my pussy. He began to pump into me and I was immediately clutching the sheets, pushing my bottom up and trying to twist round to kiss him all at once. As his mouth met mine he went deeper still, his taut belly slapping on my bottom cheeks, his hands snatching at my breasts.

We clung together, fucking like two wild animals, me squirming on his cock as he rode me, harder and faster, kissing until he broke away, panting, then gasping. His hands locked on my breasts, squeezing hard and I was gasping too, breathless as he pushed into me in a wild flurry of hard thrusts, and came, deep in me, holding himself there as I wriggled beneath him, right on the brink of orgasm.

'Lick me, you bastard, now!'

It took him only a moment, his penis slipping free as he gasped for breath, his hands moving lower, to take my hips, lift me, and bury his face in my bottom. My eyes and mouth went wide as his tongue touched my aching sex and he was doing it, lapping up his own juices and mine, from my pussy, between my bottom cheeks and on my clitoris. I was screaming seconds after he began to lick, brought back to the edge of orgasm, and over, writhing my bottom in his face, snatching and chewing at the sheets, gasping and swearing. Peak after peak hit me, Stephen still licking, until at last my pleasure broke and I was begging him to stop.

He obliged, taking one last lick from me all the way up between my bottom cheeks and letting go. I slumped down, done, and he rolled onto the bed beside me, gasping for breath and sighing in pleasure. At last I summoned up the energy to pull myself close and kiss him, before it all became too much and I collapsed.

Stephen was still with me in the morning. I did not feel good at all, and gratefully accepted his ministrations as he propped me up on my pillows and made me coffee and toast. My head hurt and my throat was dry, while I could feel the dull ache of bruising on my bottom and one hip. I was surprised Stephen was even there, let alone fussing around me like an old mother hen, but that really wasn't my problem.

By the time I'd washed and changed Snaz's clothes for some of my own I was feeling at least vaguely human. Stephen had gone into the main body of the church to look round, but came back while I was making the final adjustments to my make-up, speaking immediately, with the same nervousness in his voice as when he'd been trying to get around me to go across his knee.

'Yes, I can see why you would be keen to see the interior preserved. There are some unusual features there, no doubt unique. If only current budgetary prioritisation ...'

'Stop talking bollocks-speak, Stephen. What's the matter?'

'Nothing ... well, a little. I was concerned that you might feel I was a little rough with you last night.'

'I'm not made out of china, Stephen. It was good, as it goes.'

'I mean er ... spanking you like that. I really shouldn't have, but ... but you were rather teasing. You didn't mind too much, did you?'

'Forget it. I was pissed, and I was winding you up.'

'Good ... good. Still, I shouldn't really have done it, especially in front of your friend.'

'I said forget it.'

'Good.'

He went silent and I returned to my make-up, wondering if I could do anything with the brilliant scarlet lipstick Snaz had left, perhaps blend it with a black outline to make it look as if I had fresh blood in my mouth. Eventually I decided to postpone the effect for a more appropriate moment. I was surprised Stephen was so nervous, but then I could imagine the headlines if it came out that he was into kinky sex. They'd have a field day. I wouldn't have told anybody, because at heart I could never be that much of a bitch, but it did occur to me that it was a good time to ask for his help with my experiment into communion.

'Stephen?'

'Yes?'

'I am cool with the spanking business, but I would rather you didn't do it in front of my friends, or at all really.'

'Oh.'

The disappointment in his voice was painful.

'Well, maybe occasionally, but it . . . it fucks with my head a bit. It just makes me feel as if we're unequal, and I can't handle that.'

'Oh no, it's not like that at all. Nothing could make me think more highly of you, I assure you. Believe me, I live in awe of your ability to cope with your sexual feelings. It's a generational thing, I know, but still . . . Besides, if, as your friend . . .'

'Snaz.'

'. . . as Snaz suggested, if you wanted to ah . . . um . . . get even, then I would accept your right to do so.'

'Thank you, that's sweet, and it does make a difference, but for now, do you remember I wanted a special favour if I won the pinball game?'

'Yes, of course. Something to do with a graveyard wasn't it? As I said, I'm all yours, just so long as it doesn't involve me in any professional risk.'

'Great. Thanks.'

'It doesn't have to be in London, does it?'

'No, not at all.'

'Good, because I've got just the place. It's . . .'

'Don't tell me. The less I know about it the better. I do need you to choose the cemetery, but not just any old cemetery. It has to have the tombs of some significant people, people I can find out about. One will do, but you must choose, take me there blindfold, late at night, and just leave me. That's really important. I need you to go away, to somewhere just within earshot, and leave me undisturbed.'

'I see . . . yes. I don't mind doing that. May I ask why?'

'No.'

'Fair enough. When?'

'Not just yet, it's . . . it's an awkward time. Perhaps at the weekend?'

'Fine. I tell you, even a cemetery is more cheerful than my house at the moment. The Designer Mannequin is on a diet. I told her she was risking anorexia, which was a bad mistake. She's not even speaking to me, that's why I came back early at the weekend. The meeting was just an excuse.'

'Ah, yes, Mrs Councillor Goulding. What an old bat!'

'She is something of a virago, yes, but whatever possessed you to vandalise the back of the Community Centre!'

I was not going to admit I'd done it to get at him.

'It's a hell of a kick.'

'A kick!? It's a hell of a risk!'

'You seduce young women. I go out writing. Same deal.'

'Well, yes, I suppose so, but you can hardly compare your need to scrawl graffiti with the human sex drive?'

'No. Sex is better. That's why I quit, sort of. The other night was . . . what d'you call it? Retrogressive behaviour. It's all to do with why I want you to take me to a cemetery, and I'm not going to explain. So the weekend's booked, yeah?'

I knew I couldn't do anything before the weekend as I would be on my period. Sure enough, it started the next day, putting an end to my mood swings and providing the perfect excuse for not fucking with Michael until I was ready. He took it as casually as ever, suggesting I should give him blow-jobs instead in the same easy manner he might have asked for tea instead of coffee.

He got what he wanted, most of the time, in between modelling sessions. With the Goat of Mendes now polished to perfection he was less specific in his needs, posing me in all sorts of ways, often wonderfully strange and just as often rude. He seemed just to be building up a portfolio, but I didn't mind posing and could never tire of admiring the end results. The money also came in useful, allowing me to invest in my renewed interest in graffiti.

Snaz had asked me to come out with her, delighted to have finally found a female artist. She was also fed up with Biggy, who was good, but was now working and starting to dislike the risks. I didn't get a chance during the week, although we talked plenty, either because I was with Michael or Stephen, who cooked me dinner on the Wednesday. He'd chosen a place, and seemed to be quite into the idea, leading me to give him the same favour I was dishing out to Michael.

We went for Saturday, to avoid the evening worshippers. It was warm and dry, allowing me to dress properly, in a short black dress, hold-ups and boots, with every piece of esoteric jewellery I could lay my hands on. It was a strong image, no question, Gothic to the edge of Satanic, and could scarcely fail to provoke a reaction. I took black candles too, the rest of my stock, and a bag of flour to mark out the pentacle. The moon would be a waning crescent, not bright, but appropriate.

I spent the morning in the church, letting the atmosphere fill my head but not allowing my thoughts to go in any particular direction. Stephen came in the early evening, nervous but in control, with everything organised. He was pleased with whatever choice he'd made, and had the whole thing planned out like a campaign, with a folder full of maps and notes, even a schedule.

He'd bought me a cap, black with a long peak, which he pulled down over my eyes as soon as we were in the car. I settled back, content to let him have complete control until I was actually kneeling in front of the tomb. When I made to talk he shushed me and put on music, a classical piece I didn't recognise.

We set off as soon as it was dark and drove for what must have been an hour or more, first with the yellow lights of London streets flickering across what little I could see of the car's interior, then in blackness. I had no idea in which direction we were going, and was unsure even of the time. When we stopped it was absolutely black outside, and as the noise of the engine cut off, silent.

I'd been growing slowly more nervous as time passed, and was trembling slightly as Stephen tied a thick scarf over my face as a blindfold and helped me from the car. It had grown cool too, but the air was still and smelt of autumn leaves. There were sounds, animals nearby or in the distance, the faint hum of a motorway, not city sounds. I was out of my element, and felt it, with a vulnerability that increased as Stephen put his coat around my shoulders.

'I'll lead you.'

'Yes.'

His hand found mine and I walked forward, cautiously, my feet on leaves and twigs, then grass. There was a stile, which he guided me over by carefully placing my hands and feet, and with not a little attention to my bottom. Ever more vulnerable and ever more receptive, I let him steer me as he pleased, across thick, springy grass, then short turf. Already I could feel an atmosphere building around me, the sweet sadness of a graveyard. I caught a dull, metallic groan as Stephen opened a gate. He helped me through. I knew we had arrived. Just a few steps and he stopped.

'Here?'

He answered in a husky whisper.

'Here, yes. Don't worry, it's absolutely safe.'

'OK. Now, do exactly as I say. In my bag are candles and a bag of flour. Use the flour to draw a pentacle on the ground, big enough for me to kneel in the central space.'

He made to speak, but didn't. I heard a rustle as he moved my bag, the opening of the flour, the soft shaking of the bag, every sound absolutely distinct. I was standing straight, and he made the pentacle around me, the five points and the encompassing circle. Immediately the atmosphere grew stronger, with hints of strong emotions creeping into my head. Yet it proved nothing. I knew I was in a graveyard, I knew I was in a pentacle.

'Now the candles. Place one at each point of the pentacle and the rest on the stone.'

'It's . . .'

'Don't tell me! Not anything. If possible, make a cross. Light them all, help me down and go. I'll call when I need you. Promise you won't come to see?'

'I promise. I'll stay within earshot, no closer.'

'I believe you, Stephen, thank you.'

I let myself slowly down into a kneeling position, my open knees meeting short grass damp with dew. The smell of lich mould and leaves was strong, then the sweet incense of my candles as he began to light them. Already my head was full of thoughts, unfocussed, but growing stronger as the candle smoke filled my head. When Stephen had finished he kissed me, and left. I heard the groan of the gate and I was alone in the night, kneeling at a tomb, my mind open to trance.

Melancholy filled me, black tendrils reaching into my mind, bitter-sweet, sadness and triumph both. I began to slip, existence drawing in to make a tight parcel of my body, the pentacle, the tomb before me and its occupant. I caught a sense of masculinity, harsh and certain, and of prayer, dull and even, a litany endlessly repeated in a droning voice. An urge came, strong, righteous indignation, to close my knees, to stop flaunting myself, to cover my legs. My defiance rose instantly, as with Eliza Dobson, condemnation of my sexuality inspiring me only to yet dirtier behaviour. A fresh shock hit me, harder, demanding I pray, submitting myself utterly though my sins went beyond absolution. Again I fought, my knees moving wider, taking hold of my breasts to offer myself as the Mother, fertile and provenant.

Anger hit me, boiling rage, murderous in its intensity, and my own fear in response, my throat tight as I struggled to scream. I fought it, my fingers clamped around the flesh of my breasts, my nails raking my own flesh, trying to hold on against the great tide of fury, and failing, clutching at the grass as my body went down. My face went to the ground as the sense of my own wrongness became too strong. I was woman, dirty, lecherous, sinful woman, a witch, a succubus, evil incarnate.

I was grovelling, my face in the dirt, prostrate before the might of a vengeful patriarch, judged and found wanting, begging a forgiveness that could never be mine, my hands clutching at the soil. Tears burst from my eyes and I was wailing in misery at the certain damnation of my soul. My body came up, arched in pain, and my hands, to slap dirt into my face, the taste acrid in my mouth as I rubbed it in, hiding my sinful, lust-inflaming features. I screamed, breaking free. My fingers were at the neck of my dress, clawing, tearing, and it was ripped wide, my breasts naked, my belly, my cunt, and I was rocking forward, spread to the altar, lewd and open.

A fresh blast of hatred and rage crashed into me, but I was laughing, my hands between my legs, fingers in my sex, in dirty, joyful, masturbation. My pleasure was rising on the wave of loathing, his hate only making me stronger, my behaviour lewder as I pushed a finger firmly up my bottom. He was screaming in my brain, clawing at me, attempting to drag my fingers from my dirty holes, to tear my flesh, to send me back to the Hell where I undoubtedly belonged, even as I came.

On the instant I was in a dim space, squatting and in myself, but on hard stone, stark naked, my belly smeared with a crude pentacle, a rune of fertility at the centre. Men stood before me, two in a shattered doorway, more beyond, holding torches, rope and swords. They cursed as they took me, dragging me out into brilliant sunlight, a village green, men and women standing gaping in sympathy, in fear, in licentious disapproval.

In seconds my hands were bound, my feet, my defiled belly displayed for all to see. Gasps rang out, the people began to crowd close, to spit on me, to scratch at me. I was dragged towards the pond, my struggles futile as they strapped me to an iron-bound pole, lifted me, held me over the water. As one began to declaim my sins I was hurled out, hitting the water, going down, the sure knowledge of death hitting me even as I hurled myself back in one final effort of will.

And I lay gasping on the wet grass, my head just over the edge of the pentacle, my blindfold down around my mouth, a candle burning just inches from my face to illuminate the great mausoleum before me with its fellows. Slowly it sank in: grey rock, lichen, twisted, terribly weathered forms, wax dripping down the breasts of a carved angel, and the name – Richard Byrne.

10

When Stephen came for me I could still barely stand. I was shaking hard, my every limb still weak, my face, breasts and belly smeared with dirt, my dress ripped wide down the front. He supported me back to the car, his voice full of concern as he babbled questions I couldn't bring myself to answer. What had happened was going round and round in my head, my fear so strong I felt sick to the stomach, yet undercut by a near demented sense of triumph.

He, the man I had met in trance, had found me an abomination to his world-view, overwhelming me with his hatred. Yet I had fought back, and won, first forcing my female sexuality against the pressure, and second breaking free of the horrid vision he had dragged me into. I was dry, but for my own sweat, and my wrists and ankles had no marks to show that I'd been bound. It had not happened, yet I had felt it as surely as any real experience, just as I had felt the cocks inside me and the coldness of my lover's sperm with Sir Barnaby Stamforth. There could not be the slightest doubt my communion had been real.

Back in the car, Stephen wrapped me in a rug and gave me some water. I couldn't drink, at first, or talk, my throat too tight, my head still swimming with emotion and dizzy from the smoke. At some point he stopped at a garage, to buy sandwiches and coffee, then at a darkened lay-by where I managed to get something down myself. With the water and food I slowly began to return to reality, and while sipping my coffee with him watching over me in alarm I finally managed a wan smile. For maybe the hundredth time Stephen asked me if I was all right. This time I answered.

'I . . . I think so. That was . . . was, like nothing else.'

'What did you do? It sounded awful, the way you screamed!'

'It was awful, in a way. So tell me, who was Richard Byrne?'

'An ancestor of mine. I thought . . . well, you asked for someone you could look up, and well, I know a fair bit already. It was a bad choice, yes?'

'No, it was a good choice, in a way. Who was he?'

'My childhood hero, I suppose you could call him. He was involved with the Civil War, a staunch parliamentarian who led one of Cromwell's troops of cavalry. He . . .'

'A puritan too?'

'Oh, of the strictest stamp.'

'Ah, anything to do with witches?'

'Witches? No, not to the best of my knowledge, although I'm sure he would have been violently against anything of the sort. He was a great one for the ideal of democracy, which was what inspired me, and of freedom of conscience too, but vehemently opposed to anything that fell outside his personal world-view.'

'Go on.'

'Well, he earned considerable distinction as a soldier, and later as a politician. He wouldn't compromise his principles either, but fled to the Continent after the Restoration. When he died the family brought back his remains for interment here.'

'Where's here?'

'Suffolk, well, Essex now, but we were in Suffolk, Hingstead, where my family had land for generations. No, Richard Byrne was my role model from well before I had any interest in going into politics myself, but as I found out more, and came to understand more, my opinion of him decreased. He believed very strongly in himself, and the rights of man, but when he had power, he abused it. He was also bitterly . . .'

'. . . misogynistic?'

'Yes. How did you know I was going to say that?'

'I've just met him.'

I had met Richard Byrne, there could be no question. Michael might doubt, but I knew I was right. I had known nothing about Stephen's ancestor, nothing whatsoever, and yet my impression of him had been overwhelming, frighteningly so, and accurate. Again and again I tried to find a flaw in my argument, but there wasn't one.

Not that I could tell Michael, because he might doubt I was telling the truth, or worse, lying simply to try and impress him. That would not do. For Michael I had to be able to show that it was real, which was not so easy. What it did mean was that I could once more let myself go with him. I was back on top.

The experience had also opened a whole new world of possibilities. I had never before experienced communion without making my own choice. Looking back, I could see that I'd always been playing it safe. The free-thinkers, the debauched, the rebels, they all liked me. The others I could cope with, even Eliza Dobson, who for all her venom had at heart been a very weak person, scared of her own sexuality. Richard Byrne was different, a real firebrand, and while the experience had left me badly shaken, it had also inspired a compulsion for more.

Stephen was very good. I told him what had happened, and while he plainly didn't believe a word of what I was saying, he had no explanation for the phenomenon. He even felt guilty, blaming himself in part for my experience, which suggested to me that he did not entirely dismiss it. Back at his flat I bathed and tended the scratches I'd inflicted on my breasts and tummy in my passion, ate and let him put me to bed. In the morning he drove me back, at my insistence, because I needed to think.

I spent all Sunday in the church, naked, with the door firmly locked and Lilitu on guard, thinking on life, death and myself. Richard Byrne had seen me as the very incarnation of evil, unclean, an abomination before God. That meant his God, and while I have never had any illusions about what the po-faced and the strait-laced think of me, the sheer force of his antipathy had been extraordinary. Did enjoying my body and indulging my wilder needs make me evil?

The answer had to be no. I have always seen myself as belonging to the dark, but as a wild-child, a rebel. Richard Byrne had undoubtedly thought of himself as a good man, yet he had no doubt killed many people and condemned many more in a variety of ways, all in the name of his beliefs. Eliza Dobson was little better. If she had not killed anyone directly, she had imposed a life of miserable drudgery on hundreds, and expected them to be grateful for it. I had neither killed nor repressed, but only exalted in breaking the taboos of just such people. I was not the evil one.

I've always known that it feels good to be a bad girl,

and never regretted it. From the moment I had rejected Christian values in exchange for more loosely spiritual ones I'd been used to making my own moral decisions. If some felt that to do so was a monstrous display of arrogance, then I could only argue that it was better than abandoning morals altogether. After all, I had no choice but to abandon a religion so moribund that many of its temples are in decay, so corrupt, so blind. Yet I adored all the trappings of that very religion, the elaborate ritual, the architecture, thus linking myself inextricably to something that was dying.

By early evening I had worked myself into a fine state of Gothic despondency, and if I was rather proud in a way, I'd had enough. Brooding naked in a Gothic church is all very well, but one can have too much of a good thing, and it's extremely cold on the bum. I'd also worked out my self-doubt and felt ready for Michael. He was in, and delighted that I was coming over, promising to make pasta and have it ready by the time I arrived.

I put on my blades, knowing it would get my adrenaline pumping, my cheekiest skirt, a tiny crop top and pads, creating a Goth-urchin look I was sure he'd like to draw, and to fuck. It worked for me, just the way people reacted enough to leave me feeling full of mischief, and I was right about Michael. The door hadn't closed behind me before he was reaching for his pad, even as the rich aromas of Bolognese sauce and red wine hit me.

'Dead cute! Goth-chick on skates, always good for a poster.'

'How about Goth-chick eating pasta?'

'Nah, too weird. Give me a good pose, like the crazy one from Gorillaz . . .'

'Which crazy one?'

'The girl, of course.'

'There's a girl?'

'Just pose will you? Like you don't give a fuck ... yeah, great. Don't move!'

I'd frozen, head cocked to one side, slight snarl, middle finger exactly as I'd put it to show him what he could do with his instructions. He sketched quickly, no more than an outline to capture position and expression, then spoke again.

'Good, now hold ... hold that broom.'

'The broom?'

'Sure. In the picture it'll be a fuck-off big gun. There's a whole market for that kind of stuff.'

I shrugged and retrieved the broom, holding it like a guitar, then across my shoulders, each time changing the way my legs were set. It was not easy to balance, but he worked fast, and I was quickly getting into it. I tried a third pose, with the broom pointing at the ground in front of me as if I was rolling forward. Michael responded with a grin. I gave him a snarl and he was sketching madly, turning a fresh sheet in just a minute or so.

'Neat, now some for the *bandes dessinées*. More innocent, casually sexy as if you don't know what you're showing ... still with attitude.'

I cocked my hip out and stuck my tongue out at him, dropping the broom. He nodded, sketching hurriedly. The moment he'd finished I spun around, making my skirt fly up.

'Hold that!'

'I can't! I'll fall over!'

'Hold onto something.'

I tried, feeling somewhat silly as I attempted to twist

169

my legs into a knot while balancing with two fingers on the wall. It was not going to last, but he finished in time, now grinning broadly.

'Cute, now another. Can you pull your skirt up higher?'

'I can roll the waistband up, if you mean you want my panties showing?'

'Yes, again, as if you aren't aware of it.'

'Sure, you boys love to think that, don't you?'

I gave him what I hoped was a wry smile as I adjusted my skirt, tucking the waistband into itself so that my panties showed front and back. It felt cheeky, suiting my mood.

'Great, now, hands on hips, knees together, kick one foot out . . . sulky . . . cynical . . .'

'I'm going to fall over in a minute, Michael.'

'Don't even think about it!'

He was sketching frantically, with me in a pose that might have looked cool but was seriously out of balance. At any second I was either going to go over backwards and fall on my bottom, or forwards and fall on my face. I went sideways. One skate slipped on the polished wood of the floor, then the other, and I was doing the splits, catching myself only just in time by slapping both hands on the floor in front of me. Michael stifled a laugh.

'Very funny! Don't move.'

'Don't move!?'

He got up, turning to a new sheet as he quickly got behind me. I struggled to lift myself a little and looked back between my legs, to find him sketching away again, this time my rear view, which was going to be all legs and panties.

'Hey, Michael!'

'Don't move ... don't move ... don't move ...'

'Yes, but ...'

'That is beautiful!'

'I thought you wanted attitude?'

'Showing your knickers is attitude. Stick your tongue out.'

'Michael!'

I stuck it out though, feeling slightly put upon, because he was grinning like mad and obviously found my position humorous. Before he was finished my legs were beginning to get stiff, but as he pressed the end of his pencil to his chin in a gesture that meant he was done he spoke again.

'Can you go right down?'

'Yes.'

'Go on then.'

I obliged, letting my legs slide slowly apart, wider and wider, my tendons aching, but at last with the crotch of my panties touching the floor. He gave a nod as I looked back over my shoulder, impressed, reached forward and flipped my skirt up onto the small of my back.

'Pervert!'

He didn't answer, sketching busily until my teeth were gritted with the pain of holding my pose. Finally I could stand it no more and pulled myself up into a kneel position, grimacing at the hot feeling in my thighs.

'Beautiful, stay just like that.'

'Michael!'

Again he laughed, and I stuck my bottom out, knowing exactly what he wanted. My skirt was still up, my panties exposed, and as I glanced back I caught him giving his cock a crafty squeeze.

'You're in a dirty mood today.'

'Just a good mood, really.'

'Why so?'

'Seeing you like that, for a start, and because ... I have my new flat.'

'Great! Now how about that pasta?'

'Not yet, the art of pasta sauce is to let it simmer for as long as possible. So I'm going to sketch you, then ... actually, could you pull your knickers down?'

I sighed in mock exasperation as I reached back to tug down my panties and expose every single rude detail of my rear view to him. Once more he adjusted his cock, then began to draw, faster than ever. I could feel the air on my pussy, and on my bottom hole too. Both were showing, a very rude position indeed, and surely too tempting for him to resist. Sure enough.

'Yes, pasta later. First I sketch you, then I fuck you.'

He put the pad aside as he spoke. One tug and his zip was down, another and his cock was out, rearing thick and stiff from his fly. I gave him what I hoped was a suitably long-suffering look back over my shoulder, meaning to indicate that while I was pre-pared to let myself be mounted from the rear, it was not really what I'd been expecting. His response was to grab his pad again and make a hurried sketch of my expression, all the while with his erect penis pointing straight at my pussy. I began to giggle, amused both at his eagerness to draw and for sex.

'Patience, Dusk, all good things come to those who wait.'

With that he tossed the pad aside, shuffled quickly forward, put the head of his dick to my pussy and slid himself inside. I hadn't realised I was so wet, and gasped in surprise as I filled, and again as he began to pump into me. He took hold of the waistband of my skirt, a firm grip, pulling himself deep in, and I was lost, delighting in my rude treatment. I flipped my top up, letting my breasts free, and closed my eyes, my whole body shivering to his hard thrusts.

A fantasy began to run in my head, of being given the same treatment in the street, perhaps teasing him by letting my skirt fly up as I skated, flashing my knickers but never coming close enough to catch me. He'd be driven mad, his cock rock solid in his trousers, burning with frustration, only for me to trip. I'd go down right in front of him, on my hands and knees. My skirt would fly up, showing the seat of my panties, which would be wrenched straight down and his lovely cock pushed up into me before I could so much as squeak in protest.

There'd be a big audience too, watching me fuck in the street, outraged, delighted, shocked, not even sure if I was willing until I flipped my top up to play with my breasts. That was me, all through, a bad girl, a rude, dirty Goth-chick, showing off her panties, showing off her bum, doing it in the street, masturbating in the street because she wanted everyone to see and she just didn't care and because it felt, so, so, so good . . .

I'd been rubbing myself as I fantasised, and I came, still with Michael pumping into me, a glorious feeling as I went tight on his cock, and more glorious still when he came inside me. For a long, wonderful moment we were together in perfect ecstasy, and then it was done and I was sighing to myself as he took hold of me and pulled me up into his arms.

We kissed, long and slow, before I sank down to take him in my mouth, tasting myself as I sucked. He gave a contented sigh and tousled my hair, but pulled away before I could get him interested again. I put it off for later, content to eat and find out about his move.

The pasta tasted every bit as good as it had smelt, and left me pleasantly full and just a little light-headed from the wine. He'd been packing, most of his belongings already in cases, but the settee was still there and we sprawled out on it, my legs on his, now barefoot. Dinner had mainly involved eating pasta and teasing me, and I wanted to know what was happening with his move.

'So what's up with the flat?'

'I'm moving in the week, to a place in . . . Coburg Road.'

'My Coburg Road!?'

'Just that, in fact, better than that. It's the top flat in number 37, which is almost exactly . . .'

'. . . opposite All Angels. Wow! Great!'

'I thought you'd be pleased.'

I was, but there was an itsy-bitsy fly in the ointment, well actually rather a large fly, in the shape of Stephen Byrne. I already felt a bit guilty, because I had used Stephen to help me to better my sex with Michael. Now I was faced with a situation where it was simply not going to be possible to keep the two of them apart. Michael went on.

'I'm not going to put any pressure on you, and I would never suggest you give up All Angels, but . . . if you like, I want you to treat the new flat as your own.'

Suddenly there was a big lump in my throat. I couldn't speak at all, but flipped myself over on the settee so that I could cuddle into the crook of his arm. I kissed him and he responded immediately, our mouths coming open for a long, loving kiss. It felt so good, tension I simply hadn't known I had in me draining slowly away, until at last he pulled back.

'It take it that's a yes?'

'It is a yes.'

'No buts?'

'Oh, plenty. First and foremost, you have to put up with my weird behaviour.'

'I wouldn't put up without it.'

'Sex on tombs?'

'Whenever possible.'

'Bailing me out if I get arrested for art crime?'

'Consider it done.'

'Kinky threesomes with other men?'

I made it sound a joke, but I was watching very carefully for his reaction. Unfortunately he gave as good as he got.

'Kinky threesomes with other girls?'

All I could think of to do in response was squeeze his cock. That set us off again, me on top this time, then and there on the settee. After that it was bed, and more sex, and sleep, and more sex in the morning. It was nearly noon before I left, and it must have taken me three times as long to skate back as it had to come over. I fed Lilitu, who was not best pleased, and collapsed onto my bed.

I woke well after dark, from a dream in which a man, maybe Stephen, was on top of me, being drubbed by demons for encouragement. After a seriously weird moment of disorientation I worked out that the thumps of their fists on his back was in fact somebody knocking on the vestry door. A voice called out, and I realised it was Snaz, somebody I could talk to. Dragging myself from the bed I went to unfasten the door, letting her in. She was in black jeans, her hoodie, her Timberland's, with a bag over her shoulder.

'Coming bombing?'

'Uh . . . no . . . maybe. Hang on a minute.'

'You look like death. What's up?'

'I've been asleep. I was shagging Michael all last night.'

'Lucky bitch!'

'Yeah, and there's more. He's asked me to move in with him, well, not exactly move in . . . Hang on, I need coffee, and food, and a new head.'

She threw herself down on the bed and began to go through the contents of her bag. I started coffee and began to wash, my senses clearing as I splashed cold water onto my face. Snaz chattered away, explaining how Biggy had finally given up writing after a two-hour chase along the lines. I was only half-listening, but managed a grunt of agreement as she finished.

'. . . it's not like he got bagged.'

I began to dress, pulling on a tatty top, my black jeans and boots. Michael wasn't expecting me as such, or Stephen, and I felt I wanted to be with another girl, to talk. The bombing I knew I'd get into once we got started. Lilitu had come in from the church, and was sniffing Snaz.

'Just tickle her behind the ears, she loves that.'

'Yeah . . . right. She's coming with us, yeah?'

'Sure, but not trackside.'

'Right, not after last night. So you're still shagging both of them? You told Michael?'

'No. I'm not sure what to do.'

'Keep 'em both, like I said, one for kicks, one to be sugar-daddy. I would, and he's not bad looking that Stephen. Bit of an old pervo, but not bad looking.'

'Yeah, but Michael's moving in across the road, and he wants me to be with him. I wish I'd told him about Stephen in the first place, because if I come out with it now, it makes me look dishonest.'

'Looks like you're going to have to choose, girl.'

'Right, and it has to be Michael. He really wants me, and Stephen's just after sex, but he's been good to me, really generous.'

'Rich is he?'

'Fairly, yeah, but I didn't mean . . .'

'I'll have him then, you can fuck off with Michael!'

She laughed and rolled onto her back, watching as I twisted my hair up into a bun. I put toast on and fixed the coffee, Snaz folding her legs under her as she drank. Lilitu had crossed to the door and was looking at me hopefully, eager for a walk.

'So if not trackside, where?'

'Somewhere hard, somewhere everyone'll see. I want 'em to know we're girls too.'

'Sure. We'll do a crew tag. What was TST?'

'Trackside Trouble, no good. How about Street Bratz, like from the cartoon?'

'Too soft but not girlie enough. Street Bitchz would be better.'

'Sounds like we've got pimps!'

'Most bad words for girls are like that.'

'Too true. She-Catz?'

'Maybe. She-Catz from Hell? No, bollocks to it, who cares what the men think – Witchz from Hell.'

'You've got it, girl. Let's go bomb!'

We smacked hands and we were gone, my adrenaline rising fast even as we walked down Coburg Road, arm in arm with Lilitu padding beside us. We had no idea where we were going, just high on life and mischief as we walked the streets. As we went we talked, ever more boisterous, swapping stories of tagging and sex, cheeking the men and teasing the boys. One guy got cheeky with us back, suggesting we take him into the park and suck his cock. We went, promised we'd suck if we could tag him, pulled his trousers down behind a push, wrote and ran, leaving him with his pants around his ankles and a rock hard erection, 'Witchz from Hell' written on his bare arse in indelible marker.

After that it was chaos, running through the streets laughing, tagging anything either of us had ever taken against. By the time we stopped to rest we were lost, on some industrial site deep in East London, where a huge rank of gasometers rose black against the sky, one great drum still risen in its mesh of iron. It was perfect, huge, abandoned, the blank face of the drum visible for miles. I looked at Snaz and she looked at me.

It was crazy, a stupid, lunatic scheme, trying to paint fifty feet above the ground, but just to know we were going to do it gave me such a rush. I had to, then and there, and there was no question of backing out as we began to walk down the side of the old gas company compound to find a way in. We were not the first there: a huge black and gold dub was sprayed across the double doors, one I recognised from All Angels. A minute later it had our tag right across it.

Another minute and we were inside, and climbing, Lilitu looking up at me as I used the ornate latticework like a ladder. I was now scared, and more scared still with every metre I rose, the black iron roses on the gaunt iron lattice passing my face one by one, but I was still more elated. I made the first cross piece, the second, and with agonising care and my arm locked tight to the strut I eased a can of black from the bag and began to paint, sharing a wicked grin with Snaz as she too reached my level.

My heart was hammering, my pulse racing. I could be seen by anyone who happened to look up from the road below, standing out like a fly on glass against the surface of the gasometer. Still I worked, the reek of paint strong in my nose as I made my rough outlines, my D, my U, moving forward to make the S, and further for the K. By then I was holding on with one arm stretched up to grip the strut, balanced high on the great iron skeleton, rooftops below me, the road, and a police car, cruising slowly past.

I nearly wet myself, clinging frozen to the strut, my can still in my hand, hardly daring to breath. The car moved on, agonisingly slowly, turned a distant corner and was gone. Again I began to paint, urgent now, but forcing myself to go slow. Snaz had her letters done, faster and more practised, and was filling in vivid pink. I finished my K, tried to swap cans, fumbled and dropped the black, watching it fall as my whole body tingled to a fresh shock of adrenaline.

My eyes closed, I forced myself to be calm, eased a purple fat-cap free of my bag and began to fill, smooth and even, telling myself I wasn't racing Snaz, and nobody ever looks up, that there wasn't really solid concrete beneath me. Another car passed, and a third, both slow, lovers or maybe kerb-crawlers. Neither stopped. I finished my can, took a second and the fill was done. A few simple low lights and I moved back to the centre, took Snaz's black, and with agonising care sprayed in my final outline. I was done, the huge black and purple 'DUSK' standing out for all to see. The black was gone, leaving Snaz to sign our tag in gold, a name

I truly felt I'd earned as we climbed back down, to hug and kiss, giggling together as she took our flicks, the huge twin dub faint in the dim glow of the street lamps, but plain enough.

All done, we left, squeezing back through the damaged gate, and off, Lilitu bounding ahead of us. I didn't want to come down: I was too high, too full of energy. We made the road, to find another dub on the wall below the gasometer, the same crew who'd done the gates, and All Angels. In a moment Snaz had her marker out, to scrawl 'Look up, Toy Boyz' across the white fill of their dub, just as the patrol car turned the corner in the distance.

We just ran, helter-skelter across the road, into the mouth of an alley even as blue light flashed off the brickwork behind us. I heard the siren moan and my heart was in my mouth, my feet pounding on the tarmac, my muscles straining. A road opened up in front of us and we were across it, then another, with a high metal fence on the far side, lorries parked in ranks, men standing around the open hatch of a caravan, the smell of burgers and onions and grease thick in the air.

I grabbed Snaz, pulling her into the shadows. The bag went over a wall, I shook my hair out, her top came off and we walked calmly across, Snaz greeting the knot of truckers with a cheeky remark. We ordered burgers, the men closing around us, most keen to get our attention, still talking and joking as the police car rolled past without so much as a second glance in our direction.

We were laughing all the way back, so pleased with ourselves. In the safety of All Angels we opened beers and collapsed on my bed, replaying the hit and the chase over and over. A second beer followed, a third, and a fourth, until we were giggling stupidly together over anything each other said. When Snaz reached across me to get her can I caught her scent, and before I knew what I was doing I'd kissed her and she'd kissed me back. Immediately we were snogging, rolled together on the bed, cuddled tight, then rude, our hands pulled at each other's clothes, eager to touch. My top came up, and hers, her bra too, our chests bare together, stiff nipples against each other's flesh, and in each other's hands and mouths.

Our jeans followed, our knickers pushed down to get at each other, and we were bare from neck to knees, her bottom in my hands, her hand between my legs, her fingers in my pussy, my tongue in hers as I climbed on, head to tail, and hers in mine. I came, with her face buried in my sex and her hands all over my bottom, but it didn't stop me, or her. We went on, kissing, licking, exploring each other's bodies in drunken, adrenaline-fuelled glee, heedless of where we touched, fingers deep in pussies, bums in faces, legs and arms entwined in a tangle of sweaty girl flesh until deep into the night.

11

I woke in Snaz's arms, sore, embarrassed, not sure why
it had happened at all. It had though, with a vengeance, and regret was pointless. As I washed I told
myself it was just one of those things, another taboo
broken. I knew I was right too, but that didn't stop me
feeling I'd done something I shouldn't, or worrying
about her reaction. By the time she woke I'd made
coffee, and as I passed her mug I was praying she'd be
cool.

She didn't say a word, just looked at me, her eyes
big and questioning as she sipped her coffee. I smiled
and shrugged. She smiled back, embarrassed, but
happy, and I was grinning. I kissed her cheek and sat
back in the bed, once more running over the events of
the night before in my head, and the highlights, tagging the man's bum, bombing the gasometer, and sex.
Finally Snaz spoke.

'You are one bad girl, Dusk.'

'Then that makes two.'

'Me? I'm not in your league, girl. Look at you, tagging
men's arses! Hitting a fucking gastank! Two men on
the go at once, and ... and me! Witchz from Hell is
about right!'

'Sorry about that, I ... I suppose I got a bit carried
away. It was fun though, yeah?'

She nodded, her throat tight with embarrassment,

her face and neck flushed pink. I reached out to touch her hair, wishing the knot in my stomach would go away and I could be just a bit more cool about what had happened. She didn't try to pull back, but continued to sip coffee. At some point we'd stripped off, although I couldn't remember doing it, and we were both naked. It didn't seem to bother her, propped up with her full breasts bare, no more self-conscious than she had been when we were swapping clothes. Perhaps she felt different, as I did, now aware of her sexually, but it was a good feeling, and one she seemed to share. I stayed silent for a long time, not wanting to make small talk, and at last plucked up the courage to ask what I wanted to know.

'First time?'

'First, yeah.'

Nothing more needed to be said, the rest was clear in the tone of her voice. It might have been her first, but it would not necessarily be her last, nor mine. I got up to make toast and cereal, now at ease, feeling good about myself, and her. She stayed in bed but watched me as I moved, making me feel sure that like me she had come to view my body in a different way.

We ate and washed and dressed, now laughing and joking as we had been the night before, Snaz even planting a firm slap on my bottom as I bent to pull my knickers on. Both of us wanted to recapture some of the thrill of the night before, and we had soon agreed to try and get some proper flicks of the gasometer. I dressed carefully, to give myself a look as far as possible from the skinny, black-clad boy I hoped the police imagined they had chased: a short, loose skirt, a purple top with a death's head motif, tights and heels. Snaz borrowed a dress, some jewellery and high-heeled boots, giving herself an instant Goth-chick look, about as far from the conventional image of a teenage vandal as it was possible for her to get.

As it was, we needn't have bothered. The industrial zone around the old gasworks was as busy by day as it had been empty by night. An endless stream of vans and lorries were coming in and out of a big parcel depot a little way up the road, a load of men were milling around on the corner for no obvious reason, and a mobile snack bar had been set up directly under our piece.

It was a piece, no question, a real burner, maybe not that artistic, but with pink and purple letters seven feet high and fifty feet off the ground it was no mere dub. When we moved over to get drinks from the snack bar I heard one man voicing surprise as to how it could have been done. His mate pointed out how the frame could be climbed, but there was doubt in his voice. I shared a look with Snaz but kept quiet.

Plenty of other people were looking at it, and our crew tag stood out clear and proud, but as we took our flicks nobody thought to question us. We even had a man photograph it with us standing by the snack bar, clearly visible but not obviously the focus of the picture. That was enough, and we headed back, not wanting to push our luck.

We said goodbye at the doorway to Snaz's flats, and our parting kiss turned very briefly into a snog, leaving me with butterflies in my stomach and a deliciously naughty feeling. I had experienced so much in the last few days, and I wanted more, more of Michael, more of Snaz, more communion, more graff. I could have it too, all of it, and I was in a seriously up mood as I walked back to All Angels, singing to myself, even skipping, and not giving a fuck for the odd looks I got from passers-by.

The only person who hadn't really entered my head was Stephen, and that changed when I got back. A parcel had been delivered, tucked in behind Alasdair Croft's headstone where I had told the postmen to put them. It was quite big, soft and flexible, fuelling my curiosity, so that I opened it the moment I was inside. A note fell out as I tore the paper, a card decorated with a picture of purple lilies and 'with love, Stephen' written neatly across it.

I tugged the inner wrapping open, revealing something black and shiny, which I quickly pulled out, immediately entranced. It was a corset, faced with black satin, the cups and hem trimmed with a single layer of heavy cotton lace. It had suspender straps, pegs at the front and eyes at the back, all brass and perfectly finished. I couldn't begin to guess what it would have cost, because it was undoubtedly custom made and no expense had been spared with the materials. Not to have put it on immediately would have been a sin.

I stripped, then and there, naked, because it seemed appropriate. It was an image I'd longed to try, but never had the opportunity, bare but for corset and stockings, a *demi-mondaine*, dark and sultry. My hair was right, long and black and silky, and a collar and long gloves would give it a Gothic touch. A quick wash, some powder and I was ready, my fingers actually shaking as I pulled it around me and closed the catches. It felt tight, even with the laces slack, pulling my waist in and making my hips and bust fuller. I added stockings, clipping them up to increase the sense of tightness on my legs, black heels, and lots of make-up in black and purple and crimson.

The gloves were black lace, reaching right up to my elbows, the collar black leather. Both added spice to my image. It felt great, and it looked great, definitely sultry, and definitely rude, with my nipples just showing over the top of the cups and my bum and pussy shockingly bare and framed in black material. Michael was going to love it, and would want to draw me in it, as he had my Goth-urchin look, increasingly rude poses until we ended up fucking on the floor.

A really bitter pang of guilt hit me. It was a gift from Stephen and I was thinking of fucking Michael with it on. I mean, what kind of a bitch does that? I was going to have to let Stephen down, but I was going to do it gently. For one last night he could have me, as he wanted me. I rang to thank him for the corset and fixed a date for the Saturday, dinner out, with me in the corset beneath my dress. The implication was that we'd come back to his flat or All Angels for sex afterwards, and I didn't intend to disappoint.

It was not easy to get into the right mood for the night. What I'd done with Snaz was very much in my head, making it harder to concentrate on anything else. Also, a little part of me was saying that I was letting myself be manipulated by accepting expensive gifts which were effectively in return for sex, but a much bigger part was telling me that I should appreciate his generosity, and show it. Then there was the thought of telling him it was over afterwards, which was not going to be easy.

Not that my ill feelings stopped me making an effort. I made up slowly and carefully, then put the corset on over stockings, but no panties. High heels, gloves and a collar, only this time a black velvet choker instead of leather, all added to it; a long black dress tied at the waist to emphasise my exaggerated figure gave the final touch and I was ready. The effect was almost as sultry as before, because although I was covered, it took no more than a glance to realise that I had no panties. My nipples showed, and I knew Stephen would be both entranced and embarrassed, just the right combination for a man.

It did a lot to improve my mood, but I knew I was going to have to get drunk. Stephen had already turned up, and watched with something approaching awe as I walked over to the Jaguar. He held the door for me, even if it was only to give himself a chance to pat my bottom as I climbed in. As he sat down beside me he was more than a little pink, having discovered I was knickerless.

He was in the best of moods as we drove out of London, chatting happily about this and that, and never once mentioning his wife or any of the subjects that got him down. It was the same over dinner, in a cross between a restaurant and a pub somewhere deep in Kent. I couldn't help but be infected by his mood, and with him driving I finished off nearly all of the wine, and two brandies afterwards.

By the time we were ready to start back I was in the mood for sex, but not for heavy conversations. He was keen, snogging me and pawing my bottom in the car park, as eager as any teenage boyfriend, also feeling the shape of the corset beneath my dress. It was impossible not to respond, and there was a warm, ready feeling in my tummy as we drove.

All Angels was nearer, and we went there without the need to discuss it. It was dark when we arrived, and cool, but not too cool to prevent me peeling off my dress for him as soon as we reached the shelter of the yew avenue. He just stared, drinking in the sight of me in the corset, bare chested and without panties, his tongue flicking out to moisten his lips as I twirled to show him my bottom.

He immediately caught me from behind, cupping my breasts and rubbing himself against my bum cheeks as he nibbled at my neck and ear. I pulled away, giggling and full of mischief from his eagerness. He came after, in among the yews, walking straight past me as I had ducked down into the shadow of Eliza Dobson's tomb. I could sense her disapproval, making me worse still, and as he turned around I jumped up, to push him back against the stone and nuzzle his cock through his trousers. He was already hard, too good an invitation to resist.

I pulled him out, straight into my mouth, to make him groan in pleasure. His hands locked in my hair and he was fucking my mouth, easing himself in and out between my lips until I pulled back, not wanting him to come so quickly. He tried to hold on, to make me take him back in, but I sucked his balls quickly into my mouth and immediately danced back as he gasped in reaction. I was laughing as I skipped away, dodging among the tombs with him in pursuit, erect dick in hand for when he caught me.

Of course I had to let him, by the Major's tomb, which he bent me across and slid himself deep, fucking me even as I sensed the lecherous fingers on my bare flesh. They shared me, man and spirit, the one in me, the other fondling my breasts and legs. Stephen came in moments, splashing hot sperm across my bottom, and just as the first time down he went, to lick me to ecstasy from behind, his face buried between my bottom cheeks, his tongue doing wonders with my clit, even my bottom hole. All the while I imagined the Major pawing and groping at my body, chortling over the sheer rudeness of my behaviour, and my helpless ecstasy as I came.

Somebody had passed the gates just as I cried out in orgasm, and Stephen and I were laughing as we ran for the vestry door, gathering my discarded dress up on the way. I didn't bother to dress, but stayed as I was, delighting in being dressed to the nines yet with everything that mattered nude. He couldn't get enough of me, his eyes fixed to my body as I moved about the room, his hands on my bottom or breasts or waist at every chance.

He'd bought a bottle of champagne in the pub and we drank it together on the bed, leaving me more tipsy than ever, and more mischievous. I wanted sex again, and began to tease him, thinking of what I'd done with Snaz and reminding him how he'd spanked me in front of her, even telling him that he should have done the job properly and fucked me too, with her watching. It hit the spot, his face pink and his eyes bright as he responded.

'So . . . so you'd do it in front of her, for real?'

'Sure, why not?'

'But together? Wouldn't you mind? I mean . . .'

'You are so repressed! You'd love it, though, wouldn't you? How about spanking us together, two naughty little brats side by side, our bums all bare and rosy. Oh yes, you would love that, wouldn't you? Or maybe you'd like to watch us together? A bit of girl on girl?'

'Oh God, yes!'

He snatched for me, but I rolled quickly away, laughing. It was so funny, just the state he was getting into, but it was going to get him hard again too, no question.

I jumped up, to look down on him, his mouth wide with desire, his face red.

'Come on, get it out and I'll tell you what we'd do for you.'

Immediately he was scrabbling at his fly, in near demented urgency. Out it came, already half stiff, but I resisted the urge to take him in my mouth again and posed, cool and aloof, looking down with amusement and just a trace of pretend contempt as he began to jerk at himself.

'Oh, yes, you'd love it, you really would! I don't suppose you've ever seen two girls together, have you? No? Too repressed, your generation, I suppose. How about two men? After all, you seem to like the taste of spunk.'

'Never mind that. Tell me about you and Snaz. Would you ... with her, really?'

'Hmm ... I don't know. Maybe ... maybe not. She's fun, and kind of cute. It might be nice to ... to lick her pussy, right in front of you, the way you do me, her cute bum right in my face!'

I stuck my tongue out as I finished, waggling it. He'd gone purple, the head of his cock as well as his face. I was grinning and laughing as I got down next to him, to take hold of his swollen shaft and pop it into my mouth, sucking firmly as I squeezed his balls. His hand found my bottom, stroking, slapping, pulling at my flesh to open me behind. A finger found my bottom hole, tickling, only to stop as I pulled up from his erection.

'That got you going, didn't it? You know something, under that cold, proper exterior, you must be the biggest pervert I've ever met. Spanking? Watching girls get off together? Any other little surprises you've got for me, maybe?'

He made a gruff sound, as much a grunt as a laugh, and his voice was hoarse as he spoke.

'Maybe ... maybe I have. How about taking it the other way?'

'The other way?'

He was still pawing my bottom, and once again his finger touched my hole.

'Up my bum!?'

'Yes ... you have the most beautiful bottom, Angel, I would love to ...'

'But ...'

'Now who's repressed?'

'No, I just ... all right, if you want to be that dirty, let's play for it.'

'Not that again! Why can't we just ...'

'Uh, uh!'

I wagged my finger at him, only to gasp as the top joint of his popped into my bottom hole. It felt nice but I pulled away, keen to tease, not minding my bum entered so very much, but not wanting to feel the way I had after my first spanking. He grabbed for me again but I swung my leg over him, straddling his body with his rock hard erection beneath me. He moaned and reached down to try and put his cock in me, but I took his hands.

'Oh no you don't! You're a bad boy, Stephen, to want to put your cock in my bottom, but I'm a bad girl, and you can, but if, and only if ...'

'OK, I'll play! Pinball?'

'No can do. I don't have a computer here, and besides, you're too good.'

'Anything then, but make it quick!'

'Quick? Oh I don't know ... how about a nice game of cricket, eh old chap?'

'Angela!'

'Oh, all right. Men, always in a hurry! OK, we'll toss a coin, best of three.'

'Fine ... great ... and if I lose?'

'Simple. If you win you get to do it to me. If I win I get to do it to you. That's fair.'

'That's ridiculous. You don't have anything to do it with!'

'Oh don't I?'

I reached out to pluck one of the old altar candles from my dressing table, a shaft of cream-coloured wax a good foot long and over an inch thick. He blanched slightly, his eyes wide, as if he'd finally decided I really was mad. His mouth opened but no sound came out. I cocked my head to one side, looking at him quizzically as I held the candle up.

'Well?'

His expression became slightly more fish-like. I put the candle down, turned very slowly, and stuck my bum out, sitting down on his cock once more as I peered back over my shoulder. His expression had become one of total awe – and pale like a ghost. I reached back and pulled my cheeks wide, stretching my bottom hole for his inspection, just an inch above the straining head of his erection. I wiggled on his cock, squirming my wet pussy right onto his flesh. The ghost swallowed.

'All right. I'll do it.'

I was smiling as I climbed off. My pussy was aching to be filled, and the thought that it might be my bottom instead added a delicious sense of trepidation and naughtiness. I was wiggling deliberately as I walked across the room, Stephen's eyes popping and fixed to my bum every step of the way as he nursed his erection. I bent to dig into my bag, making his view even ruder, and pulled out a fifty-pence piece.

'You call.'

'Tails. Hopefully yours.'

I flipped the coin high, both of us looking up to watch it turn in the air, and down as I caught it and flipped it over onto the back of my hand – tails. My bottom hole twitched in anticipation and my throat was suddenly dry. Stephen grinned and began to tug more firmly at his cock.

'Again.'

'Tails again.'

I flipped, caught, turned my hand up and felt a strong stab of relief and disappointment, all at the same time, as a head was revealed. I showed Stephen.

'Heads it is. Last time.'

My stomach was churning as I flipped the coin high, Stephen calling out tails right at the top of its flight. I caught it, my bottom hole pulsing and my heart hammering as I squatted down by Stephen and lifted my hand.

'Oh shit.'

His face had gone suddenly white, more ghost-like than ever as he gaped at the coin on my hand, with the head showing plain in the light. Again I felt a stab of disappointment, but triumph too, and I was grinning as I stood up. As I took the candle Stephen began to babble.

'I . . . I really don't know if I can – physically, I mean.'

'You expect me to.'

'Yes, I know, but . . . but . . .'

'But I'm a girl?'

'No ... yes, dammit! You're a girl, you ... you're designed to take it.'

'Not up my bum, anymore than you are.'

He was not getting off. If I'd lost I knew I'd have taken it, down on my knees with his big erection up my bottom, however painful and undignified it was. I'd won.

'Yes, but ... but you ... you're so beautiful, so lovely ... the corset really brings out the shape of your bottom, and well, I'm nothing special. It should be you!'

'Stephen, darling, it really is time you got over these old-fashioned ideas. It's terribly dull, after all. It doesn't matter a bit if my bottom is prettier than yours. Besides, you have a nice bottom, good and firm, and if you feel I should be prepared to take your cock up my bottom, then surely you see that you should be prepared to take something equally large up yours, if it amuses me, and it does.'

'No, I mean, yes, technically, but ... but it's a homosexual act for goodness sake!'

'Nonsense! Do you see any other men around? I don't. Besides, I thought you might be quite into that?'

'Me? Good heavens, no!'

'I'm not quite sure you're telling the truth, but never mind. For now, it's just me and the candle. Down you go.'

'But ... but ...'

'Stephen Byrne, you will get on your knees now, just the way you like me, everything showing. Then I'm going to stick this candle up your bottom, nice and slowly so it doesn't hurt, and I'm going to bugger you. That or you go now!'

He could have refused, walked out and never come

back. My difficulties with Michael would have been solved, but it was not what I wanted. He hesitated, for a moment I thought he was going to back out and disappointment began to well up, only for him to suddenly make a wry face and roll over, buttocks up. My disappointment vanished, replaced by a truly wicked urge, to really deal with him properly.

'Kneel up, I said, I want to see, just like you like to see.'

For a moment he looked back, doubt showing in his eyes, then he had closed them and was going up, leaving his cocks and balls hanging beneath his legs and his bottom open and ready. I went for the chrism oil, watching him as I smeared it over the rounded base of the candle. It was a little big for a bottom hole, as I knew from experience, but he was just going to have to put up with that.

His eyes stayed closed, and he was trembling badly as I knelt down beside him. A shiver ran the full length of his body as I touched the candle between his cheeks, and he gasped as I smeared the thick oil between them and onto his anus. His muscle tightened in reaction and I found my mouth twitching up into a cruel grin as I pressed. Again he gasped, and again his hole went tight, struggling to keep me out.

'None of that, Stephen! Relax.'

'Ah! It won't go, Angel . . . it won't!'

'Oh yes it will, just relax.'

He gave a little sob and shook his head, but made no effort to pull away as I pushed again, and felt a wonderful, savage exhilaration as it slid deep up his bottom. He cried out, a loud gasp, but there was no pain in it, and he was immediately shaking his head and panting as I began to feed the candle in and out, as if he couldn't come to terms with what he was feeling. I wanted to laugh, and to come while I did it to him, and to watch him come too. It was just so satisfying, and there was no reason to hurry, at all. I stopped, holding the candle deep in.

'There. Does it feel good?'

He didn't respond, his head hung low, his fingers bent, clutching at the bed. His erection had gone down a little, and I wasn't having that, so I slid a hand under his stomach and down, to take the silky soft pouch of his balls in my hand, stroking, then his cock, still heavy with blood. He was growing instantly, and sobbing as his penis swelled once more, quickly reaching full erection in my hand. I laughed at his blatant excitement and began to tug more firmly, and to push the candle in and out again. He began to whimper as he was buggered, then to pant, his erection now a solid bar in my hand, his balls tight in their sac. My pussy was aching, but I knew what I wanted to do, to come as I watched him in his helpless ecstasy, and to know.

'Tell me how good it feels, Stephen ... tell me!'

He shook his head, but he was panting, and more as I stuffed the candle deeper in for his trouble.

'Tell me, Stephen! I know it's good for you, I know it is, but I want to hear it, I want you to tell me!'

All he managed was a groan, but as I began to push harder still he suddenly began to nod, and to gasp and pant again, more urgently than before. Suddenly I could no longer hold back my laughter. I was cackling like some kind of demented witch as I buggered him and played with his cock, and suddenly he was babbling.

'Yes, Angel. I do, I do. Make it harder ... deep in me,

really deep ... and ... and ... oh God, you're wonderful. Bugger me, Angel, hard, really hard.'

I pushed the candle home, now jerking furiously on his cock, in pure, wicked elation as his buttocks began to tighten and his gasps took on the urgent, uncontrolled note of climax, words still spilling from his mouth.

'Yes, use me ... hurt me ... bugger me ... really use me. Oh that feels so good.'

He grunted, his body tightened and his cock jerked, spraying come over my hand and the bed to the sound of my truly demented laughter. Even as he slumped down I was snatching at myself, determined to come, then and there, while he still had the thick candle shaft sticking out from between his buttocks and his face set in shame and ecstasy. He made to move, but I pushed him down with my boot, spreading my thighs wide as my hand went between my legs as he looked round.

His eyes came wide, staring at me as I began to masturbate, rubbing at myself in frenzied pleasure, my eyes fixed on the thick candle shaft between his buttocks, my mind on what I'd done to him, buggered him, reduced him to grovelling, squirming ecstasy at the penetration of his anus.

I cried out as I came, loud and high, breaking to a gasp as my body went into spasm, my pussy and bottom clenching over and over, my breasts bouncing in the corset's cups, and Stephen staring, his eyes wide, his jaw slack in reaction to what I had done to him.

I didn't tell him that it was over between us, I just couldn't. He was in a seriously vulnerable state, and wanted to talk about it, to express his feelings, and to understand mine. It was hard to know what to say, because for all my arousal a great deal of my pleasure had come from penetrating a male, as much as an abstract thing as a physical one. It had felt good to put something into him as he liked to into me. It had felt good to know I was riding roughshod over what had to be a powerful taboo for him, something he saw as a homosexual act for all that he wanted it, but I didn't feel I could ask him just what else he might want, deep down. It had felt good to be wicked too, dirty, a demented little witch, a real witch from Hell.

What I told him was a half-truth, that doing it had made me feel empowered, and also uninhibited because he himself was being uninhibited. That made him feel a lot better, enough for him to put me across his knee and spank my bottom in revenge before we finally went to sleep.

It was impossible not to feel good in the morning. We'd shared a night of wonderfully rude, open sex, holding back nothing, and in the morning he was more attentive to me than ever, making coffee and toast, then going out for chocolate croissants and milk and cereal and dog food, everything I needed as I lay back and relaxed.

Again I was unable to say anything, and I didn't want to. Instead I wanted them both, to share me, to take turns, whatever. It could have been so good, if only, but I simply could not be certain of Michael's reaction. When I had jokingly suggested an open relationship he had turned it around on me, but I couldn't be sure he had been joking. He certainly liked the idea of a man being buggered, as I'd seen with the Goat of Mendes. Possibly he would be up for it, or at least would be up for it if he didn't feel he was getting the raw end of the deal.

That, at least, I could do something about, or try, and by the time Stephen eventually left I had abandoned the idea of ending our relationship. It was a cowardly choice anyway, and the choice society expected me to make. That wasn't me. I would take the daring, outrageous choice, and if it all came horribly unstuck, then it wouldn't be the first time, and probably not the last.

12

The bunch of roses that arrived the next morning was quite simply huge. There were three dozen, beautiful fat blooms of the deepest possible crimson. I knew they were from Stephen before I'd even read the card. I just couldn't see Michael sending me roses. Lilies, possibly, but not roses.

Sure enough, they were from Stephen. The note read 'My Angel, for taking me somewhere I have never been before, with love, S'. It was sweet, and it made me giggle to think how strong his reaction had been to something he'd been so scared of. He was obviously going to be back for more, too.

The vestry didn't run to much in the way of vases, but there were plenty of urns, and I spent a happy half-hour's flower arranging before I was satisfied, not in the vestry, which was too cluttered with my gear, but in the church itself. It worked beautifully, vivid yet solemn, and perfectly in keeping with Foyle's interior. I was still admiring the effect when Lilitu's barking alerted me to somebody's presence. I went to the door, expecting Snaz or just possibly Stephen. I got Michael.

It was more than a little awkward. The place was littered with bits of rose stem, wrapping paper and urns, also Stephen's card. I'd left the door open too, so there was no hiding the bunches in the church. The place was full of roses, he hadn't sent them and there was just no bluffing it. In fact there was nothing I could think of to say at all. I just smiled, hoping I looked more foolish than guilty. He stepped in, puzzled.

'An admirer?'

'Well, yes ... sort of.'

'Sort of?'

'Yes, er ... you met him: Stephen Byrne.'

'The MP!?'

'That's the one.'

'I wouldn't have put him down as the romantic type. Wow!'

'Yes, he's ... he's ...'

What could I say? 'Persuasive' would sound as if he'd already persuaded me, which he had, but no more than I had persuaded him. 'Persistent' would sound as if he was pestering me, which was a blatant lie, and I had a distinct feeling the truth was not going to stay hidden anyway.

'... perverted.'

It just came out, from somewhere inside me, because it wasn't what I'd meant to say at all. I'd had no idea what I meant to say. I was already blushing, and the instant I'd said it I was wishing I hadn't, and trying to explain myself in a great, clumsy rush of words.

'I ... I mean, he's really into ... me, and ... the way I am, and being free, and not having to be stuffy, and ... he likes to pamper me, and he sent the roses, because ...'

I'd told myself I would do it, and now I had to, only even as my mouth came open the choice was taken away from me. Michael had picked up the card, his head cocked to one side as he read it. I shrugged, unable to speak for the huge lump in my throat. It was out, and he was going to be furious, and that would be the end. I braced myself for the storm, feeling small and guilty, my normal defiance no more than a tiny spark deep within me. He spoke, cool and calm.

'So what did you do to him, to take him where he had never been before?'

'I . . . like it says, I . . .'

'Just say.'

'I . . . er . . . I buggered him with a candle, OK.'

'You buggered him with a candle!?'

'Yes. It wasn't like that though . . . OK, so it was. He wanted to do me . . . up my bum, and I didn't want to, and I was a bit drunk, so . . .'

'So you made him take a candle up his bum instead?'

Suddenly he was laughing, a full-throated roar of mirth that echoed around the interior of the church and startled the pigeons from the beams. I just stood there, biting my lip, far from sure just what he thought so funny, or even if his amusement might be the prelude to anger, until he reached out to tousle my hair, his eyes shining as he turned to me.

'You are something else, Dusk, you really are! Any woman I've ever known, any woman I can think of, would have gone one of three ways. She might have refused, she might have accepted it and hated it, or she might have accepted it and loved it. Not you, not my Dusk, you turn the tables on him and bugger him until he's begging for more!'

I was blushing furiously, but I couldn't help but smile. Relief was flooding through me, because while there was more than just amusement in his voice, I couldn't detect any of the anger I'd expected. I still felt bad, and in an odd way I wanted him to be cross, but it was a far better reaction than I had expected. He went on, shaking his head as he re-read the card.

'When was this?'

'The night before last. Sorry.'

'Don't be. Maybe I shouldn't have tried to stake a claim on you.'

'No, really. I ... I want to be with you, Michael. It just happened. I'll ... I'll make it clear there won't be another time, OK?'

'No. Play it that way and you'll feel resentful from the word go. Come on, Dusk, where's your spirit? You're not going to go all Christian on me, are you, not the girl who fucks to Satanic fantasies?'

'How do you mean?'

He laughed.

'You're into all this stuff, stuff most people couldn't handle at all. You fuck on tombs, you bugger men, of course you're going to do as you please. I'd be disappointed if you were any other way!'

'Oh.'

'What was it you said to me, about creating an abstract temple in which you could be honest with yourself. Well to me you are that temple, and I suspect to Stephen Byrne too.'

'To you?'

'Yes! Don't you see? You're what a man needs, what I need anyway, not some thin neurotic designer bitch, but a free, unbroken spirit, somebody he doesn't have to hold back with, somebody for whom he doesn't have to wear the mask. For me to attempt to crush that spirit would be a terrible thing. No, I aim to help release it.'

He walked rapidly into the church, leaving me flushed and confused. I'd never seen him so emotional, and nobody had ever said anything so wonderful to me. I'd been expecting angry recriminations, the sort of stupid shouting match on which so many relationships

203

end. Instead I was being praised, almost worshipped in a way, something of which I felt utterly unworthy. I followed him, to where he was standing in the nave, staring at the rood screen. He spoke as I approached him.

'Old Isaac Foyle really could have been thinking of you when he carved his Lust. You represent everything a weak man is afraid of in a woman: aggressive sexuality, an element of spirituality which he can never share, much less control. It's all there, in Foyle's carving.'

'Stephen's not weak.'

'No, no, anything but. To judge by that note he craves what you can give. He might be submissive, but never weak.'

'Submissive?'

'Somebody who likes to be dominated during sex.'

'I suppose so ... maybe, but more a sort of all-round pervert, I think. He likes to ... to spank me too.'

'Somehow that doesn't surprise me.'

'So what? You're saying I deserve spanking?'

'With your bottom and your attitude?'

'Thanks! What happened to me as a temple?'

'A temple in which a man may freely express his lust, which in the case of a cheeky, round-bottomed imp like you and an English public-school boy means you get spanked. I take it Stephen did go to public school?'

'Yes.'

I'd come close, and I slapped his bottom, feeling the firm muscle beneath his trousers. He immediately smacked me back, catching me across both cheeks with a firm swat and snatching my hand as I tried to protect myself. I gave in, and let him squeeze me through my dress, wriggling away only when his finger began to delve between my cheeks. I couldn't help but smile, now at ease, and thinking how it would feel to show off for him with Snaz, perhaps for Stephen too. It appealed, a lot, something both naughty and seriously pleasurable, while for me it would also be atonement. He still had my hand, and led me down the nave towards the door, and Foyle's chapel. With Stephen out in the open, I wanted to admit everything

'He wanted to watch me with Snaz too.'

'That definitely doesn't surprise me. Any man who says he wouldn't like to watch two girls together is either gay or a liar.'

'So you would too?'

'Of course.'

'Then you should have been here the other night. We went out bombing, and got drunk afterwards, and well . . .'

He blew his breath out sharply. I laughed, pleased to have punctured his armour of cool once more, and went on.

'I didn't tell Stephen, I just teased him, telling him what we'd do, but in fact it was what we'd already done.'

'I bet it got to him just the same.'

'And then some. That was when he suggested letting him put it up my bum.'

'You do let yourself in for it!'

'What!'

'You drive men mad with lust, so of course they're going to want you!'

'Yes, I know that, but I don't expect them to want to spank me and stick their cocks up my bottom! You don't.'

'I'm not anally fixated.'

'Stephen is, obviously!'

'And you'd have let him?'

'I ... yes, I would, if he'd won. We tossed a coin for it, you see, because I was a bit scared, and I don't know ... I didn't want to feel I was surrendering to him.'

'You were scared? It would have been the first time?'

'Yes ... no ... yes, with a cock. Remember when I told you about my experience at Sir Barnaby's tomb? I had candles around me, and I put one up my bottom. It felt good, rude, improper, nice too, really full. And other times. When we fucked the first time ... no, the second ...'

'I remember.'

'I was imagining it was the Devil, coming up behind me and sticking his cock in while you were inside me too – that came from my experience on Sir Barnaby's tomb as well.'

He blew his breath out again. Talking so openly was obviously getting to him, and it certainly was to me. There was the same blend of fear and anticipation I'd experienced when the fall of a single coin had meant the difference between having my bottom fucked and fucking Stephen's. Had it gone the other way it would have been me kneeling on the bed with my bottom cheeks pulled apart, me panting and gasping in wanton, dirty pleasure, me ...

Michael sighed.

'Sodomised by the Devil. That I have to draw.'

'I'll pose, just find me a Devil.'

He laughed. We'd come to Sir Barnaby's tomb, and he was looking at the knight, as if expecting to find some clue in the intricate carving. There was a prickling sensation between my legs, and at the back of my neck, which went with the sense of disapproval emanating from the tomb and made me feel naughtier still. I couldn't help but wonder if Michael would be able to feel it, perhaps at orgasm, perhaps.

'Turn around, I'm going to suck your cock.'

Not surprisingly, he turned. I went down, squatting on the tiles, knees wide in front of him. Talking about rude things had already had its effect, his dick swollen in his trousers, and I quickly released him, into my hand, then my mouth, taking in the scent and taste of man as I began to suck. He took my head, stroking my hair as his cock grew in my mouth and the sense of pompous disapproval grew in my mind, but also regret and lust.

As I sucked I worked on Michael's trousers, opening them and tugging them down, to get at him properly, my hands taking his neat buttocks, my mouth working on his cock and now his balls too. He gasped as I took them in my mouth, sucking deep and licking, my passion rising at his taste, and the feel of him, and the delicious rudeness of what I was doing.

I was trembling as I slipped my fingers down between my legs and into my knickers. As I entered myself I took his cock back into my mouth as deep as I could, thinking of how it would feel inside me, and wondering if I dared invite him to penetrate my bottom. The answer came immediately. Not to was prudish, weak, and unadventurous. I wanted it. My pussy was wet, ready for cock, my fingers already deep in, and coming out juicy. The naughtiest possible feeling hit me as I pushed them back, to find the tight ring between my cheeks and to open myself, slipping in, and up.

The sense of outrage that hit me as I penetrated my

own bottom pushed away the last of my indecision. I began to finger myself and to suck harder on Michael's cock, now fully erect. He was getting urgent, his fingers locked in my hair, maybe ready to come. I took a last, lingering suck and pulled back, leaving his beautiful cock rock hard and shiny wet.

He looked impossibly thick, adding a fresh thrill of fear I rocked back. For a moment more I was playing with myself, Michael watching and toying with his erection, and then I was pulling my panties down, kicking them off, pulling my dress high to bare myself completely. He took me in his arms as I stood, his cock rock hard against my belly. We kissed as his hands went lower, to cup my bottom, lifting me, and I was on his cock, sighing into his mouth as my pussy filled.

I took a firm hold, bouncing on his cock and thinking of my bottom hole, open and juicy behind. It would have been just the moment for the Devil to appear, right behind me, Michael holding me tight as my bottom was stuffed full of thick hot cock. I had to do it, as best I could, now, before Michael came in my pussy. I began to wriggle, trying to get off, but he had me tight, his pushes now urgent as he fucked me. Suddenly I was gasping.

'No, Michael, not yet. Bend me over ... do it ... do it, Michael, up my bottom.'

He grunted, his teeth gritted as he lifted me from his erection. I'd asked for it, surrender, and it was going to happen, now. He turned me over, so easily, my body a toy in his hands, and bent me down, across the stone knight, the marble cold against my breasts and belly. My bottom came high, open, his cock touched between my cheeks, to my anus, and I was shivering with fear and desire, my head hung down, my breathing heavy and my mouth wide as he pushed and for the first time in my life I felt my bottom hole spread open around the head of a man's penis. I was gasping immediately, overwhelmed not just by the sensation, but by the delicious, rude, inappropriate act, something good girls just do not do, only bad, dirty little imps. It did hurt, as he put the full length slowly up, a numbing heavy pain that had me clutching onto the statue and Sir Barnaby laughing in my face. I clung on, determined to take it, whimpering into the cold stone, my teeth gritted, until at last I felt his balls push to my empty pussy and knew he was right in.

My mouth was wide, my jaw shaking uncontrollably, my whole body loose, helpless as he began to push into me. Slowly my pain began to die away, leaving me feeling so full, and so wanton, holding the thought of what he was doing to me in my head, a man's cock actually up my bottom hole, and bent across a tomb as I was buggered.

It could as well have been the Devil, dark and handsome like Michael, or huge and red, demonic in his passion, laughing as he buggered me, as he came up my bottom. Suddenly I was snatching at my pussy, the image bright in my mind. Sir Barnaby's cruel laughter turned to outrage as I focussed and began to rub, imagining Michael as the Devil, my bottom hole stretched taut around his huge cock shaft.

He was pushing hard, his balls bumping my pussy, helping me up towards climax as I dabbed and flicked at my clit. I pictured myself, spread bare over the stone knight, bottom high and penetrated, a big, powerful man working himself into my straining anus, his face set in demonic glee. Michael or the Devil, it didn't matter. They were one and the same, in me, buggering me, about to come in me, up my bottom . . .

As the orgasm hit me I screamed with all the force of my lungs. I felt myself tighten on his cock, and then I was bucking frantically against him, wriggling my bottom and snatching at my pussy, clawing at the stone and screaming over and over, on and on. I heard him grunt, felt the final jerk of his cock inside me and I knew he'd come too, kicking my ecstasy up one more notch, my screams louder still, and dying, my body going slowly limp to the sound of Michael's breathing and the alarmed fluttering of the pigeons.

Even when it was over and he had pulled out I felt too weak to stand. He helped me up, taking me into his arms for a long lingering kiss, until my legs stopped shaking. I was dizzy with reaction, sore and trembling, and let him support me back to the vestry. Only when I was in the sink with my poor bottom immersed in cool water did I manage to turn my mind to anything but the immediately practical.

Michael was watching me as I washed, grinning, thoroughly pleased with himself and by my reaction. I was feeling a little shy, but generally happy, for the sake of my pleasure, the experience, and the new bond of intimacy it made between us. It did occur to me that given what we'd done, and what had been in my head, I might have expected to repeat my Satanic experience, but it was Michael who posed the question.

'Did you feel anything? Spiritually, that is?'

'Yes, Sir Barnaby, but only as I expected to. I was picturing you as the Devil when I came.'

He laughed.

'I am the Devil, haven't you figured that out yet?'

'I wish. Didn't you feel anything of Sir Barnaby? Maybe a sense of moral outrage, or his amusement at my pain?'

'No, sorry. It hurt then?'

'Of course it hurt! But … in a nice way, at least once you were in. I'm glad we did it anyway. It's only a pity you don't seem to have my empathy. I wish I could convince you.'

'Oh I believe you experience what you say, absolutely.'

'Yes, but nothing more. You think it's just in my head, don't you?'

'I wouldn't put it that strongly. I just feel you should examine alternative explanations for your experiences.'

'Whatever. You made me doubt myself anyway, because what happened with Sir Barnaby related so much more closely to your Goat of Mendes story than to his personality.'

'Right.'

'I looked, and I could find no evidence whatsoever to suggest that he was a Satanist, or anything of the sort. So I set up an experiment. Stephen helped me, by taking me to a cemetery I'd never visited before.'

'I would have taken you.'

For the first time he sounded a little hurt.

'Sorry, Michael, I would have asked you, normally, but I couldn't. I … I feel too intimate with you, and I had to be safe, but alone. You'd have put ideas into my head too. Stephen was right, because I knew he'd do as he was told but it wouldn't mean anything to him. Other than the kinky stuff, he's very straight down the line, candlelight dinners and soft music. Anyway, he set everything up for me, black candles, a pentacle. I was blindfolded, and he left me to commune. It worked.'

'It worked! For certain?'

'Absolutely certain. I didn't mean to tell you, I'd hoped I could prove it to you, just now.'

'I'm sorry, Dusk. You have no idea how much I yearn to be able to experience something like that, but I can't, not me. I've tried everything, believe me, seances, ouija board, I've even attended a Black Mass, of a sort. I've never felt anything, but if my doubt has made you explore further, that can only be a good thing. So what happened?'

'The man was an ancestor of his, Richard Byrne, a fanatical puritan. To him I was a witch, which is presumably the way he would see me. I felt his hatred, so strong it almost overwhelmed me. He pulled me in too, the same way I was pulled into the Satanic ritual, only to a village where I was to be drowned, for heresy I imagine.'

'And you had no idea it was his tomb?'

'None at all. I didn't even know where I was. Sure, I'd tried to second guess Stephen, I couldn't help it, but I know his sense of humour, and I thought it would be some politician whose principles he disagreed with. Do you believe me?'

'I don't doubt you for a moment, and I certainly can't explain it, although I admit I'd like to. So you have some empathy with ... with ghosts, some resonance people leave when they die perhaps?'

'Something like that. It's certainly not physical, or I'd have been soaking wet and half-drowned. It was pretty scary.'

'I can imagine, like a nightmare only more real.'

'Exactly, like a dream, but only once I'd been pulled in. Normally I'm very detached, otherwise it doesn't work, but I'm aware of myself, and of the person who's in my head.'

'Like thinking to yourself, perhaps when you're trying to decide whether or not to go somewhere, buy something perhaps?'

'No, clearer than that, more as if somebody's talking to me but I can't see them. No, that's not right, because it's the emotion I feel.'

'There are no words?'

'Never.'

'So it's as if it's the essence of the person that's in your head?'

'Yes, usually. Always in fact, except for that once. My first experience with Sir Barnaby still makes no sense, and when I tried to reproduce it I couldn't, not just now, but as a communion, mounted on the knight.'

'You didn't feel anything?'

'No, I felt plenty. I just didn't feel anything relating to Satanism.'

'OK, let's look at this from a scientific point of view. In what way did your first experience differ from the second?'

'Two ways. The second time I kept my head clear and I had doubts about the reality of my experience.'

'But you felt something?'

'Yes, what I'd have expected to feel from Sir Barnaby as I understand his character: pompous disapproval and a desire to control. So it was inconclusive.'

'And you've ... communed you call it, with your head clear before?'

'Yes, lots of times. On Eliza Dobson's tomb, for instance.'

'I remember we spoke about it. So was there any other difference, however slight? What do you put in black candles for instance?'

'Nothing heavy, just a blend of incenses.'

'Nothing hallucinogenic?'

'No. I did try skunk, but I can't really afford it. It spoils the scent too.'

'So that shouldn't make any difference, unless it's auto-suggestion.'

'Auto-suggestion?'

'Making people associate two things by habit rather than because they are actually associated. Like when you hear a particular type of music you know there's an ice-cream van about, but you don't need that to make ice-cream, or the ice-cream to play that music.'

'You could say that, sure. I've got used to the incense when I commune, so now the scent makes me ready for communion. OK, but that doesn't account for the Satanic bit.'

'No, not really. What else? You weren't ill at all? It wasn't an exceptionally hot day? Anything odd in the environment the first time? Anything different in you?'

I tried to think, and he was right. There was a difference.

'Yes. The first time I'd been trying to commune with Isaac Foyle, as an act of atonement, but I was overcome by a need to be dirty, and cruel to myself. It was only afterwards I realised I was against Sir Barnaby's tomb. The second time I rode the knight on top of the tomb.'

'So your experience might not have related to Sir Barnaby at all, but to somebody else?'

'Yes, I suppose so, but who? There's no stone there, just bare tiles, if you're thinking there might be a grave beneath the floor. There's the crypt, of course, but it doesn't extend that far out, only under the nave and chancel.'

'Let's go down anyway.'

'Sure, just let me dress.'

I didn't expect much, but still hurried to dress. Michael's grin was truly demonic as he watched me apply cream to my sore bottom, and I made a point of pressing a big altar candle to the seat of his trousers when I was finished, just to remind him that he was not inviolate. Once in my cleaning overalls and old boots, I got together as many candles as I could, lit two and we trooped down to the crypt.

As ever, after the Gothic glory of the main body of the church it looked depressing and sleazy. I hadn't been down since showing Michael when we'd first met, and in the meantime another section of the false ceiling had come loose, making it more dilapidated than ever. Michael lifted a candle to peer into the space, illuminating the original bricks with flickering orange light, the fourfold curve of a ceiling arch and a boss carved as a star.

'Take all the crap out and this would be wonderful, but it's very open. Was it never used, or did they clear stuff out?'

'It was never used as such, I don't know why.'

He moved on across the floor, stopping at the wall in a pool of yellow light. I busied myself with the rest of the candles, melting the base of each and sticking them to the floor, in a pentagonal pattern from sheer force of habit. Michael spoke as I fixed the last in place, pointing as he did so.

'If the tower rises there, Foyle's chapel must be there, and Sir Barnaby's tomb roughly here.'

'About a metre into the wall, yes.'

'OK. So if somebody had been buried in a niche it would be somewhere along here.'

He began to pull at the hardboard facings, which came away easily enough, but revealed only blank, unadorned brick underneath. I watched, hoping he might find something but fairly sure he wouldn't. I knew from early plans that the crypt had never been used, yet his idea did make sense.

There was nothing. By the time Michael had stripped three panels away a long face of brick wall was exposed, all of it absolutely solid. He began to inspect it, peering closely at the mortar and prodding it with a key, but to no avail. Finally he stood back.

'Damn! It made perfect sense. No, it does make perfect sense. Imagine your Satanist was a relative of someone perfectly respectable, maybe even Sir Barnaby. He'd have been an embarrassment to his family, and they'd have known that if they gave him a proper tomb it would become a magnet for every follower of the black arts from here to New Orleans. So they'd have stuck him down here, in holy ground, but safely out of the way. Unfortunately, unless he was actually interred during the construction of the church, that doesn't seem to be the case.'

'No.'

I stood back hastily as Michael reached up for the sagging edge of the false ceiling. It hid only the curve of the arch, which would have been a bizarre place to make a niche, but he pulled anyway. The whole section came away with a snap, to send him sprawling and leave three of the original arches exposed, each with its central boss, a green man, his mouth flowing vine, a coiled snake and a goat's head. No, not a goat's head, the goat's head.

13

I had to know, and so did Michael. We spent the rest of the day in the crypt, heedless of the fact that he was supposed to be moving into his flat, or of anything else. For hours we were pulling at the rotten facings and the false ceiling, pausing only for water or coffee and for him to buy a paraffin lamp.

By mid-afternoon every single piece of facing and the whole ceiling had been torn down, fittings and all. We'd piled it into the middle of the crypt, exposing the walls and the ceiling. The walls yielded nothing, every one solid, plain brick with no evidence of openings made into them, no inscriptions, nothing. The ceiling was a different matter, or rather, the bosses were. Before I had only seen one, a star, but that, along with green men, snakes, assorted astrological and occult symbols and, of course, the goat's head, were each and every one of significance. There was no pattern, as such, beyond the twelve zodiac signs being arranged in sequence, and the only explanation we could come up with was that they had been meant to have specific rituals performed beneath them.

It was fascinating, but had done no more than whet our curiosity. We wanted to know who was responsible, and why. We wanted to know if the crypt had been left empty specifically to make space for the rituals to be performed. I, more than anything, wanted to know why the goat's head could have inspired such strong emotions in me if there was no burial associated with it.

We paced the distances out, and discovered that the goat's head was beneath the pews about two metres to the side of where I'd masturbated in front of Sir Barnaby's tomb. Now I knew, I could feel it more strongly still, both in the crypt and above, more so above. Just standing there made my senses swim and my head fill with bizarre and dirty thoughts. Only the state of frantic energy I'd worked myself into prevented me from masturbating then and there, but I promised myself I would not delay the pleasure long.

Oddly, none of the other bosses had any effect on me at all, even those with supposedly powerful occult symbols. The nave followed the line of zodiac symbols in the crypt beneath, so that as people entered the church or a bride might have walked to her groom's side, she crossed each symbol. I had never noticed anything beyond the normal effect of the church before, and could not, despite several trials. The goat's head was like a hotspot of emotion, just as if it had been a tomb.

By the time it had begun to grow dark we felt we'd done everything we could. The crypt had been investigated from end to end, the floor above mapped out, the walls tested for hollow spaces. More tests were possible, such as running a metal detector over the floor, but we both felt the answer was more likely to come from research. The crypt had been built for a purpose, an occult purpose, and therefore those with responsibility for the construction of All Angels must have known. More than that, they must have been responsible.

The answer hit me as I sat among the packing cases

in Michael's new flat across the road. Suddenly it was clear, both who our Satanist was and why the goat's head gave me such strong emotions. Like any church, no one man had been responsible for the construction of All Angels, but the guiding hand had been its first priest. Michael was in the kitchen, spooning out a Chinese take-away onto plates, and I told him as I came in.

'Our Satanist was James O'Donnell.'

'The priest?'

'Yes. At least, he must have been a leading light among them. His name is on the deeds, letters discussing the commissioning of the rood screen with Foyle, all sorts. He could have directed the carvings in the crypt.

'What about Foyle?'

'He was no Satanist, I'm sure, but if he could carve imps and green men, why not goats' heads and occult symbols? He'd have seen that sort of symbology as a warning of Satan's might. They were keen on that.'

'And you think James O'Donnell went the whole hog and switched to Satanism.'

'Yes. Do you know about his heart?'

'His heart?'

'Yes, his body was taken back to Ireland, but his heart was buried here, under the floor. I've tried to find where it is lots of times, looking for physical things and trying to find a spot with a strong air of sanctity. I never could, and now I know why. What I should have been looking for was an air of the satanic. Which is exactly what we've found.'

'You think his heart is in the goat's head?'

'Where else?'

* * *

It made sense. Over the next few days Michael and I spent hours digging into the career of Father James O'Donnell. There was nothing overt, but plenty of circumstance. His rapid rise in the church had come to an abrupt halt when he had declined promotion from his post at All Angels. He had remained there for the rest of his life, with the same two curates. One of those curates had later broken away from the church and had ended his life as an Adeptus Minor in the Golden Dawn. O'Donnell had also been reprimanded for stressing the power of Satan in his sermons, and there was a letter to him from his bishop that contained a gentle hint on the fate of the Albigensians. By the look of things O'Donnell had gone far beyond the idea of a balance between God and Satan. The name of the other curate was Albert Dawes, so close to the Satanist in the Goat of Mendes it gave me pause for thought, only for Michael to laughingly dismiss it as coincidence.

There was evidence enough for me, and more than enough when coupled with my own experience. Father James O'Donnell, a priest respected by thousands, had held Satanic rituals in the crypt of All Angels, rituals involving not just Devil worship, but sex, even sodomy. It was a magnificent irony and a masterpiece of Gothicism.

If I had felt love for All Angels and everything it stood for before, now it was tenfold. It was a church, but also a temple to Satan, an expression of all the impossibilities and contradictions of church teaching, the clash of the beautiful and the macabre, the solemn piety and the talk of hellfire. It was me.

Now I understood the strength of my empathy for the place when my feelings for its parent religion were mixed to say the least. It was no shrine to pious hypocrisy, but a place in which a full-scale Gothic nightmare had been played out. Michael was equally delighted, and immediately wanted to work the story up into a graphic novel, following the life of James O'Donnell from his original doubts to the burial of his heart in a carving of a goat's head. I was all for it, keen to help as best I could, by modelling for him.

I hadn't seen Stephen, despite a couple of phone calls. He was busy, either that or starting to get cold feet about our relationship. I was even wondering if the roses had not been an attempt to let me down gently rather than a genuine thank you when he called to ask if I'd like to come over in the evening. I was actually with Michael at the time, drinking coffee in his flat, which made it more than a little awkward for all his apparent acceptance. The only sensible choice seemed to be completely honest. I took the phone away from my mouth and turned to Michael.

'It's Stephen. He wants to give me dinner, at his flat.'

The answer was immediate.

'Why not invite him over here?'

'Here?'

'Why not? He can take you out, and I'll see you later. Besides, I bought you a little treat this morning, something you rather seemed to want.'

I threw him a puzzled look as he leant back to delve into a black carrier bag on the floor. Puzzled, I told Stephen to hold, then my jaw dropped open as Michael pulled out a thick leather strap set with steel rings, and a monstrous black rubber phallus. He held it up, grinning, then put his finger to his lips. His intention was all too obvious, and spoke straight to my wicked side. I was trying not to giggle as I once more put the phone to my mouth.

'Stephen, hi, sorry about that. Would you rather come over here?'

He put up a bit of resistance, but not much. Two minutes later I'd arranged for him to come over at six, take me to dinner and bring me back. I was grinning maniacally as I put the phone down.

'You are so wicked, Michael! So, you like the idea of me buggering Stephen, do you?'

'It rather appeals, yes. Your suggestion of having a man's virginity taken for the Goat of Mendes story turned me on to it.'

'Only that?'

'Well, OK, so the idea appeals full stop.'

'Would you do the buggering?'

'I might. Why not?'

'No reason. I'm glad you've the strength to admit you'd like to.'

He was grinning, and his eyebrows rose a little as he passed me the dildo. It was, if anything, more grotesque than the one he'd drawn in the illustration. The harness was like a pair of leather pants, with one strap to circle the waist and another to go between the legs. They met at the front in a ring, which accommodated the phallus itself. It was a jet-black rubber penis, obscene in the exaggeration of anatomical detail. The head was swollen and bulbous, the neck thick and taut above the rubbery mass of the rolled-back foreskin. The shaft was gnarled and criss-crossed with veins standing out like tree roots, the scrotum fat and wrinkled. It was big too, bigger than either Michael or Stephen.

'Well?'

'You want me to fuck Stephen with it?'

'If you like. Ideally I'd want to watch.'

'I don't think he'd go for that, not in front of another man, and it's pretty big. Where did you get it!?'

'In a gay sex shop near Liverpool Street.'

'A gay sex shop?'

'Sure, they have all the best stuff. And if you think that's big, you should see some of the butt plugs.'

He held both his fists together and gave a meaningful nod. Both my pussy and bottom hole twinged in instinctive reaction and I grimaced. Michael laughed.

'Obviously it's for lesbians rather than gay men.'

'Obviously.'

Just holding the thing was making me feel ever more wicked. I knew Stephen would love it too, remembering the state of wanton ecstasy I'd put him into with the candle. Michael, I was beginning to see, fancied himself as something of a Svengali figure, a motif he frequently used in his stories. Not that his heroines usually needed much persuasion, if any. I certainly didn't.

'OK, I'll see how it goes. Thanks, for this, and for being understanding. I'd better go over to wash and change.'

His response was an enigmatic little smile. I gave him a kiss and left, taking the dildo with me in my bag. Stephen wasn't due for quite a bit, but I wanted a leisurely wash and to choose my look carefully. Discovering about James O'Donnell had been something of a resolution for me, making me feel more confident and assertive. So had Michael's understanding of my gift, Stephen's ecstatic response to being sodomised by me, even having my piece on the gasometer played a part. I felt strong, and I wanted to reflect it in my look.

Stephen saw me as naïve, or he had. He liked me on

skates, in mini-skirts and crop-tops, in fishnets and no bra, preferably no knickers; anything sexy yet innocent. It made him want to spank me, which was not the result I was after. What I needed was a more refined look, Gothic of course, but not overstated, a long black dress, stockings and heels, my corset underneath.

I was halfway through when I changed my mind completely. It was much better to be just as cutesy as I possibly could, all bare flesh and giggles. I could tease him, let him think I was up for spanking, maybe even buggering, then turn the tables on him at the last minute. It was a much better idea, so I stripped off and started from scratch, no panties, no bra, a mini-skirt so short the slightest puff of wind was going to flash my bare bum to the whole world. I added a little silver bell in my tummy button, a crop-top tight enough and thin enough to leave my nipples poking up like a pair of acorns, my hair loose, no more than a touch of make-up, bare legs, rolled down socks and skates.

Looking at myself in the mirror, I knew it would drive him nuts. In fact, he was likely to whip me straight over his knee and spank me until I howled the moment he set eyes on me. However much he'd enjoyed my treatment of his bottom, there was every chance he'd be out for revenge, and the way I looked was quite simply an invitation to take it. I would be the one who ended up getting my bottom filled, and heated first.

By the time I'd stripped off again the vestry looked as if a dozen cats had had a fight in it. Just about every dress, skirt and top I owned was out, along with boots, shoes, my rollerblades, bits of jewellery and gauze, and more. Both ideas had been good, but they weren't perfect. I wanted to turn him on, and to lure him into a false sense of superiority, but I needed to be a little more subtle about it.

Lilitu was looking at me with an expression suspiciously like despair. For her it was easy. Her beautiful black coat covered all eventualities, all occasions. I would have been happy to follow her example and go out stark naked, but I couldn't see even the most bohemian of places letting us in. Simplicity was the answer, a simple black dress over nothing, barefoot and with just a touch of make-up, a Gothic waif. Stephen would be charmed, but entirely unsuspecting.

I'd just begun to make-up when Lilitu alerted me to somebody approaching. It was getting on for six and I was preparing to tell Stephen to mooch around the graveyard for a bit when I caught Snaz's voice. I'd seen her a couple of times since we'd got off, but always with Michael there. We'd exchanged the occasional knowing look, but nothing had been said, and I'd yet to have a chance to tell her what had happened with Stephen. I opened the door to find her in black jeans and a hoodie, her bag of paints slung over her shoulder.

'Hey, Dusk, what's up? Want to come out?'

She tapped her bag, which was bulging with aerosol tins. I answered with genuine regret.

'I can't, Snaz, sorry. I've promised Stephen he can take me out for dinner.'

'Blow him out, or he can drive us around.'

'No way! That he would never do!'

'Nah, suppose not.'

'I have to tell you something though. You would not believe what he suggested the last time I went out with him. He wanted to watch us together!'

'You told him!? What we did?'

'No. He got off on smacking my bum in front of you.

He wanted to do it to both of us, then have us get it on together so he could watch.'

I wasn't being strictly accurate, but it made a better story than me teasing Stephen. It got the right response, shock and delight.

'The dirty old pervo!'

'That's not all. He got seriously horny, and he asked to put it up my bum.'

'Oh, you didn't!'

'No. I told him we'd toss a coin for it. He lost, so I did him with a candle, one of those.'

Her mouth came wide as I nodded to the altar candles.

'You are one mad bitch, Dusk! So what, did he get off on it?'

'Yup.'

She was laughing as she threw herself down on the bed, a sound so full of playful, uninhibited joy I immediately found myself wondering if I should go out tagging with her after all, and to bed afterwards. I was sure she'd be up for it, after a few beers, maybe without even that; maybe she'd be up for a quick cuddle before Stephen arrived.

I glanced towards the door. She was completely casual, lying on her side, propped on one elbow, her knees up, a slice of creamy flesh and the waistband of bright pink pants just showing between her jeans and her hoodie. All I needed to do was make the right move and those jeans would come down, her knickers too, the hoodie up, for a feel, maybe a lick.

The low purr of a car from outside brought my dirty thoughts to an abrupt halt. Lilitu had pricked her ears up but not bothered to rise, so it had to be Stephen. Sure enough, I caught the heavy thump of the Jaguar's door, the crunch of leaves from the yew avenue, and he appeared in the doorway. He gave me a big smile, the quality of which became abruptly quizzical as he laid eyes on Snaz. I could tell exactly what was going through his mind. He looked at me.

'Sorry if I'm a little early. Shall I wait outside?'

'No, don't be silly. I'm ready, anyway, just about. Do you like it?'

I gave him a twirl, which pulled the dress against my body, making it quite clear I was naked underneath. He swallowed and gave an appreciative nod. I sat back down at the table and started on my lips again. For a while he was silent, and when he did speak he sounded nervous.

'I um ... I was thinking of this rather nice little place I know in the Chilterns, very tucked away. I er ... I don't suppose you'd like to come along too, Snaz? That is, of course, if you ... you don't mind, Angel?'

'Why? Do you want to take us into the woods and spank our naughty bottoms for us?'

He went from pale to purple in maybe a second. Snaz burst out laughing as he began to stammer.

'No. I ... er ... I just thought, that ... well ... maybe dinner?'

Snaz shifted lazily on the bed.

'Yeah, great, I'm up for that – if you're cool, Dusk?'

I hesitated, then gave a smile and a shrug in acquiescence. It was quite obvious that Stephen wanted to get us into bed together, and Snaz knew damn well what was going on too. I could play dirty as well as either of them, so it was fine by me. Besides, if it did happen, there was just a chance he would end up getting rather more than he had bargained for. So might she.

'Yeah, fine. Just let me sort my make-up and I'm with you. Borrow some gear if you like, Snaz.'

Stephen was fiddling nervously with his tie and pretending to look out of the window as Snaz quite coolly kicked off her shoes, pushed her jeans down and peeled off her hoodie and top. She began to look through my stuff, crawling in nothing but a pair of pink panties and her bra. Stephen was getting redder and redder, but she took not the slightest notice, trying on one dress, then another, each time turning to admire herself in the mirror. On the second attempt she was satisfied, and after a moment patting her pink hair into place declared herself ready.

We looked a fine pair of urchins: punky, Gothic, full of attitude and cheek, which was just how I wanted to feel. Stephen was wavering between embarrassment and arousal, and while he hustled us quickly into the Jaguar I did notice a passing man give him a look compounded of envy and disapproval. He responded with his blandest politician's smile and quickly climbed into the driver's seat.

It was long drive, painfully slow up through east and north London, and not really picking up speed until we were well into the country. Snaz and I teased Stephen, not just by flirting with him and each other, but by talking about graff and shoplifting and all the other things to which he devoted so much professional disapproval. He'd been flustered and horny before we left, and he got worse, but we were well out in the country before he finally snapped. Snaz had found a soft spot, his car.

'Yeah, right across the bonnet, Snaz and Dusk, big pink and gold dubs, and Witchz from Hell underneath, so's everyone sees who's done you.'

He blew his breath out.

'It shouldn't be me who's done, young lady, it should be you, and yes you would be on the bonnet of the car, bent over it for a spanking.'

'Ooh! He's threatening us, Dusk! Do you think he means it?'

'Nah, he hasn't got the guts.'

'Haven't I?'

'No, you haven't.'

He didn't answer. We were driving through a deep cutting, the sides dirty white chalk, with woods at the top on either side, so I knew it couldn't be far to the restaurant. Sure enough, we turned off at the next exit, and immediately after, down a tiny lane between huge beech trees. A new piece of wickedness occurred to me.

'Snaz, shall we tell the people at the restaurant that we're his nieces?'

She burst into giggles, but it was Stephen who answered.

'Don't you dare, and I mean that.'

'Now he is threatening us, the big bully!'

'What're you going to do about it, Stephen?'

'We'll see, shall we?'

He was pulling off even as he spoke, into the mouth of a track overgrown with weeds. There was sudden silence as the engine stopped. Stephen turned, his face flushed red, but grinning.

'Out, both of you.'

'Here? What are you going to do?'

'What I said. Spank you over the bonnet.'

'You are, are you?'

'You and who else?'

'I'm sure there are an awful lot of people who'd be

only too glad to help me, railway staff for one. Now out you get.'

'And if we don't?'

If his expression had hardened I'd have stuck to my guns, but it showed doubt for just one moment. I winked at Snaz.

'Come on, girl, let's let the poor old boy have his fun.'

She made a face, a lot of her cheek gone even at the suggestion she be spanked, perhaps thinking of how far it was to get home. I took her hand and pulled her after me as I got out of the car. Stephen followed, taking his jacket off and laying it carefully on the roof. For all that I knew what I was doing, it was hard not to pout as I went to the bonnet and bent over. Snaz hesitated.

'It's a bit public, isn't it?'

Stephen answered her as he rolled his sleeve up.

'Best get it over with quickly then.'

She made a sulky face, still biting her lip in indecision. I gave her another, more urgent wink. She bit her lips, then came beside me, bending as I was, her hip just touching mine, her flesh warm through her thin dress. It was rather open, the car and high chalk banks concealing us from the road, but the old track disappearing behind us into the woods, our bums on plain view to anyone who came along it. Even Stephen glanced down it before he stepped up behind us.

'Bottoms out.'

We stuck our bums up. My tummy was tingling, and I felt a flush of shame as I made myself available for punishment.

'Dresses up.'

I shut my eyes as his fingers found the hem of my

dress. Up it came, and I was bare, my naked bottom stuck out to the woods. I had to peep to watch Snaz given the same treatment, her face pink, giggling nervously as her panties came on show.

'And I think we'd better have these knickers down.'

Snaz gave a little gasp as her knickers were whipped smartly down, and we were both bare, and ready. Stephen didn't waste time, taking her hard around the waist and laying on a volley of hard slaps, only a dozen or so, but enough to set her squealing and kicking her legs. Then he'd let go of her, I'd been grabbed, and I was given the same treatment, a dozen hard swats to set my bottom bouncing and leave me gasping and cursing him. Snaz was rubbing her bum, panties still down around her thighs, her flesh red and her face set in consternation.

'Ow! That hurt, you pig!'

Stephen's answer was positively smug.

'Well deserved.'

He was trembling, his cock a hard bulge in his trousers, his face redder than ever. I stood, embarrassed, my bottom smarting, not sure if I wanted to slap him or go down on him. It might have happened, both of us with our bottoms rosy, Stephen hard and ready, but as a car drove past the moment was lost. Stephen climbed back in, starting the engine even as we followed.

It had really put him in the mood, and I could see why, with two spanked girls in his car and the prospect of more later. Snaz was quiet and fidgety, unsure of herself in a way I'd only seen when she'd been hurt, and my own feelings were pretty mixed. I held her hand as we drove on, Stephen doubling back, and stopping after just a mile or so.

As with all the places he took me, it was discreet, a little country pub that made an effort with its food and wine but was hardly going to attract anyone who might recognise him. We didn't play the niece joke, and maybe it was because our bottoms were smacked, not for shame, but because I could feel the heat in my cheeks and pussy and it was making me horny.

We ordered steaks and Stephen got us a bottle of strong red wine, declining any himself because he was driving. I needed it, and the first glass barely touched the sides of my throat, or the second. As soon as the bottle was empty Stephen ordered another, sweet this time, and even stronger, which Snaz and I downed as we tucked into sticky toffee puddings and ice-cream.

Stephen was in a lavish mood, ordering us huge Irish coffees with whipped cream on top, another bottle of the sweet wine for the journey back, and one of brandy. He had us where he wanted us, horny and drunk, ready to play, and ready to do as we were told. I didn't care, drinking from the bottle as we drove, in the back, warm and drunk and giggly, acutely aware of being bare under my dress, of my smacked bottom, of Snaz cuddled up beside me.

The roads had cleared and we drove fast. In no time we were back among the lights of London, then pulling up outside All Angels. I was dizzy with drink. Snaz worse, leaning heavily on me and giggling at nothing as we staggered down the yew alley. Lilitu greeted us as we pushed into the vestry, whining softly and snuffling at our legs. I patted her head, holding the door as Snaz and Stephen came in, and pushing it to, almost.

I knew what I wanted, and it was going to happen. Stephen was urgent, Snaz drunk and horny. I let my hand stray to her bottom as we stepped fully inside, feeling one rounded, meaty cheek. She purred in response, called me a bad girl, and kissed me, full on my mouth. For a moment I let my mouth open beneath hers, tasting her lipstick and the sweet wine, then forced myself to pull away.

'Not here. Michael might come over. Down in the crypt. Stephen, take the mattress.'

He didn't hesitate, spilling my things off it and dragging it through the door. I grabbed up the bags I wanted and my new black candles, and followed, nipping ahead of Stephen in the nave. Down in the crypt I began to set my candles out, spacing them beneath the goat's head in a distorted pentacle. I could immediately feel O'Donnell's presence, a gleeful lust urging me to be dirty, to indulge my darkest passions. I made a quick genuflection to the goat as Stephen and Snaz appeared with the mattress.

'Put it here, Stephen, darling, and make yourself comfortable. Snaz and I are going to give you a little show.'

I'd pulled the old chair up to the edge of the circle of candlelight as I spoke. With the mattress in place among the candles, Stephen sat down. Snaz threw herself on the mattress, her eyes glittering in the light, her mouth a little open, drunk and aroused, ready for sex. I poured a brandy, half a coffee mug full, and passed it to Stephen, bobbing him a curtsey as he took it. He replied with a cool, superior smile, and adjusted his cock in his trousers as I skipped away.

'Come on, Snaz, let's give him a good perve over us.'

She was ready, opening her arms to take me in without the slightest hesitation. I kissed her mouth, cuddling into her, her body warm against mine, her breasts pressing to my chest. Folded in each others arms, our mouths came open together, kissing with real passion. I let my hand stray to her bottom, feeling the full softness of her cheeks and thinking of how she'd been spanked, her bottom bare in a lonely wood, and mine, side by side together. She responded, inching my dress up my legs, and higher. I paused, kneeling to pull it off, my sudden nakedness sending a new thrill through me. Snaz pulled me down, to kiss my face, my neck, my breasts, taking my nipples into her mouth.

I was lost, my passion beyond the point at which I could think of anything but my friend's soft, yielding flesh, and the fact that we were being watched. It was real, no show, and as I began to tug Snaz's dress up it was because I wanted her more than to show her to Stephen. She let me, giggling as the dress was pulled up over her head and away. Her hands went straight behind her back, to snip her bra catch and let her breasts free, straight into my waiting hands, full and heavy. I took a nipple into my mouth, sucking as she had done to me, even as my hand fumbled for her panties.

They came down, pushed roughly off her hips and kicked away. We were bare, our bodies together, warm and urgent. I'd meant to hold back, but I couldn't, twisting around and pulling her on top of me, head to toe. Her thighs came open above my face, her pussy right in front of me, moist and ready, her scent strong in my head, and James O'Donnell, urging me to lick, to stick my tongue right in, to kiss her bottom, to make her come . . .

I didn't need the encouragement. I buried my face in her even as my thighs came up to pull her head into my own pussy, and we were licking. Her full bottom was in my hands, her cheeks and thighs spread wide, my mouth open on her pussy, feeding on her, clumsy and urgent in my passion. She slid fingers into me and I returned the favour, up her pussy hole, and her bottom too, making her shudder as she was penetrated. I felt my pussy tighten and suddenly I was going to come. She sensed it, dabbing at my clit, and I was there, licking frantically at her pussy, my fingers jammed deep in her body, my thighs tight around her head, a long moment of blinding ecstasy, rising to burst in my head, falling, only to rise again, and again burst.

It left me panting and dizzy, my head back, gasping for breath. Snaz was having none of it, and sat up even as I pulled my fingers out, giggling as my face was smothered beneath her bottom. Stephen gave an ecstatic groan as I once more began to lick, tonguing Snaz's pussy as she wiggled into my face and laughed in sheer delight at what she was doing. I could barely breathe, but busied myself with helping her to the same exquisite pleasure she had given me, lapping at her clit. She moaned, I felt her bottom tighten in my face, and she was there, crying out as she came and squirming herself hard into me. I took it, licking until she'd finished and dismounted, to break into fresh giggles as she saw the state of my face.

I slapped her bottom for her and rolled over, propping myself on one elbow to see what Stephen was up to. His eyes were glued to us, his erect cock sticking up from the fly, the head purple and glossy with pressure, the shaft squeezed tight in his hand. I smiled and beckoned. He stood, starting towards us, but I immediately wagged a finger at him.

'Uh, uh, not so fast. If you want to join us you strip too. All the way, and you only do as I say. OK?'

He nodded immediately, as if his head was on a spring, and I was in charge, simple as that. I lay back as he began to strip, naked and content, warm with drink and sex, full of joy and wickedness. Snaz snuggled into the crook of my arm, also watching as Stephen peeled off. He did have a good body, and the state his cock was in made me want to open my mouth for it, and my legs.

I held back, twisting round as he knelt down on the bed. He was looking eager, but a little uncertain, holding himself and eyeing our naked bodies. Snaz saw, and cupped her breasts in a gesture at once insolent and inviting. He gave me a single glance, I nodded, and he had taken them in his hands, his face set in rapture as he felt them, sending her into fresh giggling. I let them get on with it, extracting the dildo and harness from its bag, faced away as I pushed one leg in, and the other. It was Snaz who noticed.

'What is ... oh fuck! Dusk, what are you like!'

I grinned down at her, flourishing the huge rubber cock. Stephen's mouth had come open, and he was staring, his hands still on Snaz's breasts. She was staring too, and biting her lip.

'What ... where do you think you're going to put that thing, Dusk?'

Just the tone of her voice filled me with cruel glee, and at that instant I realised why men are always talking about shagging girls and never shagging *with* girls.

'Shut up and bend over. I'm going to fuck you.'

She swallowed, but she went up on all fours to present me with her bottom, her cheeks wide, her pussy ready, her bottom hole showing, all of it pink and moist, an open invitation to fucking. As I knelt down she looked back, her pretty face full of lust but so uncertain. I put the cock head to her pussy hole, her mouth came wide in a gasp as I pushed, and in it went, stretching her wide, filling her. She was moaning and grunting as I began to fuck her, and I was laughing, watching the thick black shaft slide in and out of her pussy, the way her flesh moved to the pushes, and the way her bottom hole twitched in her pleasure.

Stephen gave me another of his guilty, uncertain glances, and as I nodded my permission he offered his cock to her mouth. She took it immediately, and she was being rocked back and forth between us, a cock in each end, a fantasy I'd had so many times, and often hoped to indulge, but never taking the place of one of the men. Again I was laughing, cackling, in evil, gleeful lust, fucking my friend as she sucked cock, in and out as she moaned in pleasure, rude and wanton, too high to care for anything but pleasure. I was watching her flesh move, admiring her beautiful, open bottom, her tight waist, the swell of her breasts as they swung beneath her, the movement of her hair as she sucked on my man's erection, revelling in every detail. It would have been easy to come, just rubbing myself on the base of the dildo, which had a little bump for just that purpose. I was going to as well, but later. I pulled out.

'Up you come, Snaz.'

She immediately came off Stephen's cock, rocking back on her heels. Her eyes were half-focussed, her chin wet with spit. Her mouth curved up into a dopey smile as she turned to me.

'That was nice, Dusk.'

She came close, to kiss me, and for a moment I tasted Stephen's cock in her mouth, before I had pulled her gently back. Stephen was waiting patiently, nursing his erection and drinking in the sight of our bodies. I beckoned him.

'Your turn now, Stevie baby.'

He shuffled forward.

'Perhaps like you were ... sixty-nine, and I can go in you, Angel? Would that be all right?'

I wagged my finger at him.

'Uh, uh, nothing like that. Not yet anyway. When I said it was your turn, I didn't mean you got to fuck me, or Snaz. I meant I got to fuck you.'

Snaz immediately burst into uncontrollable giggles. Stephen went beetroot, his jaw dropping, along with his eyes, to leave him staring at the huge black phallus protruding from my crotch. I smiled sweetly.

'Over you go, just like Snaz.'

'But ... Angel, I ...'

'Uh, uh, no nonsense. You want to play with me and my friend you do as you're told. Behave, and you might get all sorts of goodies. Misbehave, and ...'

He nodded vigorously. I leant into the bag again, to pull out a tin of the chrism oil. Snaz was still giggling, and had moved to the side, chewing on one finger in delighted anticipation of seeing Stephen buggered. He got down, slowly, never taking his eyes off the dildo as he turned his back. I opened the oil, stuck my finger in, making a deliberate show of greasing the fat black head of the dildo. Stephen went down, his buttocks spread to me, his erect cock sticking down, the skin so taut it seemed about to break. I took the dildo in hand, pressed it to his bottom.

'Snaz, be a sweetie and attend to his cock while I bugger him.'

She shuffled close, still giggling as she reached under

his belly to take his cock in hand. I pushed. Stephen gasped as his bottom hole spread and I was filled with savage glee as the head of the dildo went in. Again I pushed, and he was whimpering and grunting, his whole body trembling as the dildo slid slowly up, bit by bit, until the full length was immersed in his body.

I was laughing again, more gleeful than ever, full of truly wicked delight, which grew quickly stronger as his moans and whimpers became more passionate. Snaz caught it too, giggling insanely as she stroked and teased his cock and balls, hugely enjoying herself. Suddenly she had begun to spank him, crowing with delight as her hand slapped down on his flesh.

'This will teach you to perve on us, Mister!'

He gasped, and then he was babbling.

'Yes ... please ... tell me ... like that ... and make me come!'

'He likes it! The dirty pig!'

'Yes, I do. Say more ... please, Snaz ... please, Angel.'

She began to spank harder, and so did I, a cheek each, quickly reddening his flesh, the dildo still moving in his bottom. He was really trembling, his muscles tight, his head hung low and shaking, whimpering with pleasure between gasps as we slapped at him. Snaz grinned at me, her eyes bright with the same cruel lust that was coursing through me. She spoke, her voice rich and thick, heavy with mockery.

'Oh, he is a dirty pig, isn't he? Imagine taking it up the bottom, the little tart! What should we do with you next, Stephen. Maybe we should put you in a dress?'

'Yes, please, yes ... do that.'

'Yeah, and panties and bra!'

'Please ... oh, please.'

I had to go for it.

'Yes, all pink and frilly, and make him suck another man off!'

Snaz exploded into drunken laughter. Stephen gave a long, hollow groan and then he was babbling once more.

'Oh God, yes. Do it ... do it to me ... make me suck your boyfriends off. Oh please ... yes, please. I'd do it ... I would.'

'Would you? Would you take their big dirty cocks in your mouth and suck them 'til they came, would you?'

'Yes ... I would. I would.'

'I wonder if he'd spit or swallow?'

'I'd swallow ... swallow. No, you'd make them do it in my face. Oh yes, please ... do it to me!'

I was going to come, just listening to him babbling in his debauched ecstasy and rubbing my pussy on the dildo embedded so deep up his bottom. It was so dirty, so funny, so exciting, and as something stirred beyond the circle of candle flames I was shouting.

'Now, Snaz, make him come! Tug hard! Go on, Stephen, do it, take my boyfriend's cock in your mouth ... suck him while you come ... go on!'

Stephen gasped in shock and tried to lurch away as Michael stepped from behind the pile of debris, naked, erect cock in hand. But I had him, and he was too close to orgasm to stop himself, giving one last moan of utter despair before he took the erect penis into his mouth and began to suck on it. As I saw it, I began to come myself, my pleasure rising higher and higher, my eyes glued to the junction of cock and mouth. Snaz gave a squeal of disgust and delight as Stephen spunked in her hand and I was there, screaming out my ecstasy as my head went back, to meet the gaze of the goat, full on, and I was gone, no longer me, no longer with Snaz or Stephen.

I was in the same crypt, a demented she demon, horned and fanged, my body scarlet, a grotesque phallus sprouting from above my hungry cunt, mounted on one man, in another, their bodies jerking as I ravished them. Men were screaming, scrabbling to get away from me, men in cowled robes, terrified, all but the man inside me, who was cackling in insane glee as he watched his colleague buggered. It was James O'Donnell, I knew, and there was one other, behind me, one for whom I held no fear, one who was about to push his great burning cock up my bottom, my Lord – Michael.

Visit the Black Lace website at
www.blacklace-books.co.uk

**FIND OUT THE LATEST INFORMATION AND TAKE
ADVANTAGE OF OUR FANTASTIC FREE BOOK OFFER!
ALSO VISIT THE SITE FOR . . .**

- All Black Lace titles currently available
  and how to order online
- Great new offers
- Writers' guidelines
- Author interviews
- An erotica newsletter
- Features
- Cool links

**BLACK LACE – THE LEADING IMPRINT
OF WOMEN'S SEXY FICTION**

**TAKING YOUR EROTIC READING
PLEASURE TO NEW HORIZONS**

LOOK OUT FOR THE ALL-NEW BLACK LACE BOOKS – AVAILABLE NOW!

All books priced £6.99 in the UK. Please note publication dates apply to the UK only. For other territories, please contact your retailer.

THE HAND OF AMUN
Juliet Hastings
ISBN 0 352 33144 5

Marked from birth with the symbol of Amun, the young Naunakhte must enter a life of dark eroticism as a servant at his temple. She becomes the favourite of the high priestess but, when she's accused of an act of sacrilege, she is forced to flee to the city of Waset. There she meets Khonsu, a prince of the Egyptian underworld whose prowess as a lover is legendary. But fate draws her back to the temple, and she is forced to choose between two lovers – one mortal and the other a god. **Highly arousing and imaginative story of life and lust in Ancient Egypt.**

Coming in June

MIXED SIGNALS
Anna Clare
ISBN 0 352 33889 X

Adele Western knows what it's like to be an outsider. As a teenager she
was teased mercilessly by the sixth-form girls for the size of her lips.
Now twenty-six, we follow the ups and downs of her life and loves.
There's the cultured restaurateur Paul, whose relationship with his
working-class boyfriend raises eyebrows, not least because he is still
having sex with his ex-wife. There's former chart-topper Suki, whose
career has nosedived and who is venturing on a lesbian affair.
Underlying everyone's story is a tale of ambiguous sexuality, and Adele is
caught up in some very saucy antics. **The sexy *tours de force* of wild,
colourful characters makes this a hugely enjoyable novel of modern
sexual dilemmas.**

WHITE ROSE ENSNARED
Juliet Hastings
ISBN 0 352 33052 X

England. 1456. The young and beautiful Rosamund finds herself at the
mercy of Sir Ralph Aycliffe when her husband is killed in battle. Aycliffe
will stop at nothing to humiliate Rosamund and seize her property. Only
the young squire Geoffrey Lymington will risk everything to save the
honour of the woman he has loved for just one night. Against the Wars
of the Roses, the battle for Rosamund unfolds. Who will prevail in the
struggle for her body? **Vicious knaves and noble gentlemen joust in this
tale of courtly but not so chivalrous love.**

Coming in July

WICKED WORDS 10
Various
ISBN 0 352 33893 8

Wicked Words collections are the hottest anthologies of women's erotic writing to be found anywhere in the world. With settings and scenarios to suit all tastes, this is fun erotica at the cutting edge from the UK and USA. The diversity of themes and styles reflects the diversity of the female sexual imagination. Combining humour, warmth and attitude with imaginative writing, these stories sizzle with horny action. **A scorching collection of wild fantasies rounds up this series.**

THE SENSES BEJEWELLED
Cleo Cordell
ISBN 0 352 32904 1

Eighteenth-century Algeria provides a backdrop of opulence tainted with danger in this story of extreme erotic indulgence. Ex-convent girl Marietta has settled into a life of privileged captivity, as the favoured concubine in the harem of Kasim. But when she is kidnapped by Kasim's sworn enemy, Hamed, her new-found way of life is thrown into chaos. **This is the sequel to the hugely popular Black Lace title, *The Captive Flesh*.**

Black Lace Booklist

Information is correct at time of printing. To avoid disappointment check availability before ordering. Go to www.blacklace-books.co.uk. All books are priced £6.99 unless another price is given.

BLACK LACE BOOKS WITH A CONTEMPORARY SETTING

☐ SHAMELESS Stella Black	ISBN 0 352 33485 1	£5.99
☐ INTENSE BLUE Lyn Wood	ISBN 0 352 33496 7	£5.99
☐ A SPORTING CHANCE Susie Raymond	ISBN 0 352 33501 7	£5.99
☐ TAKING LIBERTIES Susie Raymond	ISBN 0 352 33357 X	£5.99
☐ A SCANDALOUS AFFAIR Holly Graham	ISBN 0 352 33523 8	£5.99
☐ THE NAKED FLAME Crystalle Valentino	ISBN 0 352 33528 9	£5.99
☐ ON THE EDGE Laura Hamilton	ISBN 0 352 33534 3	£5.99
☐ LURED BY LUST Tania Picarda	ISBN 0 352 33533 5	£5.99
☐ THE HOTTEST PLACE Tabitha Flyte	ISBN 0 352 33536 X	£5.99
☐ THE NINETY DAYS OF GENEVIEVE Lucinda Carrington	ISBN 0 352 33070 8	£5.99
☐ DREAMING SPIRES Juliet Hastings	ISBN 0 352 33584 X	
☐ THE TRANSFORMATION Natasha Rostova	ISBN 0 352 33311 1	
☐ SIN.NET Helena Ravenscroft	ISBN 0 352 33598 X	
☐ TWO WEEKS IN TANGIER Annabel Lee	ISBN 0 352 33599 8	
☐ HIGHLAND FLING Jane Justine	ISBN 0 352 33616 1	
☐ PLAYING HARD Tina Troy	ISBN 0 352 33617 X	
☐ SYMPHONY X Jasmine Stone	ISBN 0 352 33629 3	
☐ SUMMER FEVER Anna Ricci	ISBN 0 352 33625 0	
☐ CONTINUUM Portia Da Costa	ISBN 0 352 33120 8	
☐ OPENING ACTS Suki Cunningham	ISBN 0 352 33630 7	
☐ FULL STEAM AHEAD Tabitha Flyte	ISBN 0 352 33637 4	
☐ A SECRET PLACE Ella Broussard	ISBN 0 352 33307 3	
☐ GAME FOR ANYTHING Lyn Wood	ISBN 0 352 33639 0	
☐ CHEAP TRICK Astrid Fox	ISBN 0 352 33640 4	
☐ THE GIFT OF SHAME Sara Hope-Walker	ISBN 0 352 32935 1	
☐ COMING UP ROSES Crystalle Valentino	ISBN 0 352 33658 7	
☐ GOING TOO FAR Laura Hamilton	ISBN 0 352 33657 9	

BLACK LACE BOOKS WITH AN HISTORICAL SETTING

BLACK LACE ANTHOLOGIES

BLACK LACE NON-FICTION

To find out the latest information about Black Lace titles, check out the website: www.blacklace-books.co.uk or send for a booklist with complete synopses by writing to:

Black Lace Booklist, Virgin Books Ltd
Thames Wharf Studios
Rainville Road
London W6 9HA

Please include an SAE of decent size. Please note only British stamps are valid.

Please send me the books I have ticked above.

Name ....

Address ....

....

....

....

Post Code ....

Send to: Virgin Books Cash Sales, Thames Wharf Studios, Rainville Road, London W6 9HA.

US customers: for prices and details of how to order books for delivery by mail, call 1-800-343-4499.

Please enclose a cheque or postal order, made payable to Virgin Books Ltd, to the value of the books you have ordered plus postage and packing costs as follows:

UK and BFPO – £1.00 for the first book, 50p for each subsequent book.

Overseas (including Republic of Ireland) – £2.00 for the first book, £1.00 for each subsequent book.

If you would prefer to pay by VISA, ACCESS/MASTERCARD, DINERS CLUB, AMEX or SWITCH, please write your card number and expiry date here:

....

Signature ....

Please allow up to 28 days for delivery.